The Tavistock Lieutenant

The Tenth Catrin Sayer Mystery

ALLAN JONES

Published by Allan Jones. allanj12@gmail.com

ISBN: 978-1-7773635-3-6

Cover: Souk at Dubai Mall (Author photo)

THE CATRIN SAYER MYSTERIES

The Chinese Sailor
The Scottish Colourist
The Falmouth Model
The Carnforth Double
The Powys Deacon
The Stratford Hunter
The Thornham Copyist
The Chiswick Chauffeur
The Pinewood Gardener
The Tavistock Lieutenant

OTHER NOVELS

Canons

*All novels are released as ebooks
and Kindle Direct Publishing paperbacks.*

CONTENTS

Lord-lieutenant. The British
Monarch's personal representative
in each lieutenancy area of
the United Kingdom.

Padparadscha. A rare form of
sapphire with pink and orange elements.

PROLOGUE

2009, Riyadh, Saudi Arabia.

Hanan Al Imani clutched the small jewel box tightly, taking a deep breath. She was convinced that her actions in the next minute or so would set the course for the rest of her life. At best, she thought, she would live financially more modestly than during her life so far. At worst, she could die in poverty, or struggle in a refugee camp. But it would be her decision alone to take that risk and find her way forward.

Fleetingly, an image of her mother came into her mind and she almost relented. It was a lecture to her daughters on the roles of men and women. Mother was speaking about their duties to each other and their different freedoms. Hanan was free not to work; she had servants. She was free to spend on herself, from within her husband's allowance to her. But all the main rules in life, her mother had noted wistfully, were set by men. It was the way, and no other way existed in their world without bringing shame on her and her family.

That is what she was gripping in her hand, she realised:

the emblem of her personal shame. Whatever the impact on others, she would discard that.

The smell in her nostrils was of new carpets, wafting from the stall near her. New carpets. A new home. Unlike her marriage eight years ago, which had brought her to this point, others had no say this time.

Hanan was standing at a junction in the alleys of the old Souq Al Thumairi in central Riyadh. It was a traditional market with rows of stalls, selling goods for locals and foreign tourists. Beside her stood her friend Querima and Querima's younger brother, Abbad. The group were only steps away from the modern shopping mall the women knew so much better.

The trio received the occasional glance, not so much for Querima or herself, but at Abbad. At nineteen, he was the male. Abbad was appropriately and conservatively dressed for a Yemeni man, but his expression of unease attracted attention. He was simply out of his depth, feigning confidence but revealing his nervousness. It was infectious, visible to others at a time when self-assurance was important. They all knew that if there were to be retributions, he, as the man, would suffer the most.

Querima had chosen the spot to let them watch the customers, to select a potential buyer for the ring. Not a local, she had said, nor the bigger groups of Europeans. Foreigners focused on the stalls selling everything from camel saddles to carpets, or the eye-catching silverware and jambiyas, the Yemeni daggers.

"Those who buy cheaper tourist goods will not be interested or, if they are, they won't pay a good price. We need a person who studies the quality items. Look for someone who dresses well and carries themself with assurance. Someone who understands quality."

The original idea was that Hanan would be with Abbad as he tried to sell the ring. Both his English and German were better than hers. Now his young face revealed his fears more, and Hanan discarded that idea. She would attempt this sale herself.

Eight years into her marriage, her husband had announced that he would avoid her bed, declare *talaq*, and unilaterally divorce her. Men had that choice, women did not; they only had the option of seeking redress through the courts. The immediate shame she felt was tinged with relief and fear. Yet, above those emotions burned the ever-present anger at the injustice. It overwhelmed her.

He was the one who travelled on business internationally. 'What happens in Vegas, stays in Vegas', they say in the USA, she thought. But what happens in Frankfurt and Tokyo, or London sometimes, trickles back. His indiscretions, the traces of other women and the parties he attended. His use of alcohol and drugs. The constant taunts about her failure to become pregnant. Their marriage had grown into a bitter existence, but it was being annulled, supposedly, for her failure to conceive.

He made it clear what would happen. After the statutory period following declaration, Hanan would leave his household. She would return to her parent's home with her dowry intact and her jewelry accompanying her. He had already spoken with her father. Hanan should not expect sympathy for her cold-heartedness and her failure as a wife.

She had left one comfortable prison for a second. Now she would return to the first one, in disgrace.

A bracelet sold to a cousin of a friend was her first step, taken two days ago. Querima had also given her some money that Hanan now secreted away. The ring in the box she grasped tightly was the second item to be sold. After this, there was no turning back. The ring would be missed, and other men than her husband would be angry at the sale.

The single sapphire in a dark silver band was valuable, she knew, but Hanan had only the word of others. It was a wedding present from Shaykh Yusuf Abrahim, in honour of her father and husband really, not her. Shaykh Yusuf had attended her wedding, coming to Riyadh with others from Yemen. He had told her the gift was a family item from his mother's line, a signal of his esteem for loyal comrades and a wish for a joyous wedding for her. Even at the time, she saw that the true value of the ring was its appreciation by her father and her husband.

Yesterday, Querima had looked at it anxiously. "It is a good stone, but you shouldn't sell it, really. Your father will be outraged. I remember the wedding. In fact, no one in the tribe will buy it; you must understand that? Don't try and sell it through people we know. They will inform your husband."

Which was the reason why she could use her credit cards only once during her escape plan, to draw cash in Berlin. They carried her name, but they were her husband's account. Any air tickets or hotels paid with them would be known by him within hours after she fled. She needed assets in cash.

Today, Hanan hoped someone unknown would buy the ring; and soon. The trip to her sister's home was coming up. Hanan's husband had approved that visit before his edict. Now he was glad to be rid of her for a week as his marriage staggered to a close. For Hanan now, the holiday flight from Riyadh to Berlin was to be the first step in a more dangerous journey still, leaving her husband, her family, and their world.

Querima pointed. "That man, the older one."

"Which one?"

There were two men, European. One was young, comfortable in his surroundings but vigilant, and from his skin he had been in Saudi for a while. The other was from Europe, pale skinned. He was interested in the souq and its atmosphere and was more a businessman than a tourist, a little older but not yet middle-aged, and well dressed.

"The older Englishman. Listen to their voices. The other has some Arabic, so can help translate, if needed. But focus only on the older man. He is being very selective in his interests. Perhaps it is worth a try?"

Hanan swallowed hard and nodded. Querima continued her instructions. "Tell them you are Yemeni, that the ring is from our culture, not Saud. That we hold silver jewelry in high esteem, so the stone is real. Europeans see silver as cheap, thinking only of metal prices. Abbad, if that is missed, you say it, reinforce that it is valuable."

As Hanan stepped forward, Querima finished with, "Remember the word, padparadscha. Take nothing less than two thousand riyals. Be firm. Abbad, you have the page ready?"

Her brother was holding his mobile phone, eager to support his sister's friend. It showed the description of the sapphire type.

As Querima watched Hanan enter the alley with Abbad a step behind her, she hoped she was doing the right thing for her friend. The ring was worth far more, but a couple of thousand Riyals would be the upper limit in a street sale for cash, she thought.

In Berlin, Hanan would have a suitcase of clothes, her

precious passport, the secret fund of cash and her jewelry. There, she would leave her sister's home, but not to return to the Middle East. Where she was destined, they agreed, should be shared with no-one.

Earlier, when Querima had tried to make Hanan reconsider the consequences of the sale, Hanan's flash of anger shut down the conversation. "I will make my way on my own, do whatever is needed. I may find people who help me, I may die in a refugee camp or clean toilets in Paris if I have to, but I will be free."

Hanan's concept of freedom seemed quite naive and alien to Querima. She seriously worried how her friend would survive out there.

She saw Abbad call to the men as Hanan opened the jewel box to show the ring. As she started talking, Abbad held up his phone. It caused the younger man to bring out his own, suddenly tapping away, checking the information being thrust at them.

For better or worse, it had begun.

It was a day later, at Querima's home, when Abbad asked her the question that had bothered him ever since the clandestine trip to the souq.

"Why did Hanan want to sell the ring only to a European foreigner? He bought it and didn't even haggle. I agree that many here would not buy it, not want to risk offending her husband. But the ring is beautiful. We could have found another buyer here, one who would pay more and would not care. Or she could have taken it with her, sold it abroad at a better price."

Querima thought about whether to tell him and decided against it. Who knows what might happen after her friend flees Berlin?

"Hanan has her reasons, I am sure. I do not pry, and

neither should you. The less we know, the better. To know nothing at all is best. Remember that please, Abbad. You know nothing."

You are young and male, she thought. You do not know the despair which turns to hate. Hanan married at the wish of her father, who agreed to the suggestion of the Shaykh. He was bestowing favours on two men loyal to him, with the expectations that brought. The ring from Shaykh Yusuf Abrahim was a handsome gift. For it to be sold to someone who would take it abroad, make sure it was lost for ever, was Hanan's wish.

Hanan now detested Shaykh Yusuf, the man who had forced her into this marriage. Her departure would bring shame and anger to her husband and father. The loss of the ring would give her revenge against an even more powerful man.

PART 1

TAVISTOCK

1 HERNE BAY

There was nothing unusual about the group. Three women, a man, and two little girls were together, enjoying the pebble and sand beach at Herne Bay, on the north coast of Kent. It was a warm summer's day in June, with a cooling easterly breeze along the water. The stretch of sand was reasonably crowded, but people remained in their clusters. Every group was keeping their distance from others, and not from a sense of quasi-privacy.

If there was a difference, it was that all parents were constantly alert to where their children were playing, and how close they were to other children. This was the second summer of new habits driven by words like Covid, pandemic, social distancing, and quarantine.

An observant neighbour might wonder why it was always one or other of the women and not the man who played with the children on the sand or in the water. One woman was now showing the girls how to catch crabs in the shadows off one of the wooden groins nearby, stretching out into the water.

The art of tying tiny pieces of bacon rind to a crab line

and dangling it in the water seemed to be a predominantly male occupation. With the exception, that is, of the woman with the two little girls.

In their cluster, the man was also masked even in the fresh air, one of a minority in the separated groups along the beach. Covid was understood better now, and people chose their own level of prudence. The adults had been vaccinated once and were close to the point of qualifying for their second shot. The girls were still too young for vaccination, the older being seven, nearer to eight, the younger looking to be around five. There was talk that Covid vaccine would at some point be offered to children below twelve; but when, no-one knew.

With the fears and problems of Covid, a summer's day in the sunshine away from London seemed a near-normal experience. It felt wonderful.

Melanie Farrell carefully picked through the small crabs in the two sandbuckets one by one, as the girls studied the colours and movements. There were overlapping questions and exclamations from the pair. But the girls were past the fear stage and now curious about the creatures they usually saw as cartoons on a screen.

Observing them from a distance, Jean Hughes, Melanie's wife, said to her companions, "Watch. They will name them. Then there will be tears and farewells later as we put them back."

She passed a container of sandwiches around, seeing if anyone else was still hungry. There were no takers, so she put the lid on and returned it to the cooler. Catrin Sayer, smiling and relaxed, looked across at the children. "The new masks in the cafe earlier were a hit, as usual."

The younger child, Mair, was her daughter with her husband, Chris Treneer, sitting on a folding chair behind her. Catrin was using his legs as a backrest.

Jean responded, "Sewing Sally, that's me."

Hughes was the only one of the three women proficient with a sewing machine. Early in the pandemic, she had made cloth masks. For the kids, bright colours and elephant images had been part of their introduction to their changing world. The gaudy masks with familiar characters were presented as a game, to keep fear from their eyes. From elephants to dinosaurs and their ever-changing favourite characters from Disney, the families made the best of a totally unexpected situation. And they all had first-hand experience of the impact of Covid.

Chris, intently watching the girls, had been one of the severe cases. A tall, fit Cornishman, a dedicated five-a-side footballer, he and three members of his work team became infected on the same day. They were all civilian employees in the e-crime unit of the Metropolitan Police in London, computer experts rather than uniformed officers.

The source was identified as a sales rep, making a site visit to test a new piece of analytical software. It was ironic really, for a job that fitted on-line remote linking more than most others. Mair became infected from Chris and passed it to her closest friend, Lili, but it hit both children lightly. Jean wasn't infected. Melanie went down with Covid but came out the other side without any side effects.

Catrin missed their common infection period comp-letely because she was away from London. She was on work leave from the Metropolitan Police, studying at Cambridge University. Most of her weekdays were spent at the Institute of Criminology there, to earn a Master of Philosophy degree in the subject; a career development step for a 'high-flyer' police officer. Catrin currently held the rank of detective chief inspector.

Once she knew her family and friends were ill, Catrin left Cambridge hurriedly to be home. There, she dealt with the consequences of sick family and friends and the isolation of her husband in hospital.

Two weeks later, all exhausted, they took stock of their situation. Chris had been released from hospital. He had spent four days in an ICU unit on oxygen and, for one on those days, was borderline for intubation. He had the longest road of recovery. For reasons unknown, he continued to suffer the effects of 'long Covid'. His recovery bounced back only so far, as he became one of the 'live and learn lab rats', as he put it. Symptoms of constant fatigue, headaches, joint pains, failure to concentrate and shortness of breath all wore away at him. Nobody knew how long it would last or how he would feel from one day to the next.

Jean and Melanie owned a pottery, the Cwmbran Kiln in Spitalfields Market, near both the Hughes-Farrell and Sayer-Treneer homes. There, they produced a range of household ceramics, from kitchen pottery and dinnerware to wall art and garden gnomes. The Kiln had closed temporarily during the epidemic lock-down with other shops in the market complex.

Jean and Catrin had been friends since childhood in Pontypridd, in Wales. Throughout Catrin's career as a police officer, she and Jean had also worked together as ceramic artists. From the early days of setting up the Cwmbran Kiln, the two Welsh friends produced a line of expensive 'one-off' ceramic art together. Though small in output, the pieces sold at far higher prices through a gallery in the West End, near Harrods. Both women were involved in the design. Jean made the pottery and Catrin was the ceramic decorator.

It was Chris who wanted Catrin to return to her studies, not drop out of the Cambridge course. It was the quiet, practical Jean who made it happen.

She confronted Catrin with a familiar look of stubborn resolve. "We bubble. There is no Chloe around to help us. The Cwmbran Kiln was closed for months. We have debts, like every other small business there."

Only months before the pandemic hit, they had said farewell to their jointly hired nanny, Chloe Keenan. With the children both in school, there wasn't the same need, and Chloe had her own reasons. She had told them, "I'm fully qualified now, thanks to all your help. But I need to stay focused as a nanny, working with babies and little toddlers. I also want to move back to Liverpool sometime soon."

Jean continued, "Melanie and I can help with Chris and Mair. And we need the money. You study in Cambridge during most of the week, then you and I take a day or so to work on new art pieces. You spend the rest of the time with Mair and Chris. Sayer-Hughes collectors still want our work. They are quarantined or locked down, or unwilling to travel, but Liz says they still want to add to their collections. Her gallery is busy with on-line and mail order purchases for most of her artists."

Jean gave a firm nod, her lips pursed. "If we pull together, we can get through this. You need your degree to get a promotion, and Melanie and I can't let the Kiln go under. We have put too much of our lives into the business."

There was no answer to that.

Catrin returned to her 'new normal' life, almost as shell-shocked as during the worst incidents in her career as a police officer.

Chris battled away doing his part. Getting through a load of laundry without resting, or Melanie appearing and taking over, was a victory for him. His regular work was out of the question. Forensic computer analysis of fraud and criminal cases requires intense concentration. Its output needs to stand up in court. A computer specialist who could not concentrate or have the energy to lead his team had to get well and stay home.

A day trip to Herne Bay together now Catrin had finished her studies was a special event, a triumph of resilience and friendship. It was marred only by the squeak of pain from Lili after she poked too close to a claw. This led to an urgent question from Mair about the crab biting off the end of her best friend's finger.

Melanie said, "No, it's just a little cut, that's all. We will kiss it better and put a 'Frozen' bandaid on it."

They started the retreat from the jetty to join the others.

Jean asked Catrin, "What do you think will happen?"

They were talking about Catrin's meeting next Tuesday with the head of personnel at the Met. The career plan had been developed before the word Covid appeared. Catrin was expected to transfer to another constabulary for a period. Where, they did not know. It was intended to broaden her experience before returning to the Metropolitan Police in a more senior role. Wales and the west of England had been mentioned originally.

"I really don't know," Catrin responded. "Barrington didn't say much when we last talked. I got the impression that everything was up in the air. The way it is, I'd be happy to just get my old job back, but that's not an option. That's clear."

Sayer had been a team lead in Operation Undertow, a part of Serious and Organized Crime Division.

"Most people seem to be hunkering down. There are a lot of temporary postings to cover for officers who are sick, so I could become a bit nomadic, switching around."

Chris said quietly, "It is a bit of a madhouse, truth be told. People fill in."

Catrin added, "I hope I stay put in London now. But there is still the agreement to transfer me out for a while, more in spirit than in writing. I may get an offer for work somewhere else for a period. But for the kids... I don't want to separate them for months at a time."

Melanie, finished with adding a bandaid to her daughter's finger, had sat down on the blanket. The girls played close by, the tragedy of a demon crab devouring a finger now behind them. She had picked up the conversation.

"That's not a showstopper," Melanie said. "These two will be on iPads to each other, just like now. They are more adaptable than us."

She was one for candour. "And a promotion is a big pay rise. You can't miss out on that. Not with this one lolling around doing sod all."

She gave Chris a big smile. The banter between him and Melanie had been intermittent over the months. It was their coping mechanism with the changes in their lives. For some weeks after Catrin resumed her studies, Melanie was effectively his carer. The insults resurfaced, Catrin noticed, when one or other of them felt the pain of Chris's dilemma.

Nothing had been said, but there was a limit to short-term disability coverage. And long-term disability meant a loss of his current role as a team lead. Chris desperately wanted to keep his current job.

"She still needs sensitivity training," Chris said to Jean, shaking his head.

Jean scrunched her face up. "It would be a waste. Melanie is missing the right neurons, or ganglia, or receptors, whatever they are. It would go in one ear and straight out of the other."

As the afternoon wore on, the looks between the women reached an unspoken conclusion that it was time to go home. "The kids have had enough, really," said Melanie, lying blatantly to Chris with a big smile.

When they packed up and moved their sandy belongings and picnic baskets to the cars, the women shared the load. Chris walked with the kids. They stopped every few paces, becoming excited about a piece of driftwood, an insect, or a strand of dried seaweed. From their cars, the girls called out their last farewells to their new arthropod friends.

But it had been a good day.

2 RED WITCH

The Red Witch was dressed in a charcoal grey suit, almost black, which was probably appropriate for the day and her mood. The last year and a half had been stressful, even in a job where stress was a daily guarantee.

Colleen Barrington was known also by other unflattering nicknames. The Director of Human Resources at the Metropolitan Police Service, it came with the job. She reported to the executive. As such, she was the individual most responsible for the strategic decisions on personnel management.

In her wildest career dreams, she had never imagined doing this job through a pandemic, particularly for an organisation with forty thousand police officers and civilian staff.

Her team were now inured to the new challenges but were exhausted by the pressures they brought. At the operating level - the area command units, the task forces, the borough units, and the specialist teams - the same pressures were felt. These varied by degree almost weekly, given the dislocation that Covid brought.

On top of that, tempers frayed more easily, both with officers and the public. That made the human resources jobs harder. Some people had modified their opinion of Barrington. Her nickname, earned for her ruthlessness during reorganisations, seemed inappropriate now. Her focus was support for staff with stress-related problems. She had mellowed, was the term that one chief superintendent had used.

Her assistant, Carlos Martin, came into her office for the morning review. Barrington had four meetings this morning and one lasting all afternoon. That one was dealing with resource shortfalls in boroughs south of the Thames.

As they reviewed the morning, he said, "The one bright spot is the meeting with Sayer, now she is back from Cambridge. Is there a decision, yet?"

Barrington shook her head. "I'm waiting to talk to her. Then I will give Commander Moore my recommendation."

She thought for a moment, focusing on that meeting.

"Did Linda do the update on a Christopher Treneer, Economic Crime Unit, that I asked for?"

It threw Carlos for a second, then he thumbed through his iPad. "It's there, further down. I thought that would come up later in the week. She won't contact him until next week, though. They are awaiting his next assessment report."

Seeing her assistant's confusion, Barrington said, "They are married, Treneer and Sayer. I can't go into details about his career with her, of course, but I need to include the implications. She has a big decision to make."

Colleen sighed. "Let's first check the details of the Judd retirement debacle, see if we can get Goldman out of the hole that he has dug for us."

~ ~

Catrin Sayer passed Superintendent Louis Goldman in the corridor leading to Human Resources. Suddenly recognizing her over the mask, he gave her a penetrating look. They knew each other from many years ago, in Brixton, but there had been no direct contact since.

"Sayer, keeping well? Cambridge, I heard, flying high?"

"Just keeping my wings flapping these days, sir."

He gave a glance behind him. "I know what you mean. Good luck."

With that, he was off.

"How's it going? Recognize anybody?"

Barrington's opening words, delivered in her Ulster accent, were less upbeat than Catrin remembered. The personnel chief motioned her to the meeting table. There were only two seats, across the diameter from each other.

Her comment on recognition tied to the face masks. Sayer hadn't been inside New Scotland Yard for months.

"A few, but others only as I passed them. As you can imagine, I have a lot of memory gaps arising from a year away."

They were assessing each other, their eyes showing similar conclusions; two women tired, but used to being that way. In the two years or so since the meeting held in the Commissioner's office to talk about Sayer's career direction, they had met quarterly. During the pandemic, most of those meetings had been virtual.

Barrington looked down and moved the file, a signal that she was getting into the meat of the meeting. "You did well, not great, at Cambridge, the feedback said. They also said it was amazing you completed the course at all. Carlos says you must have worn out a complete set of tires and an engine between Cambridge and the East End."

Catrin smiled; it was in her eyes and her voice. "He's right about the tires. The engine is 'sweet', the service people said. It was a lot of driving. But yes, I wasn't the leading light of the criminology course, or there to soak up the 'mature student' life in Cambridge, but I have my M.Phil."

Her meaning was clear. She had held to her part of the career plan deal; to complete the prestigious postgraduate course at Cambridge.

Barrington said, "Now what next, you ask? When we talked three months ago, I told you that a placement in Wales, either North or South, was looking 'iffy'. Too much is changing, in one sense. In another, key senior people are hunkering down. No-one wants unnecessary changes currently. Anything that came up there would be a windfall, not planned."

Catrin said nothing, seeing as Barrington was nowhere near finished.

"And now we must add Chris's Covid status into the mix. How is he doing from your perspective? And this is just between you and me. Nothing will get back to his file officer unless I agree it with you beforehand. It is your situation I want to understand at this meeting and your family is part of it."

Catrin took in a deep breath and held it, thinking.

"It is hard to say from one week to the next. Long Covid is a new learning curve for the medics as much as the patients. He's gone from a guy who played a football game in the morning and still had enough 'go' to keep up with Mair all afternoon. Now he has little energy. Early on, there were some days it was all he could do to get out of bed and move around our apartment. There are more good days than bad of late, so it is getting better. I am hoping he gets it all back. I have a lot of hope."

Colleen nodded, showing her understanding. "You have a plate load to consider, I know."

She took a deep breath. "Here's where I am at. Within the Met, there are two superintendent level positions I could see you fitting. I'm not trying to sell either one hard. First, a borough superintendent. Finchley, diverse general duties. You have been in stations, so you know about that from the front end. Mostly an office job and you'll get reasonably regular hours, which could be valuable, given Chris's situation. However, we want someone there who will stay for a while, give some stability.

"The second option is with the Central Task Force, an acting superintendent position with Commander Wood. You know that field. Drug dealers, gun traffickers, that mob. With your work in Operation Undertow, you have prior experience which qualifies you. But, like that role, you will work all hours and run from one critical issue to the next. And it would be acting until you prove you are up to it. Commander Wood knows your competency, but you haven't won his heart, being so close to Moore. You could end up there staying at DCI rank."

She sniffed. "I shouldn't say that, really, about Karen, should I? He never said that, but it was what he meant."

The battleground between Commander Karen Moore and John Wood was well known.

Catrin grimaced. "That was Jackson's job, right? He took early retirement, I heard."

"Yes; it was that or stress leave and a shift sideways. It is a high-pressure position."

21

She paused. "Neither position quite meets the original plan to stretch your experience fast. But I have one more possibility, not solid, but I want to see how it feels. No promises."

Catrin nodded but said nothing.

"We originally said either North or South Wales, or Devon and Cornwall as likely placements for two to three years. Then we would pull you back at a possible Chief Superintendent level. Well, the Devon lot have a job they would take you for, but only for one year at most, based at headquarters in Exeter. They want a superintendent to lead a strategic reorganisation task force."

Catrin's eyes rolled.

Barrington pressed on. "Yes, no-one wants a job like that. You get new names, like 'The Red Witch', for example. My opposite number there sees some plusses in a temporary like you. One of them is that your head is full of the current thinking from the criminology course. That's an asset.

"The second is that you are from Wales, not London. You could appear human to them, rather than an arrogant London prick bringing pearls of wisdom to the yokels. The real underlying reason is that they can get rid of you afterwards. Once the Task Force reports and closes, you come back. You don't become their Ancient Mariner floating around waggling your albatross, getting more evil looks behind your back. Which will happen from day one, I guarantee."

She paused, assessing Sayer. "From your face, it doesn't appeal."

Catrin responded, "You aren't exactly selling it to me. But I'm thinking about it. What do you like about it?"

"It would be a hell of a stretch for you in the personnel and organisational logistics areas. So far, your biggest team has been around thirty officers, not the span of an entire constabulary. Also, Chris could take an enforced leave of absence tied to your temporary assignment. That would freeze his short-term disability coverage period. We wouldn't visit the subject of long-term disability kicking in, at least until you came back. The union agreements require us to hold his current position open. We would be filling it with a temporary."

Catrin smiled. "Now that is a crafty one you are pulling."

Colleen shrugged. "I'm just following the rules carefully. Why it appeals to me is the experience you would have there. Tough as it will be, it is the sort of thing that the Commissioner wants people to gain by moving outside the Met. Only a year at most, and you would come back as a lateral transfer at superintendent level. If you perform well, you would be in a position for a Chief Superintendent post here sooner than either position I mentioned earlier."

She looked at her watch pointedly. "Think about it. But, not for too long. The two positions in London would have you stay at home. Finchley might be easier, given the other demands on your time. The Central Task Force role would be like Operation Undertow, familiar ground. The Exeter job is the most challenging, but it may have some family benefits. I understand Chris has family down there?"

"In Falmouth and Penzance. His sister and her partner, and his mother. We get on well with them. They would be very supportive."

Barrington added, as she stood, "And a one-year assignment would mean you could sub-let your current home for the period. The Met and Devon and Cornwall would foot the difference in accommodation cost if you rent a home down there. You will have an assigned vehicle you could flog to death between Falmouth and Exeter, if it worked."

Catrin stood too. "I appreciate the thought and effort you have put into this."

Barrington smiled. "Nice to please someone these days. You take care now. Look after yourself."

Two days later, Sayer called Barrington. "In principle, subject to terms and more information, I want to pursue the position with Devon and Cornwall. Chris is with me on this."

Barrington seemed happy with the outcome. As they talked about next steps, she threw in the comment, "Perhaps the Devon and Cornwall lot will call you 'The Welsh Witch'."

Catrin responded, "Or worse. And you weren't the Red Witch when you arrived."

"No, I wasn't. It was 'Axewoman' then, I know. Yours could be worse still."

3 REALITY

The decision to transfer to the Devon and Cornwall Police was both easier and harder than Catrin expected.

In the 'easier' camp came two items. Thankfully, Lili and Mair accepted relatively quickly their temporary separation. Melanie, picking up on her prediction in Herne Bay, was instrumental in that challenge. Once the first bout of tears and anguish had been dealt with, an offering of two new Samsung tablets, in pink, with matching cases, were a deal maker. The children negotiated hard. Time together online was additional to their normal game time. Lili was promised a a visit to Exeter, to be with her friend and see the sea and the crabs down there.

Mair was largely silent until the end. "When we come back, when I am home, do we still keep the new computers, or do we give them back?"

"You keep them." The adults were almost in chorus. It clinched the deal.

The other surprise was the ease with which they sub-let

their apartment, through Jean's network. A boutique owner at Spitalfields Market and her husband were having their home in Leytonstone modernised and had to vacate for five months for the builders. They wanted to rent a home nearer to the city than further out. Within a few phone calls, it was agreed in principle. They would take the full lease period even if they moved back home sooner. It was ideal for the boutique owner and fine for her husband, who worked in the Stock Exchange.

"I knew they weren't short of money," said Jean. "She seems OK. Are you sure they won't mess you around?"

Catrin gave her a stare. "It's not us. The Met has a firm they use for relocations and moves, the facility management side. I think the contract won't allow any room for either side to mess the other around."

The Devon and Cornwall Police Headquarters are in Middlemoor, on the outskirts of Exeter. The reality set in for Catrin during the interview there. The two-storey brick buildings made a stark contrast with the Curtis Green building of the Met. The refurbished headquarters of the Metropolitan Police on the Thames Embankment was a landmark, a piece of history. The Exeter HQ reminded her of a well-worn high school that had seen too many students.

During the first week of August, Chris's sister and mother traveled from Cornwall to their new home, to help them settle in. Catrin spent two days in headquarters for her initial orientation. Their belongings they needed arrived in a removal van. That excited Mair. Chris did well through it all, albeit with more breaks and rests than he liked.

The following week, Catrin spent three days in Birmingham, at the offices of the consulting firm,

Wherry, Keefe & Otley Ltd., engaged to support the organisational review. WKO were specialists in public institution reorganisation, having clients across the UK. It had a staff of twenty, led by three partners.

Catrin met first with the managing partners, and then spent time alone with Dr. Ursula Otley, the partner who would lead the team supporting the work in Exeter. Otley was a founding partner of the firm, a former CEO of a public agency that had moved into management consulting. The team assigned to the exercise was brought in and introduced.

It was when Otley asked her to share her own professional experience with the team, in confidence, that she became a little apprehensive. She talked briefly about her development from a new police officer through to her last role, as a detective chief inspector. Then she spoke about the management elements of the course at Cambridge.

She closed with a comment about the special nature of police work; that she had been injured on duty, pointing to the scar on her face, and three years ago she had dealt with the violent death of fellow police officer. These were realities for police officers, she told them, aspects that were not dealt with in the dry analysis of job descriptions, but when it came down to decisions on individuals, needed handling with sensitivity.

Otley responded with, "So you are used to investigative work, leading a team you need to depend on, one where everyone knows their role. And keeping a professional distance from others, including the public, to maintain the objectivity of your investigation and keep information confidential."

It was a statement. Catrin nodded.

"For the next months, this is your team. None of us

are in uniform, but you can rely on us and our expertise. We are there to support you. You will find as this exercise starts you will be keeping a professional distance from just about everyone else around you even though they are your colleagues in uniform. People will be doing that to you, anyway."

Catrin grimaced. "I expect something like that, I must admit, having been through reorganisations at the Met. To be kept arms length, a bit like the police officers in internal investigation units."

It was a team member called Daniel who smiled at a colleague, then spoke up. "We heard that analogy from another client. He later said at least the Internal Review people only had to be face-to-face on issues with people accused of breaking the rules. He had to deal with every-one."

A second day was spent on process outline, the expectations for the Task Force work program and the roles of the individual consultant team members. The final part of her preparation was an hour-long Zoom call with a police chief superintendent in the Midlands who had fulfilled two years earlier the role she was about to com-mence. His experience confirmed the consultant's prediction. She would be isolated, even wearing the same uniform. It was like no other role he had undertaken.

"I was offered at the beginning a chance to move constabularies or stay with Leicestershire Police. I moved when I finished. It was a great people management exper-ience that catapulted my career, but very hard to go through. It may be easier for you, given that you have no existing relationships with people in the Devon and Cornwall Police."

Or I may be even more isolated, thought Catrin. I won't even feel on home ground.

She had a three-hour drive back to Exeter that afternoon, and a lot to think about.

When she arrived at their new home in Exeter that evening, after catching up on their day, Chris's sister, Jen, took Mair to the park, to give Chris a rest and some time to talk with Catrin. Chris's mother was preparing supper. She and Jen would depart the following morning.

Chris looked at her. "It has become real and daunting, hasn't it?"

Catrin nodded, finding herself unable to speak. After a moment she said, "I hope I can handle it all. It's not the policing I know. Intellectually I knew that when I talked with Colleen but, you are right, it is a lot more intimidating now."

He held her hand. "You will do well. I know that. It will be easier once you get started."

I hope so, thought Catrin. At least this position had a reasonable daily work schedule and a convenient commute.

They had rented a home in Colleton Crescent, in the town centre, with a park across the road and behind that, the drop to the narrows of the River Exe. Her commute was at most fifteen to twenty minutes, much less than in London. After years in crime investigation there and her recent 'mature student' life, the domestic arrangements were a welcome change.

The following Monday, in her new superintendent uniform with the Devon and Cornwall Police insignia, she turned up at Headquarters for the inaugural meeting of the new Task Force. For a reason she now understood, having absorbed the blueprint for the process, it was referred to as the Keystone Two event.

In the months head, she was aiming for Keystone Five,

the meeting where she would provide the Task Force report and recommendations to the Chief Constable. In her mind already was the presentation of that report and her return to the Met, hopefully to police work she knew.

4 TAQUIL'S

Taquil's Restaurant on the Old Brompton Road in London offered authentic Yemeni cuisine and 'creations' based on cross-cultural tastes. Its signage was discrete – Taquil in Arabic and underneath that, the name in plain, Calibri-font English. Other restaurants in the area used banner style signage halfway up the building, modeled after the nearby pub, the Duke of Clarence.

Although it was a wet night in mid-November, business was good, as most nights. The owner had built up a loyal clientele over the years and the quality of fresh ingredients with lively but efficient service was appreciated.

It was nine-thirty when Taquil talked briefly to the chef and then approached Nabil Jaber, one of three sous-chefs. His face looked concerned.

Nabil had been busy. He took in his manager's expression and stopped, wiping his hands.

"A man called Assad, Bital Assad, is in front. You know him?"

"Not personally. He works for Mr. Rahman in Paris, I

think. Mr. Rahman... you know Mr. Rahman."

"He wants you. It looks like custom is easing off. I said you would be free by ten. He will wait. Do you want to meet him or not?"

"No, but I should. Mr. Rahman has been good to my family so... I should."

"Finish ten minutes earlier than that and clean up. Nabil, we are small people, a small restaurant. I like being small. I don't like involvement with big people. Whatever it is, keep us and my restaurant out of it. That is all I ask."

As Nabil, ready to leave, came through to the restaurant he usually saw only across the serving bay, Assad stood and pointed at the car across the road. As he left the table, Nabil saw that Taquil had provided hors-d'oeuvres and juice for the man while he waited.

Outside, as they walked to the vehicle, Nabil, tall and thin in his late twenties, watched the shorter, burlier man carefully. Dressed in a quality suit, Assad was twice his age.

"How is Mr. Rahman, Mr. Assad? In good health, I hope."

"In excellent health, Nabil. A happy man. All is well with him." He looked Nabil directly in the eyes. "You owe him much. And your sister. She enjoys London, too?"

"Yes. We are very fortunate to have the opportunity to be here together."

Assad pressed the car remote, unlocking the doors and pointed at the front passenger seat for Nabil.

"This is not about Mr. Rahman. It is someone more important again who we all owe. Someone who is not a happy man at present. But you and I will change that."

The emphasis was on all. The tribe.

"Shaykh Yusuf?"

Assad gave a slow nod. "Our beloved shaykh. Yes. Get in."

Assad talked as he drove, appearing most comfortable with that. Nabil wondered if it was because no-one could observe or overhear them. Assad had a reputation as a hard man. Rumour had it that it was not Mr. Rahman's choice to hire him on to his company's team in Paris, that Assad was Kahn's man, the Omani now living in Germany.

"You were in your teens when the Al Imani insult occurred. The wedding gift. But teenagers hear more than they admit. You know this story?"

Nabil's immediate thought was to deny knowing anything. It would not help, he realised.

"The wedding present to the Imani woman in Riyadh, the ring that was lost. Vaguely, yes."

"Stolen, not lost. It troubles our shaykh, particularly recently. Like the prodigal son, what is lost has been found, or at least located."

"I am happy for Shaykh Yusuf that this has happened."

"Located, but not retrieved. Yet. I am entrusted to complete that task. And I have chosen you to assist me. Our Shaykh agreed; you are honoured by him."

Nabil looked lost. "I am not a financial man, if it is a matter of purchase, or negotiation."

Assad gave a small, cynical laugh. "It is too late for that. Mr. Khan had people go that route. The current owner dismissed the suggestion of a sale out of hand. And he is the man who bought the ring from the Al Imani woman, we discovered. And there is worse, but that does not concern you."

As he accelerated away after a traffic light turned green,

he said, "You enjoy being a sous-chef?"

"I enjoy my work, yes, but would like to be my own chef. Any chef would."

"And where will you get the financial support for such an investment? Not an English bank. Leave here without plans and finances, you might be lucky to have a similar job in Paris or elswhere."

He stared momentarily at Nabil, assessing his reaction before refocusing on the road.

"You need a benefactor. One more influential and generous than Majid Rahman."

Nabil shot back, "Mr. Rahman has been very good to my family. I will not hear him spoken of with such lack of respect. He is your own employer!"

"Enough! There is no disrespect. Rahman has his limits, his financial limits. The shaykh does not."

They drove in silence down one of the streets near Earls Court for a minute or so. Nabil was astonished. A little over thirty minutes ago, his focus was on the restaurant dishes he had to prepare. Now he was resisting the demand to become embroiled in some plan involving the recovery of a jewel.

"Why me, Mr. Assad?"

The older man looked at him momentarily then sighed as he drove. "The butcher in your village, Nasir, had two kids, Adil and Rahem, didn't he? You grew up with them. They were your friends."

His home village. All he could say was, "Yes. But I haven't heard –."

"Rahem was killed three days ago, in Uzullah. He was shopping. The danger is always present back home, is it not? As in any time of war. You were fortunate to escape that life and are doing well, like myself. You want to get on. Although you have a benefactor, you could have one more generous still, the man who has honoured you with the role of assisting me."

He paused and his tone of voice changed.

"Don't turn soft and weak with me. We were both soldiers. I told Taquil you will be away tomorrow but back at work the following day. That's all it takes. One day. All the preparations are made – by me, except one that you must do."

It was as if Nabil had already said yes. By not asserting himself with this man, saying no and demanding Assad to stop the car, he may have already given that answer. Nabil was stunned by the sudden realisation that Shaykh Yusuf, whom he had seen only once as a boy, standing by a big luxurious foreign car, had such control over his life. His shaykh had never seen him or spoken to his family.

It's London, he realised. It makes you think differently, being in the west. As if you are free. It is an illusion.

His shoulders slumped as he suddenly realised Assad had just given him an instruction.

"What?"

"You call your sister. She is to rent a car for us early tomorrow morning. Tell her Mr. Assad and you are spending tomorrow discussing business, the business of restaurants, and are looking around at potential opportunities."

He pulled over, stopping near the Kensington High Street underground station.

"Nabil, you are a man with more fear than bravery, but you have the desire to make something of yourself. I have more bravery than fear, which is not sometimes a good thing, I admit. But I want the same future, too. Together we will honour our shaykh by addressing his problem of the Al Imani betrayal. We will be rewarded well."

5 VICTORY HOUSE

Victory House stood on the hillside on the outskirts of Tavistock, Devon, along the A390. The tall steeple of the Roman Catholic Church of Our Lady of the Assumption was a nearby landmark.

The house in Tavistock had not been named by its current owner. 'Victory' referred to its origins, built by a wealthy soldier, Major Rupert Gaumont, following the First World War. A large home, once with a larger garden still, it had stayed in the Gaumont family until the line petered out. Later, a section of the land was parceled off and sold for development.

Fifteen years ago, Victory House had been bought by William Harding, a mid-level civil servant in the Department of Trade and Industry. He and his wife had their own family wealth. They improved the property and later raised their two children in it. His wife had lived all but her final week there; she died three years ago of ovarian cancer.

By then, Trade and Industry was changing its name, scope, and functions at regular intervals, tortured by short-term political opportunism. Harding, recovering from his grief, was now a single parent. He declared his own victory and took a severance package that he called his early retirement. No more weeks in London, or time on overseas trips pushing British commercial interests.

Long involved in the world of business development, he secured work on a variety of boards of governance in the county. Those earned him an adequate supplementary income, leaving time for similar volunteer work with several charities. For all that effort, his service was recognized by a royal appointment, as a deputy lieutenant of the County of Devon.

At 5.16 p.m. the day after the two Yemenis had driven away from Taquil's restaurant, a Lydia Thompson called 999. Her voice shaking and broken by tears, she reported the sighting of two bodies at Victory House.

Until then, it had been a bright, late-autumn day. She, with her daughter Estelle, had stopped at the Harding home to collect Ashley Harding, Estelle's friend. They were going into Tavistock for a visit to a pizzeria, a reward for their involvement in a volunteer project a week earlier. Now it was a horror story that had Lydia in shock.

Two minutes into the call, as the emergency operator tried to elicit more details, Lydia repeated her opening statement.

"I don't know. As I said, they are on the floor, dead, Ashley and her father. There is blood everywhere. We need the police, now."

"Lydia, stay on the line. The police and other emergency responders are already on the way. Are you sure the people you saw are dead, I asked? Do they need help?"

"I'm a nurse. I checked. I sent my daughter back to the

car. This is terrible, I'm shaking; it's the shock. And I'm a nurse, as I said."

The operator noted the repetition of her profession, for the third time. For a nurse to be so flustered, the scene with the fatalities must be terrible.

"Go back to your car now and lock yourselves in. The nearest responder is three minutes away. It won't be long. Just stay on the line and talk to me."

"But there is Adam, the son. He's ten. Unless he is doing something else, he should be home. I need –."

"No. Please stay there with your daughter. Lock yourselves in your vehicle and leave the rest to the first responders."

Lydia could hear a siren now, which helped steady her.

Within a couple of minutes, a fire engine pulled up, the first response to the call. It was a fireman, Harry Cassidy, who found the boy alive, shaking and traumatised. Adam was still in his school uniform, with his pants soaked in urine. He was hiding in the wardrobe closet in his bedroom.

Cassidy pushed the boy's sobbing face into his shoulder as he carried him out of the house, past the room with the mayhem, as the first police car appeared.

It normally took around an hour to drive west from Exeter to Tavistock. Detective Chief Inspector Michael Hicks took forty-five minutes to get there. Hicks held a senior role in the Devon and Cornwall Police Serious Crimes Division. A home invasion resulting in two fatal injuries is a priority response and this week he was the senior duty officer on call.

On arrival, he found one of his team, DI Oliver Wastle, who had beaten him there by ten minutes. Wastle had been closer, in Plymouth when called.

Wastle greeted him with, "Scene is secure, boss. Both dead, with gunshot wounds. The duty doctor from the Tavistock Hospital declared them, a father and daughter, but had to leave. Dr. Simon is about five minutes away, behind you."

"The boy?"

'Taken to the hospital with trauma, not wounds. Two officers are there. His aunt and uncle in Plymouth have been contacted. I have sent a car for them, as they are too shocked to drive."

"Anyone else?"

"No signs. DS Tydman is here and is organizing a search of the vicinity, just in case. And I've called for any signs of suspicious vehicles speeding or showing erratic driving to be tracked but not stopped. With the guns."

"The wife?"

"She died years ago. Harding is - was - a widower."

"SOCOs?"

The forensic team, the Scenes of Crime Officers.

"Three based in Plymouth are in there, setting up. The full team is on its way. But we can cover up and get a first look, they said. The caller is a nurse, so she has been into the scene. She's being processed for prints and DNA, and her daughter is with her. The girl can't stop crying. She and the dead girl were close friends."

Hicks seemed satisfied with the initial steps, Oliver thought.

The available SOCOs had set up stepping plates as far as the study, the scene of the carnage. They, too, were not going near the bodies until the pathologist arrived on site.

Hicks took it all in slowly. The room was not trashed, which was useful. Two picture hooks on the walls showed where items were missing. He turned slightly, seeing a third vacant space on the wall beside him. The reflected light there revealed a slight shading difference, a rectangle below the hook. A painting or a mirror, perhaps, had hung there, protecting the wall behind from fading.

In the corner of the room, a panel covering a floor safe was leaning against a nearby desk. They could see only the hole from this angle. He wanted to know if the safe had been opened and relocked, or the door just dropped back. But that could wait.

The bodies were the focus of his attention. The girl lay spread-eagled on her back, face up, in a pool of blood emanating from a hole in her upper leg. The entry wound was visible. Michael knew immediately that the shot had taken out the femoral artery. Her father lay across her chest and head, appearing to have toppled over her as he fell. There was a bullet hole and an area of blood on the back of his head. The face was hidden, resting in another pool of blood.

Michael had to resist the impulse to pull the girl's legs together. She was in tight-fitting pink leggings and, legs akimbo, seemed vulnerable and exposed. But he knew better, had seen similar scenes before. Violence leaves victims doubly impacted, losing life and dignity.

"Other than Tydman, who else is here now?"

As Oliver listed the Serious Crime team members already arrived or nearly at the scene, he said. "Ask Erica and Sam to talk to the boy as soon as possible; very gently. She now has interviews and forensics. You lead the search for the perpetrator or perpetrators. Dr. Simon will pin it down, but these deaths are very recent."

DI Erica Kendrick was less experienced than Wastle but held the same rank. DC Samesh Ray was one of two family liaison officers assigned to the Serious Crimes team.

Hicks continued. "All home security cameras on the road, and others in the vicinity; get their data. Door-to-door follow up. Get cars checking all vehicles in and out of the A390 at the east and west junctions. It may be too late, but whoever did this will probably have blood spatters."

He turned, hearing the footsteps incoming as Wastle left. The pathologist, Dr. Annette Simon, gave him the 'we start all over again' look as she took in the scene. She shook her head. "A girl. I hate the ones with young victims." Then she glanced at the man. "Her father, I gather?"

"Indeed. William Howard Harding, D.L."

She looked at him. "Doctor of Letters?"

He shook his head. "A deputy lieutenant of Devon. A ceremonial position, a royal appointment. He was a former civil servant, I gather. Forty-three, born in Tavistock and a widower, now with one son in trauma. That's all I know, at present."

She was crouching now, on one knee near the bodies, opening her case. "Do this one right, Michael, and you get a knighthood. Mess it up and you are in the Tower."

Hicks' phone rang and he answered instantly, listening after identifying himself. A minute later he said, "I'll be back shortly to get an approximate timing, if you could? They've just arrested two bikers eight miles from here with a stash of drugs."

She nodded, saying nothing, lost in her work.

Hicks's parting words were, "Two bikers, a spitting distance from two murders. Either God likes to give us strange coincidences at the worst possible time or something very strange is going on here."

~~

Twenty-five minutes earlier, DC Steve Rollins was driving to the incident, heading south on the A386. Just north of Okehampton, he came around a bend near the aptly named Folly Gate to see a Harley motorcycle dead ahead, coming at him on his side of the road. He felt the kerbside tyres on his Fiesta bump and complain as he moved hard towards the shoulder. The motorbike flashed past him at speed within inches, tilting away as it forced a path back to the correct lane.

It was the emblem on the crash helmet, not the plain black motorcycle coat, which gave him the clue. The two bikes in his wing mirror were reforming into one line as they headed north. Neither was wearing leathers, but the insignia was the D-Crew, a gang operating in the West Country.

Steve had once spent three months assigned to team on a case against the D-Crew, one which had fizzled out. After cursing the pair, he drove on. He had more urgent things to do, in Tavistock. But he called it in, doubting anything would come of it.

It was a pair of uniformed officers behind him who had the sighting of the flying biker.

They had been in Hatherleigh, at a junction, waiting to turn north on the A386. Two blaring horns and a sound of crumpled metal drew the officer in the passenger seat's attention. A hundred metres away, the biker flew in an arc, narrowly missing the evergreen in the centre of the roundabout. The police officer winced as he saw the rider land on the surrounding concrete border. The police car turned south instead of north and called in the accident.

The lead rider had been looking back at his buddy. As he refocused on the road ahead, he was blinded by the sun reflecting off the windshield of a vehicle on the roundabout. At his speed, he knew he would need to bank the bike to get around the curve of the roundabout. God help anyone who got in his way.

On the roundabout, now in the shade provided by the tree, he ignored the blaring horn of the vehicle that had right of way. He pushed the Harley into the turn – too far. His rear wheel lost traction and he slid into the road sign, a chevron of arrows pointing the direction around the circle. There, he parted company with his bike.

His partner behind braked hard. Traffic already on the roundabout cleared the crashed vehicle and left, other than a lorry, which braked and put on its flashers. At least this prevented other vehicles behind him from hitting the bike. The rider who had braked, hesitated. A car behind him blocked that exit route as the police car came on to the roundabout, lights flashing, stopping beside him. He was penned in and going nowhere.

The female officer said, as she got out the car, 'Switch off the bike. Now." Her colleague was moving to check on the injury and she wanted to assist him. The rider looked around, trying to see an easy escape as his bike died. She had reached across and killed the ignition as she removed the key.

"Nice bike. My brother has one. In the back, now."

He stared her out for a second, and then did as he was told.

Her partner, the driver, walked on to the roundabout where the trucker and another motorist were attending the injured rider. His immediate fear was the sight of the face. There may be no face to see.

Courtesy of a good helmet and faceguard, that wasn't the issue. His face was intact, other than the gory tip of his nose. They all could hear the combination of swearing and pain. Both wrists were broken, and the leather riding gloves were oozing blood. There were injuries to his legs also, but the biker was conscious and alive. It was a miracle, the officer thought.

As other officers attended the scene, along with an ambulance to deal with the crash victim, Rollins' message about the pair had been passed on. They searched the men and the bikes. In the saddlebag of the uninjured rider, they found a plastic shopping bag. Inside it was a polythene bag, closed with tape, holding a neatly cut half of a '1008 brick'; half a kilogram of heroin.

Back at Victory House, in the middle of the disciplined movements of people in white coveralls and police uniforms, DI Oliver Wastle stood waiting. Hicks was talking on his phone to someone, a superior officer. From the tension in Hick's voice, it clearly wasn't Superintendent Kettle, Hick's boss. They were on first name terms, no 'sirs' involved.

When he closed the call, DCI Hicks stood still, staring into the distance. Wastle looked on, waiting.

'Deputy Chief Constable Billings, Oliver."

"Dougie wanted an update?"

"Yes, in brief."

He paused, obviously mulling over whether to say more. He looked at Oliver. "And he mentioned Catrin Sayer; our new Superintendent Sayer."

Oliver recalled Sayer as he first saw her years ago, a detective sergeant. He had collected her from the hotel in Falmouth during the Janis Mitchell case. They were equal rank then. Now she was way ahead of both him and Hicks.

In Falmouth, after initially getting on the wrong side of Hicks, which it was easy to do back then, the team had solved the case. Sayer was a good copper. They had worked well together. Catrin had seen the clues in the art involved. Then she had disappeared back to London, to be followed shortly thereafter by one of their techies, Chris Treneer.

Oliver responded, "Catrin? I saw her around a few times since she started. We talked once, caught up a bit."

Hicks grimaced slightly. "She's come a long way."

Oliver said quietly, "I wouldn't want her current job, though, despite the pay and rank. Or her name."

The Grim Reaper. Where the nickname came from, no-one said. But it was an ominous prediction of her assumed role with the Devon and Cornwall Police.

Hick's face was unreadable. "For you, as you know her. Not for others yet. Billings had caught up on your first report, about the safe robbed and the art missing. He is giving her the case, instead of Kettle."

Oliver's eyes widened. "We'll report to Catrin? That's a turn-up for the books."

"He is just off to ask her to do it."

"Ask? Since when did choice come into it? You and I get told to come to this, at the end of the normal day. We'll be here half the night."

Hicks smiled at his colleague's expression, carefully making sure only Wastle saw it. You don't smile around a murder scene.

"Since you get to be a VIP from the Met, I guess."

Oliver wondered how his boss was taking it.

Michael gave a questioning look. "And only half the night? You're always the optimist. Let's check in with DS Lough. See what lies those bikers are telling Luffy."

6 BILLINGS

Three months into her project, Catrin Sayer was finishing work in the police headquarters in Exeter before heading home for the weekend, trying to refocus on the evening chores ahead.

It had been a tough Friday, and she had spent enough personal energy on her new job for today. Yet, she sat in her car and couldn't drive off.

Even the sight of the late-autumn flush of coppery and gold leaves falling didn't raise her spirits. Frustration led to tears as she sat there, wondering again why she had not chosen the position offered in Finchley. That would be something familiar, something which provided her some respite for a while.

She was her own worst enemy, Catrin decided.

The morning Task Force meeting had reviewed the year one phase of the proposed restructuring plan. In preparation, the consultants had run the numbers through their system. Ursula Otley kicked off the team meeting with their top conclusions. The current proposals would never give a basis for progress to the three-year financial goals. In one area, it amounted to excessive reduction, but in two other areas it fell short.

By the end of the morning discussion, tempers had flared. Two team members were in conflict. A disparaging remark was made about the competence of the consultants. As chairperson, Sayer had to use her leadership skills repeatedly to bring things back on track.

One of the Task Force members, DCI Hayden, had put his concerns about her own role politely, but brutally.

"Ma'am, my objection is that you know nothing of our operations, or some of our challenges. This isn't London. The coastline policing framework was developed over many years, a decade at least. We have hundreds of miles to cover. It shouldn't be touched."

Catrin had shot straight back at him. "I'm here because I can ask those questions. I am not saying the framework is right or wrong. Given the results we reviewed earlier, I am asking if it is effective and efficient. How can we increase that efficiency? That is our remit."

She looked around the table, at the mix of officers holding chief inspector and superintendent rank. Finally, she glanced at her vice-chair, Chief Superintendent Leslie Henry. Police officers read faces well. About half of the table, leaving out the consultants, were onside with Hayden.

In the momentary silence, Dr. Otley said quietly, "The questions are about numbers, not individuals or teams. We need them to process our options for discussion at the next meeting, not to argue their merit. Please give our consultancy a chance to do our job and support you."

She sounded so reasonable and confident; most heads nodded. They moved on.

Sitting in her car now, Catrin wondered if she would

ever develop the conciliatory skills that Otley kept demonstrating. Catrin was a team player, happy with people around her. Several years ago, her teams in Operation Undertow had moved quickly through their wariness about a new, younger boss with a Welsh accent. They warmed to her, supported her, even when decisions were tough. She had supported them, too. But they knew from day one that she was the boss.

Here, her authority was different. It appeared no-one had overcome the wariness, not the Task Force members nor her peers. People wondered if she was a twelve-month wonder, a stranger from London full of Metropolitan ways. The general population of HQ kept their distance. A sudden turn in a corridor revealed the watchers and finger-pointers. She wasn't one of them, the signs conveyed, despite the uniform. They weren't sure what she was, other than someone assigned to run a team that would change the lives of many of them.

Her office administrator, Clarissa Saunders, had called her 'Ma'am' until Catrin said, "You can call me Catrin. I would prefer it."

Saunders had looked serious for a moment. "Super-intendent Lowell always liked to be 'sir', Ma'am."

"I like to be me. So Catrin, please."

"Yes... Catrin. Then I am not Clarissa. Everyone calls me Clarry. Just in here, though?"

Catrin looked at her. "Just everywhere. We talk twenty or thirty times a day, for heavens sake."

Clarry smiled, to herself it seemed. "Right, Catrin. Now, I came in to see if you wanted more coffee?"

Catrin shook her head, looking at her mug, one third drunk, with signs of it going cold. "My last team discover-ed I have a mission in life; letting coffee get cold. I'll stick with this, thanks."

It helped to be normal with Clarry. But she was only one person.

In the car, she dabbed away the tears of frustration, blew her nose, then sat up straight. She had a job to do, and get through it, she decided. In these times, she should be grateful that she had a job at all. She took a deep breath and set off home.

Chris had claimed he had a good day, when she checked in with him just before leaving. She would judge that herself when she saw him. She could tell from the eyes and the breathing rather than his statements. Mair was being good, too, he told her. He had even started preparing the dinner, in as much as they subscribed now to a meal delivery service. That rankled him a bit. In London, he had been fussy about preparing meals from scratch when he cooked.

Tomorrow would be another day, and the bright spot was that she had the weekend off.

Several hours later, those thoughts came back, then evaporated into the distance, where they vanished. Within minutes, she knew her life was going to get a lot harder again.

Deputy Chief Constable Douglas Billings had called, asking, "Can I stop by? It will save you coming back, but we need to talk urgently."

He was on her doorstep within ten minutes.

Catrin had just come downstairs after reading to Mair in bed, watching her fall asleep before the end of the chapter. Kids had hard days, too.

When Doug Billings entered, he declined tea and coffee, but focused on Chris.

"How's it going? Do you miss us?"

Whether it was through briefing or from memory, he knew Chris Treneer had once worked for Devon and Cornwall Police, Catrin saw. In his response, Chris seemed far more at ease with Billings than Catrin felt.

The senior officer suddenly focused on her. "Two things bring me here. First, your profile includes art crime expertise. No, don't go, Chris, just take this as if you were back in harness."

After stopping Chris from moving, he focused on Catrin. "You won't have heard, but we have a major incident, a double murder and art theft near Tavistock. One of the victims is a member of the county lieutenancy, a deputy lieutenant, William Harding. The other is his twelve-year-old daughter, Ashley."

She shook her head. "No, sir. People aren't exactly chatty with me. We have discussed that. I have been in meetings all day."

He focused on her. "Yet you are – or were – one of this country's top art crime investigators, I am told. At least, one who is not working in the private sector."

She wasn't quite sure what to say.

Chris said, "She is that."

Catrin responded, "I have been away from it for well over four years now. But I do have a lot of experience with art crime, that's true."

"Hicks hasn't identified the art that's missing yet, but he will."

"Michael Hicks?"

He nodded. "DCI Hicks. You worked together, he said, years ago, on the Mitchell case."

It took her back.

Billings went on, "The girl was shot in the upper leg, the father in the head. If they had both been executed, I would see it differently, but currently we see this as a robbery gone wrong. Early days, I know, but if I'm right, the items stolen will be a primary focus of the investigation. An art theft with disastrous consequences."

Cluing in that he wanted her involved with the investigation, she was interested, but thrown. A murder of a senior county dignitary had its own ramifications, of course. Art crime was her main experience in terms of her years at the Met but involvement in it now wasn't the reason she was in Devon.

Before he clarified his intent, he switched back to Chris. "It would screw up any regular hours for a while, or longer. How does that sit with you, and your health, your recovery? Like, this weekend will be all work."

He moved his eyes constantly between them as he addressed Catrin. "It was an element of your decision on moving here, you made that clear."

It was Catrin's expression that made something in Chris respond so strongly. For months now, he had been 'the patient', supported by his wife and friends. His mood, fired by fatigue and pain, had run the daily gamut of gratitude and frustration. He focused on her.

"Catrin, you should do this, no matter what. You are a detective at heart, a good one. This is something familiar, and needs doing. Right, Doug?"

Billings nodded slowly as Catrin's eyes widened slightly at the sudden familiarity. He was still focused on Catrin. "I think so. Some regular police work might ground you better here."

He smiled. "My wife's a Treneer. They are like the mafia, Treneers, thick as thieves."

Chris added, deadpan, "It will stop her mollycoddling me." He turned serious. "I'm so bloody tired of... this, of being tired. We will handle whatever comes up. Won't we?"

Catrin looked at her husband, seeing his resolve, then turned to her senior officer.

Billings continued, "I want you to take overall charge. Michael will continue as the SIO, reporting to you. Rank matters. So does the complexity of this crime. Two deaths, art theft and already some additional elements; bikers with drugs."

There was the difference, thought Catrin. Hicks would be the Senior Investigating Officer. She would direct him.

He paused. "We will have Chief Superintendent Henry take up the slack on the Task Force. Les can stand in for you for the first day or so next week, but you will still lead it. Once this investigation is up and running, you will handle both operations."

Seeing the surprise on her face, he added, "And I know you never had a leadership role in a major homicide investigation before. Michael has no prior involvement with art theft either, he said. This case will be highly visible to the media and a lot of others in this county."

He stood, checking his wristwatch without any subtlety.

"The Met said they wanted to stretch your experience. Leadership of two entirely different projects; well, that will do that. Will you take it on? Yes, or no? I am giving you the choice right now before I talk to anyone else."

Catrin gave the only answer that would work. "Yes, I will." She bit her tongue. This man wouldn't want caveats, or qualifiers, or 'I will do my best'.

He stood there, nodding, the weight of it all on his shoulders, she could see. "Thank you. I'll leave you to your supper now. I'm on my way to meet up with the Chief Constable, to head over to see the Lord Lieutenant. I'll let them know and fill Michael in on the way over."

As he turned, he added, "Don't do anything on it

tonight, other than sort out your agenda. It will give Michael Hicks time to adjust and do what he does best, the management of a crime scene and the response. He is up to his eyes, as you can imagine. This will test him as much as you."

He gave a bleak smile. "The Task Force is about change and adaptation to future needs. Well, I guess I am doing some of that myself, now. Be at their morning briefing at eight-thirty tomorrow and prepare to be with Michael as you lead the press briefing at ten."

As he shook hands with Chris, he wished him a speedy recovery. "Sorry for ruining your plans. Life is like that, at present, isn't it? You just get well, or that sister of yours will be on to my wife, giving me hell."

As he reached the door he said, "Catrin, call Les Henry, tell him you have talked to me, but ask him to take over the Task Force until you find yourself free. It will give you a window to rebalance your workload. And thank you again."

He seemed to gaze out from the doorway, not at his car but out across to trees at sunset. The reflections off the river below enhanced the silhouettes of the trees.

"This will be one of the largest investigations in our patch in a while."

With that ominous prediction, he was off into the darkening night.

Left alone, it was Chris who spoke first. "You can do this, I know. I hope Michael Hicks can."

He had worked on cases with Hicks and knew the man to be territorial and controlling. But neither he nor Catrin had any contact with the detective in recent years.

She said, "I'll be working all hours, this weekend and beyond. There is Mair to consider, I had no time to think."

Chris responded firmly, "My mum is in Penzance and Jenifer and Mason are in Falmouth. We have a spare bedroom if someone stays to help. And long Covid symptoms can't last forever. At least, I hope not. I'll deal with all that. You do what you need to do."

Suddenly there was the old pre-Covid Chris in his voice and eyes. It caught her by surprise. His energy may not last the evening, she thought, but she was stirred by it, encouraged. As she hugged him, she whispered, "Right. You are right, as usual."

He gave her a suspicious look. "As usual. Don't you mean, 'for once'?"

She smiled. "This time, anyway."

Seconds later, Catrin pulled out her phone and called Clarry. Could she come in early tomorrow, unplanned?

Clarry Saunders found her weekend in upheaval, too. But, she noted, there was an energy in her boss's voice. Hearing about the developments, Clarry felt like she was working for a police officer again, not a reluctant administrator.

7 BRIEFING

Ironically, apprehensive about the changes, Catrin slept like a log.

The following morning, as she walked into the Serious Crimes Operations area, over twenty officers and support staff were present. Some were in uniform but most dressed in plainclothes. A few looked as fresh as her, while others were tired, still wearing the clothes they wore yesterday. After the briefing, those officers would be heading home, grabbing some sleep and a shower.

The noise level dropped as she entered, but the expressions gave it away. If any uniformed officer at her level and not part of the team entered, the conversations would pause momentarily. In this case, she was already typecast as the outsider, part of the structural review. Several of the faces showed momentary displeasure.

She ignored it, heading over to Hicks, standing talking to two others. He gave her a mix between a smile and a look of pity.

"Ma'am. These are DI Erica Kendrick and DI Oliver Wastle. You know Oliver. I have informed them."

As she shook hands with the two officers, he asked, "Shall I announce it, or you? We can start whenever."

They were watching for her reaction, she saw. Hesitate, and she was lost.

"I'll open, thank you, Michael. Let's get going."

Keep control of the agenda, she thought.

DI Kendrick called out for silence and attention, letting the teams know they were getting started. As people focused on her and then Michael Hicks, the noise dropped completely. Some took seats and others stood, leaning on desks or against walls. Hicks gave Catrin a look, then a small hand flourish.

Catrin moved forward a pace.

"I am Superintendent Catrin Sayer. Most of you won't know me, but DCI Hicks, DI Wastle and I have worked together before, years ago. From some of your faces, you know already that I have another job here. As of last night, I also have line responsibility for this investigation, led by DCI Hicks as the SIO. Michael, who will take us through the update, you or one of your team?"

Hicks responded, "I'll kick it off and pass it to Oliver and Erica."

Catrin turned to face the operations board. "Let's get going."

No speeches or rallying calls. Straight to work.

It was the expression on the face of a young female constable in uniform that stopped the flow. The appalling sight was the image of William Harding's head. DI Kendrick was in the process of reviewing the forensic reports and had commented on the angles of the two gunshots. She had moved on to the probable position of the shooter at each point.

A colleague near the young officer asked, "Are you

alright, Deanna?"

PC Deanna Burrows, white as a sheet, nodded, "It's not the same as training, though... but so much blood and other tissue. I'm OK."

Part of the man's skull and face were missing, the fracture and fragmentation caused as the round exited the front of the head.

They made Burrows sit down in a freshly vacated seat.

The older officer who had observed Deanna's reaction looked at Sayer. "And you, Ma'am?"

His face was more impassive now, more a challenge; it was a question about her rather than any concern about nausea.

Catrin responded clearly, at a level all could hear. "I am horrified by it – the apparently deliberate executions of an unarmed man and a girl."

She focused on DI Kendrick. "Any read yet on the possible weapons?" Her voice was even, showing no emotion.

"No, Ma'am."

Catrin asked, "Do the calculations you just mentioned give an approximate height for the shooter?"

In theory, it should, she recalled from her training.

"I was coming to that, yes. Tall, just under six feet. They are refining it now."

Catrin thought for a moment. "Enough facts. Can someone give us the run through, as the pathologist and forensics best see it, please?"

Erica Kendrick looked at Michael, who said, "Erica, you do that. This is all still provisional."

Catrin said, "I know, Michael. But I want people to have the same picture of the crime."

It was a fair point, Hicks knew. He would have done that later anyway and Erica had belaboured the forensic details somewhat. With Burrows' response, moving to the big picture was appropriate.

Erica Kendrick pointed at the image of the scene.

"There were two guns and two shooters, or one who moved about a lot and used two weapons. Ashley was standing near her father, at the safe. First, while the safe wasn't open, an assailant shoots her in the leg. She falls this way, thrashing with pain or shock.

"Later, seconds or perhaps a minute or so, but not longer, the assailant then moved here, or a second assailant came forward. William Harding had opened the safe by then. Ashley's blood is on his fingers, but none of it transferred to the keypad, so he had opened that first. He then turned back to help his daughter. There are no blood traces inside the safe, so Harding didn't remove anything there. The shooter did, later.

"There are marks on Ashley's leg of two sets of fingerprints opposite each other. Harding and another person, perhaps the first shooter or another person present, were trying to stop the bleeding. Then that person pulled away hard, shown by the blood streak here, and the gunman shot the father. Harding was focused on helping his daughter. The bullet entered the back of the head and exited through the side of his cheek. Over here it penetrated the flooring. Once we have the bullets analysed, we may know more about the weapons."

It was DS Tydman who said, "It seems as if Ashley could have been unconscious or in pain, witnessing close up her father's death."

Kendrick said, "I just pray she was gone by then, or unconscious, at least."

Catrin looked around the room as the faces, seeing the reaction. She had wanted the explanation given that way. The dry formalities of bullet trajectories and blood splatter patterns did not capture it for her. This crime was about people, not abstract victims. She sat for a moment, thinking about that, then looked at Hicks. 'What next' her eyes conveyed.

Hicks said, "Erica, your team stays on the forensics. Nothing has come out of the area search yet. Let's move now to the stolen items, then to the bikers. There is a time limit on charging them."

Into the art, then. Catrin's area of expertise.

Oliver Wastle took up the brief again. "We now have a list of items stolen, perhaps incomplete. John?"

He added as an afterthought, "DC John Peart, Ma'am."

Peart stood. "Around five hundred pounds in notes were usually kept in the safe. We will check Harding's bank withdrawals for any identifiable serial numbers. Also missing was a ring in a box. It belonged to his late wife, a gold ring with a precious stone of some sort. He was saving it for his daughter, Harding's sister said. Papers in the safe were scattered, as if thrown out."

Willam Harding's sister, Eve Wansbury, and her husband, Trevor, had traveled over from Plymouth to look after Adam Harding.

Peart continued, "On the walls were three paintings. PC Reimer has the details so far. Jan and I got all this all from Harding's sister, too. Jan?"

The uniformed constable stood and looked at her notes. "No images of the art yet, I am afraid. The sister said there was a Wallis, a Cornish artist, Alfred Wallis, valued at £8500 when bought, but worth quite a bit more now, I think. It is a harbour view and will look like a child's painting; it is what's called naive or primitive art. I'll follow up. The two others were more recent purchases from a local artist called Nana Lee, so we will check with her after the briefing; again, to get images for your use."

As she finished, DC Peart asked, "Any questions?"

Catrin had been impressed with the concise but accurate summaries on the works by the uniformed constable. She had questions and observations, but time was passing.

Reimer sat down as Hicks stood. "Peart, you and Reimer stay with the art theft and the ring." He looked at Sayer, who nodded. "Talk to the superintendent later, after the briefing, she may have more input. It's her expertise."

He focused on the group. "The superintendent used to do art crime investigation at Scotland Yard."

He pointed at a middle-aged man. "Jason, the bikers." He looked at Catrin, as the newcomer. "DS Jason Lough, Ma'am."

DS Lough brought forward three photographs. One was a police record image, another clearly taken earlier of a sullen man, his head on a pillow. The third image showed the drug haul found on the bike.

Lough started with the photo from police records. "Ryan Smith, a full patch member of D-Crew. He has been inside once for drug possession and distribution. He was the one who stayed on his bike."

He looked at Sayer and pointed to the map on the board. "They were sighted here, riding dangerously, at high speed. His pal 'Stu', Stuart Bains, was just made a D-Crew half-patch member. He came off his bike in the middle of the mini roundabout, here."

His finger stabbed another point on the map.

"Two broken wrists, a broken ankle, and some repair work with skin grafts needed on his knees and nose. He wore a proper helmet. It saved his head. He is now at Derriford."

The big hospital in Plymouth, Catrin recalled.

"The funny bit is this. Well, strange, for me." He put up the photo of the drug pack. "The half-brick packaging isn't anything we have seen before, the drug people say. A sample of its contents is being analysed. Hopefully we will track down the source, but it may be someone new to us."

"Also..." His finger stabbed again at the photo. "This edge is just taped over. That's crap, carrying heroin, unsealed. Nobody does that. His pannier had the narcotics dog in full reaction two yards from the bike. This biker gang knows how to ship drugs. They don't move unsealed packages."

Hicks intervened. "The big question is, are the two crimes linked? As Luffy said, this one is not a usual catch, in terms of the drug packaging. And it was only eight miles away from the scene of the murders."

He stood, looking at the team for a second before adding, "Something is off."

Catrin was watching the group now, waiting for someone to raise the issue on her mind. No one did.

She spoke up. "How often have we, and I mean any police service in the UK, taken a full patch biker into custody holding half a kilo of heroin?"

"Exactly!" said Lough.

There was silence, then a young officer said, "Luffy, there have been raids where bikers had lots of drugs on the premises."

He had responded to his partner, Catrin noticed, not to her.

She nodded. "True enough. But on the road?"

She had been keeping an eye on Lough. She gave him her full attention now.

He pursed his lips. "You are right, Ma'am. We don't. They may ride to keep tabs on the drug shipment, or on the carrier set up to do the job, but they are off out of it as soon as there is any sign of trouble."

Hicks asked, "And what does that mean to you? To anyone?"

Lough gave as good as he got. "This wasn't business as usual, wasn't a normal operation for D-Crew. It was different somehow."

Hicks added, "Different enough, perhaps, to give it a link to the Victory House deaths in some way. But we won't be getting much out of either Smith or Baines, I think. Lough, you lead on the interviews of the bikers. We need medical clearance for Baines before any interview, but you handle those aspects."

Catrin checked the time, then said, "In any event, Michael, we will talk to CPS and lay charges for possession of the drugs against Smith and Baines and oppose bail. That will be after the press briefing."

Hicks asked, "Do you want to follow up on the art directly?"

Catrin restrained herself. "No. I will meet with DC Peart and PC Reimer to give input as I see it, but they report in here, as you see fit. But that will have to be later today. I want to meet with the family after the press brief. Who is handling that?"

It was an older female officer who raised her hand. "DC Perry. I'm handling the family liaison. Currently my partner DC Samesh Ray is with the boy and the aunt and uncle."

"Sort it for me and DC Hicks as it works for them and my timeline, and let my assistant, Clarry, know. Michael, set them on their way, then you and I will prepare for the press. In my office with media relations, in fifteen, please."

Catrin moved forward. They were all looking at her

now. "No speeches. You know this is a big one. Be vigilant for the press out there when this breaks, how you act, look. I want an update on all areas of the investigation by late afternoon, through DCI Hicks. Thank you."

She turned and walked out of the room.

8 PRESS

"I am Superintendent Catrin Sayer. On my left is Detective Chief Inspector Michael Hicks and beside him is Detective Inspector Erica Kendrick.

"Yesterday, a deputy lieutenant of Devon, William Harding, and his daughter Ashley, age twelve, were killed. The crime took place in the family home in Tavistock. We believe that one or more assailants were present. Several items were stolen, including artwork and jewelry. At this point, we have no suspect or suspects identified.

"The murder of two innocent people in their own home is a shocking and tragic event, doubly so given the death of a child. William Harding devoted much of his life to the service of the people of Devon. He was recognised for that by his appointment as a deputy lieutenant of this county. Our condolences go to the family of the deceased.

"A major investigation is underway to find and arrest the person or persons who committed this crime. We seek the cooperation of the public, asking for any information that may help us. Anyone in the vicinity of the A390 and the A386 near Tavistock College between noon yesterday and seven p.m. may have seen something. If you have information, or dashboard camera recordings made in the area, they could assist our inquiries. Also, anyone else with any relevant information should come forward now. There is a telephone number on the screen for you to contact us. I emphasise that all information, no matter how trivial you think it may be, will be welcomed. DCI Hicks?"

Catrin sat still, her face serious and impassive, as Michael went into more detail of what he wanted. The press turnout, fuelled by rumour, was large, given they were in Exeter, not London. A lot were freelancers, she thought.

Then she opened the session for questions.

A young journalist asked, "Given the appointment of Mr. Harding to the lieutenancy, has the Palace been informed?"

Michael opened his mouth and shut it again; it was out of left field.

Catrin filled in. "The Chief Constable has spoken with the Lord Lieutenant, Sir Neil Trotter. There are procedures in place."

"How did they die? Can you tell us?"

Michael responded, "Both victims received gunshot wounds. We will know more after the pathologist completes their investigation."

An older reporter asked, "During the pandemic, Devon and Cornwall has had a lot more people move here. Is this an example of big city crime moving in, and if so, how are the police dealing with that?"

Hicks turned to look at Catrin.

She stayed clear of that one. "This was a violent, absolutely tragic event, whatever its origin. The team assembled to investigate this crime will have all the resources it needs. We will be diligent in our efforts to track down the perpetrators."

"Jenny Ko, for the BBC. There was an incident nearby, a road accident, around the time you mentioned. Is this connected?"

Hicks answered that. "Officers responding to the incident in Tavistock did encounter two motorcyclists in a road vehicle accident, yes. One man was taken to hospital and both riders are currently in custody. No charges have been laid at present."

Sensing that the main questions had been addressed, Catrin closed it down. "We will advise you of any significant developments in this case. Again, we encourage the public to come forward with any information they have by calling the number given. That will be all for the present. Thank you."

She stood and, with her team members behind her, left the room.

Ten minutes later, Catrin found the time to be alone with Michael Hicks for the first time. She simply beckoned him into her office and closed the door.

She asked, "How do you feel about this? Me instead of Kettle?"

Hicks paused a moment. "Tim Kettle and I work well together. I know him. You and I – well, we got on fine at the end of the case we worked together. But that was years ago. I am concerned about your relevant experience, or lack of it, despite your career progress. You did ask."

He kept his face neutral.

She kept her eyes on him. "Fair enough. Between you and me, it's still Catrin. And yes, I went to Cambridge for a year. I've done the senior management courses at the

Met. I know my role with you on this case, but I haven't lived it before. What I have done since we last worked together is spend over two years leading a team of around thirty officers in the Met's Serious and Organized Crime Command, mainly in undercover work. That's about the size of your current resources."

Hicks nodded, obviously not swayed much by the news.

"I tell you this because my boss throughout that time was a Superintendent Gerry Lauder. The first thing Gerry told me was that it wasn't his job to lead the team, that was mine. What he did was give me my operating boundaries, which could change. Then he made sure that no one else got in the way of me doing my job, inside or outside the Met. It worked for me; does that work for you?"

Hicks nodded slowly. "Not quite the formal job description, but that's more or less how Tim and I work, so yes."

"Fine. I saw your look when I pushed Lough on the heroin packaging. I apologise; it was not my place to do that. I recall how prickly you were back on the Mitchell case at the outset. So that we are clear, I won't do anything to usurp your authority. But I will throw in ideas if they occur to me, just as you would expect any team member to do."

Hicks nodded and seemed to relax a little. Clearly it had been a bugbear. "Hard to give up the reins as a DCI?"

She smiled ruefully. "A little. Now I am leading a group where conciliation is the watchword, not command, but that's another matter."

A memory surfaced of a comment about Commander Moore, years ago, being too inclined to get 'hands-on', wanting to do interviews. Now she knew how Karen felt.

Her face turned serious. "Gerry Lauder had one iron-bound expectation of me and the other team lead who reported to him. There was to be no blindsiding, ever. Keep him in the loop on the good and the bad, always. I want that from you, too."

"I can do that. Yes."

"Then let's work well together to get the bastards who killed the Hardings into the cells."

~~

In the Wansbury family home in Plymouth, they met with the survivor of the attack and his aunt and uncle. The ten-year-old boy was looking as desolate and bereft as Catrin expected. Adam Harding was sitting on the sofa, leaning into his aunt next to him, his eyes fixed on a photoframe he was holding. Family photos rotated through at intervals.

Trevor Wansbury, his uncle, hovered nearby. DC Ray, the family liaison officer, introduced them. "Adam, this is Superintendent Sayer and Detective Chief Inspector Hicks. They are leading the investigation."

Adam looked first at Hicks in his suit, then at Catrin in her uniform. He took in her face as she said hello, shaking hands with the relatives before moving closer to Adam.

She asked softly, "How are you holding up, Adam?"

"I don't know. Numb, mainly. You are Welsh, are you, not from here?"

She nodded. "Yes, from South Wales. My husband was born in Cornwall, though. He used to work for the Devon and Cornwall Police."

Adam nodded, accepting that as the logic for her role. He looked at Hicks.

"You are going to get them, aren't you?"

He had only been released from the hospital a few hours earlier and hadn't been interviewed yet. That interview was set for the afternoon, with two people. One was an officer with specialist training in interviewing children in trauma. The other person present would be a child psychologist.

The uncle spoke up. "They will do everything possible, Adam, I am sure."

Catrin responded, "We have a lot of experienced people working to do that right now, yes. We all want to catch whoever did this."

He had shifted his focus from Hicks back to her, searching her face, as if that would help in some way.

"How did you get that scar; in a fight?"

Catrin's memento of a run-in with a gang enforcer many years ago was a white line on her left cheek. It was more visible now, standing out from her suntanned face.

Eve Wansbury said quietly, "Adam–," as Catrin responded anyway. As she did, she sat at the other end of the sofa and turned sideways to face him.

"It was a long time ago. I was a police constable. A man hit me with a metal bar as I tried to arrest him. But he was put in prison for what he did to me and to others."

She didn't take her gaze off Adam. She wasn't breaking eye contact until she saw he was ready to.

His eyes teared over. "You must have been brave. I couldn't help. I hid in the closet as the man told me. You fought someone and I couldn't do anything. I was so frightened."

Catrin reached out and took his hand, holding the photo frame with him.

"From what we know so far, Adam, I don't think there

was anything you could have done. But you can help now. Two of DCI Hicks' team are coming to see you, to talk to you about what happened. If you can do that, tell them everything you remember, even the small useless bits, it could help us a lot. Will you do that? Even if it is scary and upsetting, will you try?"

He nodded, suddenly eager. She knew his emotions would be all over the place.

She said, "Bravery is not as simple as we see it in movies and TV shows. Helping us now will be very brave of you."

She squeezed his hand slightly and let go, standing again, looking at Hicks, who was just taking it all in.

Adam put the frame down and stood himself, holding out his hand to shake theirs. It was a sudden politeness, formal and unnecessary, first with Hicks and then her. As Catrin took his small hand and let him lead the handshake, she placed her other hand on his shoulder. She turned her head suddenly, averting her eyes from the child and his relatives behind.

DC Ray was face-to-face with his new superintendent, met for the first time, her eyes moist but with a look he could not read at first on her features. Not anger, nor sympathy, he thought. Then he understood what he saw, the eyes narrowing, the compression of the lips. It was resolve, a very intense resolve.

He had seen it before. Whatever resolution Superintendent Sayer was making, it tied to this boy. That could only be about seeking justice for Adam.

The moment passed. Her face returned to the neutral expression of a professional police officer.

As Catrin looked back at Adam, blinking, she said as lightly as she could, "You didn't see anyone, did you, Adam? Not a glimpse at all?"

"No. A man, a foreign man in a balaclava, shouted at me to get in the closet. The bedroom door was open. He already had Ashley's phone; I think. I heard it bang in the bathroom. I think he threw it in the toilet. Then he told Ashley to go downstairs."

He can recognize the voice perhaps, she thought, and the man's size and figure. And the eyes. She turned to DC Ray. "Look after him. Michael?"

Hicks nodded, "I've put a car on watch here."

Sayer said to the relatives, "For the media attention after the press coverage. Our call lines are very busy at present. There is a lot of interest from the public, wanting to help us."

DC Ray understood her deflection to the aunt and uncle, and why Hicks had placed a security watch on Adam Harding.

It was the uncle who took them to the door. He said, "Thank you. We are all still reeling. I did the ident-ifications of the bodies earlier, and I am still absorbing that. I hope you make some headway, but I am sure it is hard to say at present."

Hicks grimaced. "We are following every lead. Yes, it is still early, too early, and speculation won't help. There is a lot of forensic evidence to go through also."

"DI Wastle seems very capable. I talked to him at the hospital."

Hicks said, "He is, I assure you."

Wansbury focused on Sayer. "He told me you were an art crime expert, but had also worked in London, dealing with organized crime gangs. I can't believe that Bill would have anything to do with that world."

Catrin replied, "There is no suggestion that he did, Mr. Wansbury. One of the first things we do is check the background of the victims on police records." She paused. "We will keep you informed of progress as best as we can. There are limitations."

She looked back at the door to the lounge. "And I promise, when we find out who did this terrible thing, I will come back myself and talk again with Adam."

9 HALLMARK

It was two p.m. when Clarry told Catrin her schedule had been adjusted. DC Peart and PC Reimer were waiting to brief her about the stolen items.

On their entry, Catrin pointed to the meeting table and as they sat down together, she asked, "What do we have, then?"

Reimer, the uniformed officer, took the lead. "We have images of all three paintings now. The smallest painting is the most valuable, a Wallis, as I said earlier."

She opened a tablet computer, turning it so Sayer could see the images, as she scrolled through.

"Alfred Wallis, yes."

Reimer replied, "Yes, Ma'am. The valuation in the safe states eight thousand five hundred pounds. And an online check suggests that it is worth around twenty thousand now. The two other paintings by Nana Lee are worth about three thousand each."

Her finger moved the images, so that the two abstracts lined up.

"Apparently, Mr. Harding knew her slightly. Lee is

shocked. We just came from talking to her. He bought one work at a charity dinner in a silent auction at a steal of a price. Later, he came to her studio to buy a companion painting, paying the full price, where she talked to him for a few minutes. She has never heard of her art being stolen before."

Catrin had been glancing at the images but also watching the two officers. "Do an inventory of all art in the house and check for anything he bought or sold recently, also. And ask if any art appraisers have visited, if you can."

She looked at the images of the works by Lee. "I don't know her work. Do either of you?"

Peart said, "I don't know anything about art really, I just drew the assignment. Jan did art at university, I knew, so I asked for her to be assigned, too."

Reimer said, "I'm glad to do this with John. No, I know of Lee, but had not seen her art. She can think of no reason for this at all."

"Do a background check on her. I can't see the link, but you need to rule out anything there."

She pointed at the photo of the painting by Alfred Wallis. "Wallis is reasonably well known in the field of British primitivist artists, so interest in this one may be among specialist collectors and dealers, rather than art sellers local to Devon and Cornwall. Check them out. I'll put you in touch with the Art and Antiques Unit at the Met. They have a database of dealer contacts and will help, I am sure, narrow down any specialising in the style."

Catrin opened her phone, to look up a number. "The other item, the jewelry you mentioned?"

Peart said, "A ring, Ma'am. The ring is more interesting; to me, anyway. There were photographs in the safe with a valuation document from 2011, from a jeweller in Plymouth. It may be worth as much as £5,000 at today's prices. It was valued at £3000 then."

Catrin phrased her feedback carefully as she examined the offered images. A gold ring with a single stone, a pink sapphire. There were the standard jeweller's marks on one section inside the band and a separate mark on the other side.

"I am sure DCI Hicks will tell you to contact the jeweller and do background checks on current and former staff. Again, we need to contact known fences who handle stolen art and jewelry."

"We are doing that now, or starting to," replied Peart.

Catrin remarked, as she passed the photo back, "I'm no gemologist, but we knew a few good ones while I was in Art and Antiques. Sapphires can be very hard to read, for valuation."

Almost as soon as she let the photos go, she asked, "That second photo of the ring, the one with the hall-mark. Can I see it again, please?"

They sat in silence as she examined it further. Then without ceremony, she picked up her desk phone and made a call.

"Mark, it's Catrin. Can you spare a moment?"

Whatever the response, she just said, "Yes, I know it is Saturday. I'm not surprised, it's a big one. I have two of my officers with me; they are dealing with the art items stolen and there is something I want to check. I'll put you on speaker. DC Peart, PC Reimer, this is Detective Inspector Mark Harper, head of the Met's Art and Antique Unit."

As their greetings crossed the ether, she went on, "We have several paintings and a ring stolen. I'd like your help in reaching out to dealers and associations. But the primary reason I called you is the jewel in the ring, a single coral pink sapphire. Set in gold, one of the hallmark markings on the band reminds me of the Arabic rings we saw in the Kellerman robbery. Do you recall?"

Mark hesitated. "No. Could it have been between my first assignment and my current one?"

"You are right, now you mention it. It was. John Obi will know about it. But there was a specialist jeweller we used to do the background check on the sapphire, someone based in the Hatton Garden area. He knows that field well. I can see his face, but his name escapes me."

"Frank Hamal, by any chance?"

"Yes, him. Thank you. That's right. Look, I'll give these two your number. If they text you theirs, can you get someone on your team to liaise with them? To go to Frank with the information on the ring? If your officer could do a conference call from there, I would appreciate it. Frank is no use unless you are face to face with him, he gets distracted."

"No problem, we can do that. Glad to help but, as I have you on the line, Catrin, could you pick up?"

She picked up the phone and listened in private. Reimer saw her face fall as she said, 'I'm so sorry. He is such a nice man. I'll get in contact. How is Isabelle doing?"

She listened again and said, "Right, I'll touch base with you in a while. Thanks again for the help – and for letting me know."

Catrin looked at the two young officers, who were clearly sensing that something was wrong. As she wrote out Mark Harper's telephone number to give to Peart, she said, "A former colleague, an American FBI officer, Morley Kerswell. He is in ICU in Paris with Covid. He worked on contract killers for a long time and then came into art crime, which is where I met him. His wife is one of my former team members."

The two officers expressed their sympathies. Sayer stood suddenly, passing the sticky note to Peart, and making the effort to be more upbeat than she felt now.

"Work with the Art and Antiques Unit and, if you can organize it, be part of the conversation with Frank Hamal. That ring marking: there may be more to it. Why would a Devon man have a hand-crafted ring with an Arabic marking, I wonder?"

As Catrin opened the door to let them go, she saw DCI Hindley and Chief Superintendent Henry from the Task Force just arriving.

She finished with, "Feedback to the team, but keep me in the loop if anything else on the art comes up."

As they left and the next two visitors entered, Reimer heard Sayer ask, "So what's the problem?" as the door closed.

John Peart was looking at the note. "She called the head of Art and Antiques at Scotland Yard, just like that, and he answered."

Jan said, "I checked: she used to be the head of Art and Antiques. He probably used to work for her."

As they walked away, Peart added, "That last bit about problems, those two going in as we came out. That must be something about the reorganisation."

Inside her office, Catrin was dealing with a new problem; a rumour resulting from a leak of confidential information. At the back of her mind was the need to call Isabelle Kerswell as soon as she could do so. She had been where Isabelle was now, waiting, with a husband in ICU.

Chris was younger than Morely. And Morely had been

a heavy smoker for years, much earlier in his FBI career. She wondered how he would respond to any treatment they were giving him.

10 TYDMAN

Catrin walked into the evening briefing in the operations room right on time, closing out a call on her mobile. There were one or two looks, but nothing that bothered her. Somehow, in a few hours, she had become accepted as a presence. Whether a welcome one was another matter.

Some of them, working most of the time since the incident, would be hoping for the evening off. None would expect a free Sunday now. Time was passing, and the pressure was on.

She had met half an hour earlier with Michael Hicks and ACC Billings for a short, high-level update, so she had the high points already. Now it was the detail and the interactions of the team members she was observing.

Hicks called for the briefing to start, and she focused on one speaker after another.

DS Lough was up first, still full of energy. Hicks said, "Luffy, you need to get off, I gather. You start."

Lough began with, "Mum and dad's fortieth; I said I would be there, so thanks, boss. Neither of our bikers were communicative – they were full of 'no comments'. Smith, carrying the heroin in his saddlebag, is sitting there, waiting for the charge. In hospital, Baines is denying everything and complaining. He knows nothing about any drugs, he claims."

He shrugged. "We need some leverage with one or other to get them to respond, but I haven't got there yet. I'll keep at it, but we need to charge them soon."

He checked with Hicks who pursed his lips and looked at Sayer.

Catrin said, "First thing tomorrow, you do it. The charge sheets are ready. Both men, for the possession of Class A drugs with intent to supply."

Lough added, "The heroin. I pushed a bit with the lab. The prelim evaluation suggests it is of South American origin. The wrapping is the same as on heroin bricks turning up in North Africa and the Middle East. We'll keep at it."

Lough walked off, picking up his suit jacket before leaving the room.

Sayer glanced across at Peart and Reimer. It was the uniformed officer who returned the look first, a gleam in her eye. Peart gave an almost imperceptible nod. An Arab ring hallmark discussed earlier, and an unusual drug packaging that could have links to the Middle East. Neither Peart nor Reimer had missed the possible link.

DCI Hicks then gave the feedback from the autopsies in subdued terms, to a totally quiet room.

"The blood splatter patterns confirm that the daughter was shot first. Her cause of death was rapid bleedout, from severance of the femoral artery. Ashley would have died within a few minutes. Fingerprints in the dried blood and pre-mortem bruising reveal that two people made futile efforts to stop the bleeding. Some of the prints lifted may be useable, but blood on flesh under pressure results in distortions and smearing. It will take some specialist work, I gather – and time. So far, there are no matches for one set; but initial match of the other prints indicate they are her father's, as we suspected.

"William Harding's death resulted from a single shot to the centre back of head. The bullet emerged from the left cheek, removing part of the bone. He would have died instantaneously. Splatter angles and the path of his collapse tie in with the father assisting his daughter as he was shot. Erica, you have the forensic update?"

Kendrick nodded. "Of particular interest forensically is the safe door, with a digital lock. The fingerprints around the door belong to Harding. The keypad and door front had been wiped quite vigorously, probably with a glove. However, there are traces of DNA other than Harding's on the pad. The current thought is that the glove touched the wearer's own skin and sweat transferred to the pad. Forensics are hopeful that the DNA might be indicative, if we have a suspect and get a DNA sample."

Hicks asked, "No matches currently, I take it?"

"No."

Hicks grimaced, then nodded. "Let's move on to the art theft." He focused on DC Peart.

Peart gave a brief update on the stolen items. "We met with Superintendent Sayer and received her thoughts and suggestions. Jan and I are making enquiries but have no results yet. Through the Super, we are now in touch with the Art and Antiques Unit at the Met, and they are assisting us. The superintendent suggested that the ring may be of Arabic origin and expensive. Someone at the Met is lining us up with a jewelry expert in that area. Nothing else so far, on the paintings."

It was short. Catrin recalled that the news about Morley

had thrown her off track. She hadn't explained her reasoning – and now was not the time to do so.

PC Reimer spoke up. "One of the hallmarks on the ring is characteristic of Arabic tribal symbols of some sort. Right, Ma'am?"

She looked at Sayer.

Cartin responded, "Yes, that's what I thought, but I don't know much about them."

Reimer added, "And we have access to an expert on sapphires now. What reason would William Harding have to be holding an expensive ring with an Arabic marking in his safe?"

DCI Hicks head nodded gently. "Rhona? How is the background check developing?"

The older woman said, "It may tie in. Between 1994 and 2011, Mr. Harding was with the Department of Trade and Industry. He visited several countries in the Middle East regularly, so he may have bought it there. But why it is in the safe when other possessions of value aren't, I can't say. His watch wasn't taken, a Longines, and that is worth a lot."

She mispronounced the watch name, making the 'g' hard, Catrin heard.

DI Kendricks interjected, "That's pronounced Long-ines, if anyone is discussing it." Her pronunciation of the French name was accurate.

"The killer may not have wanted to touch the body," came from someone.

Rhona persisted. "May be. But checking the house, a burglary for the paintings doesn't fit for me. They spent the time to take three paintings from the same room but did not take a watch there, nor other equally valuable items in other rooms. I think they came for something specific, the ring or another item held in the safe. They may have added the paintings simply to confuse the investigation."

The officer at the whiteboard wrote, 'Art theft a cover-up or items snatched in panic?'. Catrin thought she was doing a good job of capturing points.

It was DS Tydman, perhaps the oldest officer in the room, who spoke next. He said, "I've been thinking about the incoming responses from the public. There is some build-up of the biker sightings. Other vehicles reported are mainly one-offs, but several calls cluster around a sighting of a red Skoda on the A390 that appears to have parked for a while. We don't have a reg number yet, but what if we have a two-part event?"

People were focused on Tydman now.

"Suppose the bikers are involved, but not in the robbery or killing? They meet with the assailants before the robbery. Their takeaway is half a brick of heroin. It's a theory."

Hicks nodded at Tydman and said to the scribe, "Capture it."

A younger officer sounded doubtful. "Bikers usually deliver the drugs and take away the money, not the other way around."

Tydman said evenly, "True. But I'm going with the facts we have, not the expectations. Bikers also move and handle illegal guns. What if they delivered the guns and the heroin was the payment, instead of money?"

Catrin could see some of the other officers nodding at that idea. Tydman was right; it could fit the facts. She spoke up. "Then we recheck the bikes, not for heroin, but for any indication of firearms being carried."

Hicks nodded. "Luffy's gone. You follow up on that, Rollins. Get SOCOs on to it as soon as possible."

It was a female officer in her thirties who spoke up next. "DC Jackie Neil, Ma'am. There is a rumour going around. Officers within two years of full-service qualification are in line for early retirement offers. If there isn't enough take-up, forced redundancies are being considered. Is that true?"

As some gave Jackie a pained look, others nodded, glad to see the rumour aired. Neil addressed her colleagues. "Well, we were all talking about it. I want to know."

Michael Hicks looked at Sayer, his eyes showing his displeasure, but she said to him, "I'll speak to that. This once."

Catrin stood and moved to a central position. "Jackie, I'll give you an answer. This morning I met briefly with Adam Harding, so my first reaction was, frankly, irritation. After this, I don't want discussion in these briefings of any issue other than the investigation. That applies to everyone.

"But you all are working hard, and I know the stress of organisational change. I've been through it more than once, at the receiving end. What I can tell you officially is – nothing. The Task Force makes recommendations to the Chief Constable only."

She paused.

"I was made aware of the rumour mid-afternoon. As you may recall from the original notice about its formation, the Task Force has a mandate to draw up a five-year plan. Our proposal must cover the needs of our counties as we go forward. Part of that process is to develop a range of short term and long term 'what if' scenarios. Each scenario requires a needs assessment, fulfilment options and costs.

"As the chair, I can tell you that no decision has been reached on any element. At present, we have no coherent plan. Many ideas are on the table. We are discussing those, but still have a long way to go. It is my job, my other job, to push that to its conclusion. And I will do that."

Catrin had moved closer to the whiteboard. She pointed. "But here, my focus is on this traumatized, bereft boy, these victims, this tragedy. My goal is the arrest of the perpetrators. Nothing else. Understood?"

As some people nodded, others looking dissatisfied. She said, "DCI Hicks, next steps, please."

Hicks took up the lead. He reviewed the developments and assigned tasks for people working into the evening. He closed with confirming that all officers would be expected to be present at the Sunday morning briefing.

As they broke up and Catrin moved to speak to Hicks alone, PC Reimer headed past. Catrin said to her, "Thank you for the input on the possible origin of the ring. If William Harding has been to the region, it may be a link, or turn out to be nothing."

Reimer paused. "I am glad to work on the theft part because of the art. I was going to say that this afternoon, but the call with DI Harper –. Well, it ended differently."

With that confusing outburst for Hicks to witness, she blushed and moved away. He gave Catrin a querying look.

"I called my old team for the support, as she said. One of them, Isabelle Howlett, retired and married a retired FBI agent we knew. He is in ICU with Covid. A lovely man."

"Catrin, it's the times. You dealt with the rumour well. Thank you. If anyone raises anything off-topic again I will shut it down immediately. They all heard your reason."

He reflected a moment. "Yes, Reimer was keen to work on the art aspects. Peart wants more of the action.

She reminds me of you, back when."

"She is interested in art, I just heard."

"Yes. Don't know what, though. But she's enthusiastic about it, like you were, when I was putting you down."

It was his first sign of humour since they had met up again.

She smiled at the memory. He had been a royal pain in the rear, then. "And I was giving you lip, in return."

She grimaced. "I'm off. A meeting to deal with the rumour."

~~

That evening, Mair was in tears after her talk to her 'sister' Lili on their tablets. "She has a Chocolate Bear and Aunty Melanie has one for me but it's at home! I miss her. I miss my room and Mr. Andrews at school. I want Lili! I want my new teddy!"

Catrin looked at Chris. The brand of fluffy dark brown stuffed bears was so popular they were impossible to find. Jean had said she would work on it, with the 'mafia'. Not the illegal variety, just the other shops in Spitalfields Market. They knew East End distribution systems intimately. It seems that Jean had been successful, but Lili had found out and turned whistleblower.

Catrin talked her daughter through the tantrum. As Chris finished preparing supper, she told Mair they would go soon to visit her aunties and Lili for a long weekend. She wasn't sure when, given her extra responsibilities, but they needed to plan on it, she thought.

Mair considered this sop carefully. "I'll tell Lili I am coming to see her. I can get my bear!"

"Let's make sure I can get away first."

She and Mair would go, by train, she thought. She

would also fix up with Jean to do some decoration of a new ceramic work they had been designing together.

As Chris called that the meal was ready, Mair relented a little. "I miss Lili, but it is more important that Daddy gets better. That's why we are here."

11 SKODA

The following morning, despite Sundays being a quieter time, the gossip in the Middlemoor headquarters was that a Sergeant Howard Fenton had been suspended. Fenton was a 'fast track' officer, one of the Task Force support team. No reason was given. Some said it was for a week, while he awaited reassignment.

He had last served at the Penalverne Drive Police Station in Penzance, as a detective constable. Part of his career development had been a promotion to a uniform-ed HQ role. Penalverne Drive was the station where the 'early forced retirement' rumour originated. Everyone knew that.

Reimer remembered Sayer's question as they left her office; 'What's the problem?' she had asked. Well, it appeared that she had found out – and dealt with it.

As Jan entered, she saw that Sayer was already there, and caught her glance. She had the suspicion that Jackie Neil wasn't going to be asking about this new item of gossip.

DCI Hicks started the briefing of gathered officers with a contained expression. "Tess? Report on the interview with Adam Harding."

DC Tess Standish stood and moved forward. "We spent forty minutes with Adam before we felt he had to rest. It was productive. He held up well, considering."

She glanced at Hicks, then Sayer, adding, "He told us he was trying to be brave."

Her eyes moved back to the team. "Adam helped us refine the description of one perpetrator. A male, about 175 centimeters tall, slim, but with broad shoulders. His eyes and surrounding skin were not Caucasian. Possibly they were Indian or Asian, but probably not Black. The pupils of the eyes were deep brown, flecked with white. The voice was 'foreign' but we couldn't narrow that down."

She paused. "We didn't push him on that. Dr. Healy and I thought that the description of the eyes might include Arabic features, given yesterday's information. Adam did hear two shots, separated by about a minute, perhaps, but the timing may not be as reliable. We felt he was over-extending then, so we cut the interview.

"Still, compared with other interviews in similar traumatic situations, he did very well. Dr. Healy feels strongly we should not ask him to do either an identity parade or be a witness. She has recommended a therapist, a child psychologist she knows well, and I feel he will need him. That's it, boss."

She moved back to her seat.

Hicks then surprised Catrin by calling up a junior staff member from the call desk. "Starr, please update the team and the superintendent."

So that was the reason for his earlier expression, Catrin thought, as he gave her an enigmatic smile. Something has developed on the public information front.

Catrin had noticed that Ivor Knowsley, in charge of the call desk team, was agitated. DI Wastle had arrived and talked with Ivor as Hicks turned up and they clustered.

The nervous-looking young Black woman from the back corner desk had moved forward in anticipation. Knowsley and another female colleague were encouraging her. Starr kept her eyes on Hicks until she turned to face the group, but somehow got stuck facing Catrin. She froze.

I don't bite, thought Catrin. "What's your first name?" she asked.

Starr looked at the Grim Reaper. She didn't want to give her name. Everyone knew Sayer was there to chop the headcount. Starr was the newest member of the support staff in Serious Crimes. Last in, first out, she reasoned.

"Starr. Starr Omari, ma'am."

It was the tone of voice. Fear. I don't have a scythe over my shoulder, crossed Catrin's mind. She smiled. "Sorry, I thought Starr was your surname. Go ahead, tell us."

Starr nodded, looked to the front, and took a gulp of air. On release, it came back with, "We went through the traffic cams last night and found something. It's like this, Bren and I – Brenda – we were at the bus stop on the way home after our shift and, well, we came back."

She pointed at the middle-aged woman who had encouraged her to move forward. Several of the officers were giving Starr a look implying, "Where is this going?"

Starr looked at Catrin again, then turned to the map of the crime scene vicinity. She pointed the pen she was holding at different points as she spoke.

"We started on the traffic links on the A386 between

the crime scene and the biker accident location. These are the closest camera points at each end. Originally, we were supposed to start that today.

"We checked every vehicle report. Our focus then moved to reports on the A390 between Callington and Tavistock during the period we communicated to the public."

She was into it now, Catrin saw, nodding encouragingly.

"After that, we did the same thing for traffic reports of vehicles flowing the other way, counter to the direction the bikers were going."

"Some of the reports fit together. One particularly does. Two people saw a red car and bikes in the car park of the Dartmoor Inn, and we have a videoclip sent in from a dashcam on that road section. We can bracket the time the vehicle was there. One caller said it was a red Skoda, because his wife has one in white, and the dash cam showed a red Skoda parked at the pub. Then we took a punt and looked up the number plates of all red cars coming off the A30 south in that window of time. The Skoda was one of them."

The A30 was the main east-west route across the county, bisecting the Tavistock and Okehampton areas.

She took a breath, looking up, collecting her thoughts. "And?" someone asked.

"We stopped and went home. But I texted Bren and we came in at seven and ran all the registrations. Bren?"

Her partner spoke up but didn't move. "We have the registered owners of the red cars. You can follow up on all of them, but the one linked to the Dartmoor Inn car park seems to stand out. It is a Budget rental, a red Skoda Octavia with a London plate, so not local. The car came off the A30 from the east and was seen parked close to the bikes. Later it went back the same way. But it must have stayed somewhere in the vicinity of Tavistock during the period of the crime."

Starr's eyes were gleaming. "It may be nothing, but a rental car? Well, the company keeps track of their vehicles automatically, don't they? A London car in the vicinity of the house – and the bikers. One that must have stopped somewhere close by between timepoints that matter to the team."

Hicks looked at Sayer, her surprise and pleasure evident. He said, "Oliver, you call Budget. Follow up. Right now. No prevarications from them, or I will ask the Met to assist."

Ten minutes later, Wastle was back just as the forensics update finished with, "So, it's clear that we have two weapons. The bullet that passed through Ashley's leg was from a nine-millimetre calibre weapon. The bullet that killed William Ashley was from the other weapon, fired from this point beyond him. That was from a 0.32 calibre Sig Sauer; the rifling is characteristic."

Hicks stopped the update and addressed Wastle. "Anything?"

Wastle said, "Yes. The car was rented by a woman, a Dalia Jaber, a foreign national from Yemen. The rental location she used is near her house, in Central London. The car has been returned, cleaned, and is now awaiting pickup by a client, but I have told them to hold it, lock it and wait."

Hicks looked at Sayer and said, "A possible Arab ring stolen. An Arab renting a car. Heroin in packaging found in the Middle East. One of the perpetrators having eyes that could fit that ethnicity."

She said softly, "Get the car, quickly. And the woman."

He nodded. "My thoughts, too. Erica, you follow up on the car."

"Will do. Rhona, with me."

They headed across to Erica's office.

Hicks raised his voice. "Is there anything, given these new developments, that is time-critical? If so, speak up."

No-one did.

"Then get on with your current roles. Be prepared for changes in assignment. If not before, we will debrief at five again."

He looked at DI Wastle. "You and your team on this woman Jaber, Oliver. Location, movements, reason for being here, the lot. We'll be interviewing her."

As they broke up, Hick called over to the art invest-igation duo. "Peart and Reimer, tell me and Superinten-dent Sayer more about this ring, and the feedback from the discussion with the London expert. In my office, now."

As Catrin stood to head there, she saw Starr and Brenda, now at Brenda's desk, talking. She walked over. "Well done, both of you. You can see the result of your work, the energy in the team now."

They smiled and looked at each other.

Brenda said, "Last night we got the bit between our teeth, rather than wait for our next shift. After we built the spreadsheet, we were flying."

Starr said quietly. "We were just talking, though. We came back, but we had no overtime approval in advance."

By the rules, their work was unauthorised. But their times were in the system as their badges had to let them in and out.

Starr left it hanging.

Catrin gave a smile. "It will be sorted; I'll see to it. Thank you again. And keep at it. Are the calls coming in still?"

Brenda said, "Oh, yes, Ma'am. We are adding to our database, almost one report on some aspect every fifteen minutes. People are really angry about this attack."

Catrin's face changed, more serious, as she thought of the crime. "They should be. Thank you again."

12 PADPARADSCHA

John Peart pointed at Reimer. "Jan can report. Halam was very cooperative on the videocall. It helped that DC Cowling mentioned your name, Ma'am."

Catrin didn't know the name of the detective constable from the Art and Antiques Unit. It showed how much time had passed.

Hicks pressed on, looking at Reimer. "The ring?"

The young constable replied, "It's a padparadscha sapphire, a real mouthful, and rare. And the ring is eighteen carat gold. The appraisal found in the safe said 'pink sapphire, good quality', but it missed the real value completely."

Peart added, "I am still getting my mouth around that one."

"That's worth how much?" asked Hicks.

Peart answered. "He is not sure until he can examine the stone, but a lot, lot more than the evaluation. Tens of thousands, perhaps. He said, if his conclusion about the inscription and the stone is correct, it is all about the story, not the price."

He looked astonished as Catrin said the same closing phrase along with him.

She explained. "That's Frank's line, and he is right. Often insufferably right." Catrin looked at Hicks. "I don't want to –." She stopped herself. "Can I suggest that DC Peart and PC Reimer should follow up with Frank directly, and anyone else he suggests? There will be people he knows in Hatton Garden or London who may know more. Perhaps Mark Harper will loan us this DC Cowling to help for the day."

Hicks looked undecided. "I'd rather have Peart follow up here on the paintings. John, I want you to continue to check around here with any dealer who might be handling the stolen items."

He looked at Jan Reimer. "If you don't mind the travel, you can go by yourself?"

Reimer looked surprised. "London? Sure, but when?" It's Sunday, she thought.

Hicks mused on the suggestion. He poked his head out the door. "Erica, what's happening with the rental car?"

Both Wastle and Kendrick came over into the doorway. Erica said, "Budget are holding it. I'm sending a team to bring it back here for forensics to start on, but that will be later today at the earliest."

Wastle added, "We have started looking into the background on the renter. Jaber's not listed for diplomatic protection, I heard."

Hicks said, "So we will need a team prepped to go to London. Talk to the Met to use a local station, but if there isn't a simple explanation, they are to bring her back here. Thanks."

The team leaders headed back to their groups.

He turned to Reimer. "Your timing is easier. Go up separately by train today if Hamal is available. Out of uniform. This ring seems more relevant now and we need as much background as we can get. Head home, pack for overnight and go. Sort it out yourself and contact this DC Cowling in the Met. John, you get on with contacting art dealers."

The two officers stood. Jan Reimer asked, "And I can stay overnight? Do more there tomorrow if I need to follow up?"

He nodded and pointed at the door. "The interview with the jeweller, and any other expert he suggests. Nothing else. Preferably have the Met guy with you. Call any findings back into Erica or Oliver."

Reimer seemed a bit overwhelmed. Thank you, sir, and you, Ma'am."

As Reimer and Peart left, Hicks gave Sayer a look. She murmured, "Sending a PC alone to London? It will get around this place."

He smiled. "It is background work, fact-finding. Reimer won't be interviewing suspects, so it doesn't need two officers together. Anyway, she seems keen enough for two. This case is getting weird."

She nodded. "I know. A red car. A red rental car, to boot. What sort of person would use that to get to and from a premeditated crime? Amateurs, not professionals."

Hicks replied, "I thought the same, as soon as I saw the bodies in the study, that it wasn't a professional job. The gunshot to Harding looked that way, but the shot to the leg on Ashley, that was a wild shot if ever there was one. Or a gun in the hand of someone who has no idea about blood circulation. Now we know they used two weapons. On top of that, there is a vehicle that would stand out, one with automatic GPS tracking by the rental company."

Catrin said, "Put a block on the renter and any family or known associates leaving the country. If she tries to leave before we question her, make it a hold and search order."

Hicks nodded, "Right. We could do with more on this 'story' of the ring. Samesh told me before the briefing that the family were trying to sleep, after a disturbed night."

He paused. "I'll check again."

He dialled a number and DC Ray responded.

"Mrs. Wansbury and Adam are still sleeping, sir. Mr. Wansbury got up a few minutes ago. They were debating about going to church later but decided against it today. I am making coffee for us."

"Can you put him on?"

He covered the mouthpiece. "You or me? As it is about the ring."

Catrin said, "I'll do it. Put it on speaker."

After asking about him, his wife and Adam, she said, "We have many officers involved now on different aspects of the investigation. We need to know a little more about the stolen ring if you, Mrs. Wansbury or Adam can help there."

"Well, I know a bit. But Eve knows more about the ring."

"Please don't disturb her. We can follow up later but anything you know would be of interest."

"Bill bought the original ring in the Middle East, but I don't recall when precisely. Nine or ten years plus, at least, may be more. He and a colleague there used to go out, walking the markets and shops and ferreting around. Most of the business teams he was part of tended to be all about work and big dinners. This man and Bill liked to get out and sightsee."

Catrin said, "Why did you say 'original'?"

"It was a present for his wife, Sylvia, he said. Sylvia

apparently liked the stone and the ring design, but felt it was a bit clunky for her. The silver band had darkened, pitted with age, and it didn't appeal. It was just before she fell ill. Bill surprised her; he had a jeweller in Plymouth remount the stone in gold, with the same design, just a little more... what's the word? My mind is like sludge at present."

Catrin suggested, "Petite? Feminine?"

"Yes. You get the meaning, at least. She loved it. He was keeping it for Ashley. I know that much."

"And this colleague you mentioned, do you have a name?"

The line went silent for seconds, then Trevor Wansbury said. "Not really. But his first name was William, too. And his middle was an old traditional name like Alistair, or Algernon, with an A. He said they joked about using middle names with each other and agreed to stick to Bill. The man was embassy staff, not from Bill's team in London."

Catrin said, "That is very helpful, thank you. We will investigate it further. Would the jeweller who remade the ring also be the one who gave it the appraisal? Could you ask Mrs. Wansbury when she gets up? DC Ray will get the answer back to us."

"Of course. I am just hoping my wife and Adam get a decent sleep. I know the police car is keeping the reporters at bay, but it is quite disturbing having them there. We are staying home today, anyway, missing church. We aren't up to it."

"They will leave in dribs and drabs as they get assigned to other stories, I am sure."

"Will we need to do an appeal of some sort?"

Catrin stopped and pointed at Hicks. It wasn't her viewpoint that mattered.

Hicks said, "Possibly yes, Mr. Wansbury. But we have had a good response to our request yesterday. An appeal would be useful when and if we have more questions and want to engage the public about them. We don't want to put you through that without a good reason."

"Fair enough."

In the growing silence, Catrin said, "Thank you for your help. We will be in touch when we know a little more."

As Hicks closed the call he said, "A British civil servant at a Middle East embassy, in the period Harding travelled there. Someone called William A. something. We'll get on it."

Catrin responded. "Update Reimer about the ring. It's Yemeni, by the sound of it. She can run it by Frank."

Hicks gave her a quizzical look.

"Yemen has silver mines but no local gold. Silver there is valued a lot more than its market value when it comes to traditional family jewelry."

He smiled. "Something you just happen to know?"

She nodded, "As a former Art and Antiques detective, yes. It is one of those tendrils of useless information that sometimes are not so useless."

She looked at her watch. "I need to go. Let me know of any developments."

~~

Her pressing meeting was with the lead consultant with the Task Force, Ursula Otley, and her deputy chair, given the developments.

When Otley entered Catrin's office, Clarry said, "Chief Superintendent Henry is on his way now, ma'am. He apologises but will be here in five minutes or so."

Catrin thanked her and closed the door.

Ursula commented on the news that Sayer was now doing double duty and asked after Chris.

"He's coping. But it is only a day and a bit. But I'm glad to have this assignment, both for its own purpose and to ground me more in this exercise."

"How do you mean?"

"Your process and ranking system, versus the reality. I'm giving you a heads up, as I am uneasy about its robustness."

She pulled up a file folder on her laptop and opened a spreadsheet. In the corner was a stamp, 'Task Force Lead Team Only'. She moved to a highlighted name.

"In the last twenty-four hours, the best original suggestion on the Harding case came from a DS Tydman. He made the investigation team rethink the meaning of some evidence. Tydman is within the two-year early retirement slot. That was experience talking. We can't lose people like that if they want to stay on."

She rolled to another page she had marked.

"Civilian staff. I am looking at the first run ranking of Starr Omari and Brenda Nugent. They will hold their current jobs, it seems. Brenda had a phase of unexplained absenteeism, which brought her ranking down. But these two women worked most of the night and, of their own initiative, they have given us a strong lead. Currently they wonder if they will even be paid overtime for showing initiative."

Ursula Otley was nodding, as if she had the answer. "These listings are raw data analysis; a first step. We cover everyone, including performance elements, at the next stage. That is when we interview the next tier in the reporting structure. It isn't missed."

Catrin said, "Somehow, that part slid by me. If I am

concerned, other Task Force members may also be. I'm putting the item on the next full team agenda, for you personally to give a fifteen-minute explanation. We will allot up to twenty-five minutes. I want us to have a common understanding of the approach well before we have to make those decisions. Can you do that, please?"

Ursula Otley noted that Sayer's decision wasn't really a request, it was an instruction. She had dealt with a lot of Task Force leads in organisations. Some proved to be inflexible. Others were too obliging or indecisive, forcing her to push them take key decisions. She felt intuitively that Sayer was somewhere in the middle.

"I would be very happy to do that, to put your mind at rest, and those of other members, if they have similar concerns. Our process does not miss the chance to keep value in the organisation, I assure you."

13 HATTON GARDEN

Jan Reimer's original plan for Sunday was her weekly grocery shopping and some laundry. Now in plainclothes and on a train speeding east, she would be in London in an hour, the first time there for work reasons rather than pleasure. Without the superintendent's involvement, this would not have happened.

Arriving at Paddington Station in the early afternoon, she splurged on a taxi to get her to the building on Cross Street in Hatton Garden, the centre of London's jewel trade. Hamal had agreed to meet her there. "We are in, anyway, as it happens," he said.

DC Cowling wasn't available until late afternoon or early evening but didn't explain why. That didn't bother her for the task assigned.

She had an urge, though, to visit the Met and say she had been to the Art and Antiques Unit. She would never tell anyone, but she knew of Sayer before the superintendent joined the Devon and Cornwall Police. It had been in an article on ceramic art.

The last day had been a bit of a dream.

Frank Hamal was in his fifties, she judged. From the Zoom call yesterday, she had imagined him to be big, but that was the voice and his computer camera angle, not the man. He was thinner and shorter than her perception, full of energy and now wearing an oversized face mask. Hamal settled her in his little office with instructions to an assistant that he was not to be disturbed.

He asked to see the appraisal photographs again. The lab had rushed high-definition enlargements of the originals for her to use.

Hamal peered closely at them for a minute or so. After that, she showed him the short appraisal note. He gave a big sniff and glared at the paper. "This jeweller missed it completely. Sayer saw it, perhaps not specifically, but she would want it followed up. What's she doing now?"

"Our boss reports to her. Superintendent Sayer has several duties."

He looked perplexed. "It's been a while, I suppose. Time flies. Pity. She should get back to Art and Antiques. Art crime is ballooning, and we have so few people dedicated to dealing with it. Tell her that and give her my best."

She looked impassive. That wasn't a message she would be reporting back; she didn't know how Sayer would take it.

He returned to the task in hand. "This is a fine one, as I thought. I gave Farida Al Araqi a call, asking her about the jeweller's mark. You should talk to her, too. Basically, this is a padparadscha sapphire of good clarity and colour. It has been superbly cut. That places the stone price up there."

"Is it unique?"

"What do you mean, precisely?"

Jan struggled for a moment. She thought the question

was obvious. "Is this sapphire distinguishable from other quality pink sapphires? Not simply seen as a rare sapphire, but a particular sapphire?"

Hamal gave her a penetrating look. "The combination of pink and orange locations in the stone, with the pattern of the cut is unique. I know cutters who, with the right uncut stone, or rather, a partly cut stone, could produce a duplicate. But an expert would still see differences."

She saw he had followed her question.

He added, "So yes, if someone who knew the stone saw this image, they could be pretty sure about it."

Reimer restated her conclusion. "The robbery could be either because it was a valuable ring, or because it was a particular ring?"

"Either is possible, yes, and supportable in court. It belonged to the deceased, you said?"

"Well, yes, we understand so. It was in his possession."

"Not his wife's? That is usually the case."

"No. She died some years ago."

He nodded, grimacing. "I really need to see the ring. The enlargements are useful. I see no –."

The door opened. "Not now, Arthur."

"It's Mrs. Fenstein. She is insisting."

Frank jumped up, as if scalded. "Excuse me, I won't be long."

Ten minutes later he returned. In the next twenty minutes he had another interruption, a shorter duration.

When he re-entered the second time, he said without ceremony, "We'll call Farida. She'll be free by now."

"Who's Farida? You didn't say earlier."

"Dr. Farida Al Araqi, at the Museum of Natural History. A gemologist and an expert on Arabic jewelry. She works on Sunday afternoons."

On the call, apart from the introduction, Frank did all the talking. The gemologist listened to him, then asked, "Constable Reimer, what do we know about the man who was robbed? Had he visited the Gulf area and, if so, when?"

Jan wasn't sure how much to reveal. "Yes, his work took him there for a period, to several countries in the region. It was in the period 1994 to 2011."

"Hmm. His travels started before the departure of President Saleh. Perhaps he visited Yemen; afterwards, probably not. This symbol, I think, is a Yemeni tribal mark, a 'v' shape with an inner line. Few jewellers there would use them, as most don't have any tribal affiliation."

Jan jumped in. "I need to find out as much as possible, as soon as I can."

Al Araqi responded, "Why not come over? Not now, I have a commitment. But first thing tomorrow, to the museum. In the meantime, I will check here, and I also have some reference material at home. I will try to find an answer for you. Say, at nine a.m.? The museum opens an hour later, but if you come to the main entrance, I will get you in."

As Jan wrapped up with Frank Hamal, thanking him, he said, "As I said, give my regards to Catrin Sayer."

Jan said, "I will – well, if I get the chance. She is a senior officer and I'm a constable."

He smiled, "I remember her vaguely from when she became a sergeant. I was in their shop when we met, not at the Met."

"Shop?"

For a moment, she misunderstood. Then her memory of the article on Sayer and Hughes art came back to her as Frank continued. "Jean Hughes' shop. Well, it's Jean's shop with her partner. But Sayer and Jean Hughes make ceramic art as well as Jean making her own lines at the pottery. They call it the Sayer-Hughes art line. The Cwmbran Kiln is in Spitalfields. It is close by."

Seeing the expression on her face, he added, "A number eight bus just outside would get you there in less than ten minutes."

14 MOORE

Hicks had texted Catrin. Although they were making progress on several fronts, there was nothing significant. She spent some time in the office reading Task Force materials then headed home to spend some time with Mair and Chris and catch up on household chores. A second text message sent later said he would like to call her this evening.

When Catrin arrived home, Chris's mother, Mavis, had arrived and was in the middle of doing laundry. From the aromas from the kitchen, she was also preparing a roast dinner for supper. Catrin knew she was arriving today from Penzance, staying for two to three days. Walking in the door, she could see Mair talking away with her grandma. Chris was sitting in a nearby chair watching them. Catrin relaxed and looked at Chris. "Well, you look a bit better, if you ask me. Do you feel that way?"

He gave a smile. "It's Cornish air coming into Devon, that's what does it. But I do. Not a lot, but I had a little more go about me this afternoon."

Mavis Treneer smiled at her son. She said to Mair, "Go

see your mum for a while and tell her about your exciting day. I'll get the rest of the dinner prepared, now she is home."

Catrin said, "I'll help in a minute –."

To be cut off. "No, you won't. I saw the TV coverage. You looked very much on top of it, but that sort of thing would frighten me to death. You have enough to do."

As she left the room, Mair said, "We went to the train station and I was the one who saw Grandma first, as she got off the train. Daddy was looking in the wrong direction!"

Chris smiled. "She paid a supplement onboard, to move to First Class. Coffee service at her seat, would you believe? So yes, I was second in the granny-spotting contest."

Catrin thought back to the time he came out of hospital. He is doing better. It's slow, but it is progress.

Mavis was reading to Mair in her bedroom when Catrin caught up with Hicks.

"We have made quite a bit of progress today, Catrin. The renter is a Dalia Jaber, 28, from Sana'a, Yemen, here for a year on a business visa. She is a junior oil technologist, a sort of technical role on a marketing team. She lives in a Yemeni state-owned or rented property in Kynance Mews, wherever that is."

Catrin responded, "Close to the centre of London and Hyde Park. It would be out of the price range of a junior anything."

He continued, "She has the use of a mews home, two bedroomed, with her brother, Nabil. He is a sous-chef at a Yemeni restaurant in Central London. Nabil Jaber arrived six months ago and has a military service background. He would know his way around weapons. We have a request into Immigration for their fingerprint records."

He moved down his list.

"The rental car is almost here now, on a secure trailer. SOCOs will do a first search this evening but leave the main work until tomorrow.

"Reimer is in London and has connected with Frank Hamal. He thinks the sapphire is worth a packet but won't commit to a price without seeing it. He has put her in contact with some other expert at the Museum of Natural History. Reimer says she will meet her there first thing tomorrow."

"We have the airports, trains and ferries covered for both Jaber siblings. I'm having checks on their phones, so we know their locations. It would be useful to have the Met do a covert surveillance on the pair; I will try to arrange that next. I've organised an arrest team to head up, leaving tomorrow morning and will try to get the Met to spare us tactical support. Hopefully they will do the front work, given the gun risk. The team is pretty tired now. So am I. We'll go at it fresh early tomorrow."

"It sounds in hand, Michael. Well done. Shall I try to get some support for you through my contacts?"

He paused. "If you think it would help move things along, without crossthreading the communications. Yes."

"Hold the line. I will try now with someone and pull you in. Don't ring off."

Hicks held for a couple of minutes, doing other things to wrap up and leave, when the line opened again.

"Michael, I have Commander Karen Moore on the line. Ma'am, this is DCI Michael Hicks."

"Hicks, good evening. You and Catrin are on the double murder, I understand."

It was a voice of authority. "Yes, ma'am. We have two

possible suspects in London."

"You want them monitored until your team can take them in for questioning. And you need some tactical support for the arrest. You have it. What's your number?"

Hicks reeled it off. Moore said, "DI Rita Matta, my aide, will call you within fifteen minutes. Whatever you need, she will fix it. Any problem, go to Catrin and she will come to Rita or me, if necessary. Catrin, Rita replaced John when he was promoted. Now, anything else? If not, best wishes with this one. A child murdered; you get anything you need, Catrin. Let me know how it goes."

Catrin said, "I will, Ma'am. Thank you."

Moore said "Goodnight, then," and there was a click as the line dropped.

"I'm going, too, Michael, you will need your line free."

Hicks said, "I am impressed, Catrin. Really."

"She is a 'take charge' person, yes. We can count on her."

"No. That's not what I meant. That you could fix this, so fast."

"She was my boss's boss for years. And we have travelled some miles together, including a hostage incident."

"Well, she laid out the red carpet for us. See you tomorrow."

As he rang off, she thought, Karen is my mentor. She puts the fear of God into me at times, but she is still my guide. Suddenly she knew what she would be saying to Dr. Ursula Otley at the next debrief, to plan for the next Task Force meeting. You keep value within the organisation with a mentoring structure, and the reorganisation needed to accommodate that.

15 SPITALFIELDS

After leaving Frank Hamal, Jan Reimer had taken the bus. She frowned about the people around her not wearing masks. London was far worse for that than Exeter, she thought. In hindsight, she wished she had walked, or taken another taxi.

She found the Spitalfields Market easily. Some shops were open, some closed. The Cwmbran Kiln had lights on. A customer was leaving, so her impulsive decision hadn't been a total waste of time.

Jan first looked in the window and then entered, checking out the pottery on display. Suddenly she saw a poster on a wall with the motif 'Sayer-Hughes Art' and went over to read it.

As she concluded that she was in the wrong place, that she needed to be in a gallery further west in London, a female voice asked, "Can I help you?"

"I'm just browsing," Jan replied, realising the obvious lie of her response. "Well, I was looking for this, actually. I was with someone who told me this is the workshop for Sayer-Hughes Art."

"It is. But it sells at a gallery, as it says. If you wish, we can look on the website and I can call Liz, the owner, to see what is available. And Jean is here, in the back. Would you like to chat with her about it? Devon, is it?"

The accent.

Jan smiled. "Yes, Exeter. And you sound as if you are from Somerset. It's harder with these masks. Sounds get muffled."

It was the look on the shopkeeper's face.

"I confess. I work for the police. Superintendent Sayer sent me to check something in Hatton Garden. They told me there that she worked on her ceramic art here. I got nosey."

Melanie nodded. "When you said Exeter, I wondered if there was a connection. This is Catrin's new assignment, then. We saw the news item on the internet. How is she doing?"

Jan said, "Well, our boss reports to her, and it is a big team. As to how she's doing, she's up there and I am down here." She raised and lowered her hand accordingly.

"I'm Melanie. Come and talk to Jean. And please don't leave until I get back. I won't be a minute."

With that, she led her through the arch into the workshop, where another woman was decorating a set of plates.

"Jean, this is –?"

"Jan. PC Janice Reimer, I should say. I am out of uniform."

"She works with Catrin. Show her some of the art you do together. I'll be back in less than five."

Jean said hello and then grimaced and raised her eyes at the retreating figure. "Are you on the train or in a car?"

"The train."

"Melanie will lumber you with taking something back

for Mair, Catrin's daughter. A teddybear. She and my daughter Lili wanted them, and we bought two. But if it not workable for you, just say."

She trailed off and smiled. "D'you like ceramics, or art in general?"

Jan responded, "I did a liberal arts degree at uni, at Bristol. That's why I volunteered – well, why I am here. Superintendent Sayer sent me up rather than do the interview over the phone. She seems to know a lot. I read about her, at Art and Antiques. I pinch myself a bit, really, to get this chance."

Jean smiled. "She has done well."

Jan continued, "I didn't develop any niche interest or any brilliant skill. I draw, ink and pencil work, cards for birthdays for family and friends, but I never show them to anyone else. I get lost in the galleries, though, and in art history. I'd love to go to Italy."

Jean pulled out an ipad and opened a file. "This is my 'top favorites' collection of the work Catrin and I have done together over the years. Have a look if you want, and we can talk about them as I work. I have a dinner set to complete."

For the next few minutes, other than an occasional remark, Jan looked at the images of the art. Some showed works with either Sayer or Hughes also in the picture. When the doorbell rang, she thought it was Melanie, but no; it was a customer. Jean went forward and served her.

As that sale completed, Melanie entered, with a little girl. She was wearing a mask and Melanie was carrying a box about eighteen inches long by a foot square. "You are seeing the art. Good. Could we ask you to take this parcel back with you, for Catrin? It's not heavy and I'll put string on."

Jan looked at Lili, who was staring at her. Lili said, "It's a Chocolate Bear, for Mair."

Jan looked at her then Melanie. "Chocolate?"

"Not real chocolate, it won't melt. It's the brand name of the toy, its colour."

Jan smiled at Lili, understanding. "I see. I promise I will get it to her safely. How does that sound?"

It was half an hour later when Jan left, after a cup of tea and a chat. She had enjoyed it. What struck her most wasn't Superintendent Sayer's other life as an artist, but an image in the set on the iPad showing a much younger Sayer, more Jan's age, smiling at a camera and holding a vase. The scar on her cheek wasn't there yet.

It would have been rude to ask, she thought. Jean had said, "We did that before she left Brixton, to become a detective in art investigation."

But it made Jan think.

DC Cowling, from the Art and Antiques Unit, called Jan mid-evening, apologising for his unavailability. She told him it wasn't a problem, and she had a meeting first thing with an expert at the Museum of Natural History.

He asked, "Would you like to meet up afterwards? I am in the office tomorrow, as it stands currently. It's only twenty minutes on the tube, the District or Circle lines to the Embankment."

Would I, Jan thought? She said, "I'd love to."

~~

The following morning, she turned up at the museum on time. Once inside Farida Al Araqi's office, the gemologist opened with, "This ring intrigues me."

Al Araqi was a small woman carrying a lot of weight on her hips. Her hair was now turning grey, almost white in places. Jan had checked her out on-line. For a fifty-year-old woman, she looked closer to sixty. The extensive wrinkles on her hands and brow accentuated the impression. Jan got the feeling that Al Araqi's life had not all been spent in London, and part of it had been hard on her physically.

She asked why it intrigued the woman.

"The only jewellers who used that mark on their work were a father and son team, Emile and Basra Ratzon. They were silversmiths."

Jan said nothing. She decided to hold back the information received from Harding's brother-in-law, that the original ring was silver. Al Araqi's comment corroborated that.

Farida took a deep breath. "It seems that the sapphire, a fine padparadscha stone from the images, could have been set in a silver ring. Frank explained the stone to you?"

"Yes."

"Someone, probably a westerner, liked the ring but not the metal. Old silver is not so valued here. I suspect that they had the ring remade in gold, complete with the mark. I can show you some images of works by the original jewellers. Both are now dead, I understand."

Jan said, "That is very interesting. It could tie in."

The expert said, "Here's where I get into trouble, if I am wrong. I must rely on you not to make my comments public unless you have separate evidence which supports them. It could cause problems."

How?"

"These jewellers sold almost exclusively within their tribal affiliation. They were local and sold locally. It was the practice. People commissioned pieces for dowry gifts or other presents. The world was different back then.

"Now, a gemstone of this quality in a ring implies an important and wealthy client. I can guarantee that such a person wouldn't part with it. It would stay within the family. You wouldn't get it sold into Europe."

She stopped.

Jan responded, "But if it was worth a bit, and they needed money–."

"It would be worth a lot. It is not our way. To sell jewelry like this does happen sometimes, but it is a loss of face, a shaming event. Other than that hypothesis, I can't understand how this sapphire ended up in a gold replica in the UK."

Jan decided she needed to be more open with Al Araqi. "We just discovered that the owner here, one of the victims, gave the original ring to his wife. It was silver, as you said. For the reasons you mentioned, she liked the sapphire and not the ring. He had a jeweller over here copy the ring in a smaller size in gold."

She could see the understanding grow on the gemologist. Then her face clouded over as a look of concern developed.

Al Araqi said, "If the family who owned the original ring became aware of the stone, and its fate, they might try to recover the piece. And they are likely to be wealthy people. Very wealthy."

"And if the owner didn't want to sell?"

Farida looked at her. "I can't say."

It was her face which revealed the concern, perhaps about saying too much.

"This group is a tribe of some sort? Can you identify that, perhaps?"

"I suggest you check with someone in the Foreign Office. Tribes in Yemen have their own substructures. According to my resources, the Ratzon jewellers sold within a sub-group of a larger tribe. The current tribal head is Shaykh Yusuf Abrahim. I cannot say more than that."

Your face already has, thought Jan. "Mrs. Al Araqi, this has been very helpful. I do appreciate it. And I will ensure we contact others on this matter. Now, it would be helpful to have some details, if possible, perhaps in any published documents. After all, those could come from any expert like yourself, could they not?'

Farida Al Araqi looked relieved.

Jan wanted to finish the interview and call this in. She might get sent to the Foreign and Commonwealth Office to follow up on the tribal link.

When she spoke to DI Kendrick, though, twenty minutes later, her plans changed. She was to start back immediately with whatever she had from the experts. The team was in the process of making arrests.

16 MEWS

The arrest of Dalia Jaber and her brother Nabil took place at 117A Kynance Mews in London, at seven fifteen a.m. on Tuesday. It was five days into the investigation.

The Met had, as promised, monitored the movements of Dalia and Nabil as they went about their lives. After a long drive yesterday, a team led by DI Wastle arrived at Kensington Police Station.

In preparing for the arrests, the most difficult element to finalise was the exact status of the mews home. By 9.00 p.m., they confirmed that the property was sub-leased to a Yemeni businessman living in Paris. The owner was a Scottish aristocrat. There were no diplomatic status issues if they needed a forced entry to the building.

All went smoothly and quietly that morning. From a firm knock on the door to the cars driving out of the narrow, enclosed road took less than three minutes.

A grey, anonymous-looking van and a uniformed police officer stationed at the door of the home were all that anyone could see after that.

Men in business attire from two neighbouring homes came to speak to the officer. Both were of Arabic ethnicity. Each left with their questions unanswered.

The most crucial point of the arrest was the safety of the team involved. Two armed officers were visible for about a minute at the door to the home. A white passenger van with darkened windows parked in front, with its rear doors open. The remaining tactical officers were inside. Once the two occupants were secured, the van and its tactical team evaporated into the morning commuter traffic.

The Jaber siblings were taken in separate vehicles to the nearby police station. There, Wastle informed them that they had been arrested under suspicion of involvement in a crime committed in Devon. Each person had the right to representation by a solicitor.

By ten o'clock, they were being interviewed by Devon and Cornwall Police staff in the presence of solicitors. The Embassy of the Republic of Yemen had arranged the legal support.

It was about that time the calls to Devon and Cornwall Police from the various powers-that-be started. These were to continue throughout the day and were channelled to Clarry and Catrin Sayer.

As Catrin dealt with the inquiries, she was reminded of times in the past when she left the room, leaving her bosses to it. Operational staff were kept away from the political minefields. Now it was down to her.

Late morning, she briefed DCC Billings.

"As expected, neither suspect is co-operating. Michael will be stopping Wastle's team soon and bringing both here. The solicitors are objecting, wanting to keep them in London unless we charge them, but they can't do much about it.

"A search of the mews home is now underway. A thorough forensic examination of the vehicle is near completion. Dalia collected the Skoda with a full tank of petrol. Michael is now working on the premise that she drove it to the mews, after which one of them drove down here. We have started looking for motorway camera records for the vehicle and its occupants. And for any people they met, or items picked up or discarded.

"The most recent development was twenty minutes ago. It seems the sister has a firm alibi in London. We are still checking it. If so, it could be the brother with another person that came west and killed the Hardings."

"Motive?"

"We are moving more to the theft of the ring as the reason, rather than the paintings, based on feedback from two experts in London. So far, we are treading gently around Mr. Harding and his time working in the Middle East. I don't want to give the impression that we are investigating the activities of a member of the lieutenancy. Not without a clear and substantive basis, at least.

"The Foreign Office has identified a former diplomatic officer for us who may have spent time with Harding in Saudi, a man called William Allingham. Fortunately, he is not overseas; Allingham now lives and works in Birmingham. From DS Tydman's conversation with him, we feel it is better to have someone talk to him face to face; Allingham wanted to check with Whitehall before speaking about events tied to his work at the embassy in Saudi Arabia. With the current activities, that will need to wait a day or so, to get people up there. It is more background material than direct evidence, I suspect."

"Quite right, to tread gently, not feed the media speculation," said the DCC. "But there are drugs linked, it seems, even if we can't prove that at present. If you find a substantive reason, don't hold back, but let me know. I don't want the Lord Lieutenant blindsided."

She nodded. "That's all, sir. Media interest is still high. I don't think we will get these two to Exeter without some spike in that interest. I have communications preparing some news release scenarios, just in case. My preference is to say nothing, though, unless we make formal charges."

The DCC seemed satisfied with the brief. He asked, "You and Hicks, are things going well? You were dropped in there with no advance warning."

"Very well. He runs a good operation, and his team are competent and motivated."

The DCC added, "And things at home? You aren't spending much time there, I know."

Catrin smiled wryly. "Not much. My mother-in-law is staying. She and my daughter are looking after Chris, who hates being looked after, as you heard. And my sister-in-law and her partner will come over from Falmouth when his mum goes home. We are coping."

He nodded then said straight-faced, "Falmouth Treneers. Always were a bad bunch, fighting authority. That probably makes him a lousy patient in recovery."

He added, with levity and an underlying seriousness, "Of course, we'll take him back, should you decide to stay, not go back to the London mob."

Catrin gave him a hard stare, then a smile. "My nickname, I gather, is the Grim Reaper. If they are feeling friendly, it is simply 'the Reaper'. When the Task Force finishes, I'd better be out of here with a bodyguard to the Dorset border."

He nodded ruefully. Every wild embellishment has a nucleus of truth. He muttered, "I overheard that one, too.

Pretended I hadn't. Don't let it get to you. The real interviews with these two from London start when?"

"We told them they will be interviewed as soon as they
get here and are fed. Their lawyers didn't want that. They
argued for a pause on the detention clock and a start first
thing tomorrow. We objected, but then capitulated.

"It works out well, really. They get to sweat their
worries overnight in the cells and the interview teams get
a night's sleep. Michael is sticking with the same teams
and seeing them on the videolink, I agree."

17 SADDLEBAGS

The following day at the hospital in Plymouth, the D-Crew member Stu Baines eyed DS Lough with suspicion as the sergeant asked after his health. DC Rollins was silent, checking that the recorder was picking the sound up clearly.

Baines's lawyer, a man called Cressington, was watching his client for the first sign he could claim that the interview needed to be stopped.

Baines responded sullenly, "It's the knees. I've got to wait for the grafts to take. Then I can go home."

He shifted his glance between Lough and his solicitor. "Can't I?" It was the solicitor who looked doubtful about that. Lough just smiled.

Stu, feeling a little more confident, asked. "Is my bike damaged badly? No one will say."

Lough responded, sounding somewhat distant from it all, lost in thought. "Mainly cosmetic, I heard, but you will need a new back wheel. But I'm glad you mentioned it, though. I have a question for you, Stuart. About your nice saddlebags. Are they saddlebags or panniers? I never know the right term."

More interested now, Baines replied, "Saddlebags, 'cos they are soft-sided, made of synthetic leather. Cost me a packet direct from Harley, not rip-offs."

Lough moved forward, focusing now on Baine's eyes.

"Was it the right one you used to transport the fire-arms? The dog thought so. The second dog, not the drug dog that cleared your bike and went wild about Ryan's Harley. This one was an explosives dog. It seemed really interested in your right saddlebag. The people in white coats are probably cutting up sections of it for analysis now. At least it's not real leather, you said."

Lough watched the expression change. Anger at the last message, about his bike being violated, to a slow realisation of the implication. He restated the question more generally.

"The guns were in your possession on the way to the meet, weren't they?"

"I know nothing about guns. Nothing!"

The panic on Stu's face seemed to contradict that, to Lough. He shrugged.

"We will see what the lab says, then. You just said you bought the bags new, so you can't claim you got them from another club member."

Lough said gently, "Think about it. And soon. Before we don't need your input. If those were the weapons that killed members of the Harding family, you will go down for a very long time. The grafts on your knees will be old and white by the time you are released. Talk to Mr. Cressington. See if you both can find a path forward to help you and help us."

Lough knew it was unlikely that a biker would talk without the prospect of a deal, so he hadn't pushed harder.

Stu turned his head away and sobbed. The combination of his injuries and his prospects were overwhelming him. He said, into the pillow, "I never saw any guns. Ryan just asked me to carry a parcel in my bag. Ask him."

DC Rollins pointed at the recorder. Lough said equally gently, "Stu, could you repeat that, I missed some of it. We will ask Ryan, of course. That's procedure."

Baines turned his head, doing so.

Lough's next question was more forceful. "What was this parcel like? Can you describe it, the size? And its weight?"

A break in the ranks, he thought. He and Rollins were going to have an interesting day after all, probably shuttling between a police station interview room with Smith and the hospital with Baines, using the 'he said, she said,' interview technique.

~~

The message late afternoon came through Clarry and pulled Catrin out of a session of the finance sub-group of the Task Force, leaving Chief Superintendent Henry to chair the meeting. DCC Billings needed her right now.

As Catrin left the meeting room, Clarry offered to take the files she had brought out with her and said quietly. "Not in his office. You go straight to the Chief Constable."

There, she found Doug Billings and Chief Constable Aiden Jessop already in a meeting with two visitors, a man in his early thirties and a woman in her fifties.

"Sayer, join us, please." Jessop pointed at a vacant chair next to him.

As she did so, he added, "This is Nathan Atkins, an assistant to the Minister of Foreign Affairs, and Sheila

Murray, from the ministry staff."

He looked at the pair. "Could you repeat for Super-intendent Sayer the purpose of this visit? She has direct oversight of the Harding investigation."

Jessop's expression was unreadable as Catrin looked from the Chief Constable across the table to the visitors.

Murray took up the offer.

"The senior investigating officer, DCI Hicks, has made several requests to us, to Interpol, and I suspect others, concerning two Yemenis you have in custody. He has included requests for background on a Shaykh Yusuf Abrahim. It has something to do with a stol-n item, a ring."

Catrin looked blank, waiting.

Murray continued. 'From our perspective, that is a problem. If Hicks is on a fishing expedition, we would like him to reel in his line. If he has solid evidence of any involvement of the shaykh in this crime, we need to know about it first. Can you give us the background, please?"

Catrin glanced at Billings, who nodded, a signal to do so. She felt on the edge of her experience, entering a new field. Years ago, as the security officer for an assistant commissioner at the Met, she and other staff were excluded from this sort of meeting. Other occasions when she found herself in the presence of political figures or a member of the intelligence services interfering in a case were led by a senior officer and she remained silent. Here she was with the two most senior ranking officers of the constabulary, in a meeting where she was now on the front line.

"The inquiries are linked to a double murder and a stolen item, a ring, yes. Our current view is that the ring probably was the reason for the assailants being there. The deaths arose from a robbery that went wrong. An expert's impression of the ring identifies it to be of Yemeni origin, probably owned by a tribal member with wealth. The jewellers who made the ring sold their works solely within that tribe, decades ago. Shaykh Yusuf Abrahim is the tribal leader of the group which includes the Jaber pair, the sister and brother."

Nathan Atkins spoke up. "That's all you've got, is it? To start rumours about a Yemeni authority figure?"

Billings responded, equally snappishly. "It's early days in the inquiry. The team is following all leads."

Catrin replied, "We aren't, to quote you, starting any rumours. We are making confidential and legitimate inquiries through official channels."

Atkins stared at the table for a moment, as if it would reveal some wonderful answer to whatever problem he faced. Then he looked up at Sayer.

"What do you understand about the Yemeni political situation, the war there? Anything?"

"Very little." She resisted the impulse to elaborate what she knew or had read recently. He wasn't a class professor she needed to satisfy.

Sheila Murray said, "It is complex, a fight between opposing Muslim factions, a bloody war and a population in need of food and medical aid. Shaykh Yusuf Abrahim is someone open to working with us and our allies. There are sensitivities."

Catrin looked at Jessop and Billings. It was the Chief Constable who broke the ensuing silence. "We have two people murdered in their home. We aren't stopping or altering the direction of any aspect of the investigation that DCI Hicks and Superintendent Sayer feel they need to pursue. That is my decision, and my instruction to her now."

They had been through this already, Catrin realised.

She saw the flash of anger in Atkins. Murray, clearly the peacemaker, said, "Nevertheless, as we said earlier, the Minister is asking – no, let's be truthful – insisting you conduct your inquiry in a manner that does not tarnish this government's image as it pursues its foreign policy."

Atkins stood, signalling he was done. "At the end of the day, you will need our support to do anything involving foreign nationals. Remember that. Thank you for your time."

Murray stood also, slowly followed by the police officers. Within a minute, the police team were alone.

Jessop pointed back at the table as he called through the door to his assistant. As he entered, he asked Catrin whether she wanted coffee or tea.

Billings muttered to Catrin, "It's not the first time we have been through this. Just a quick visit for a 'quiet word'. If it's not them – Aiden, we aren't going to find SIS turning up for more quiet words, I hope?"

Jessop shrugged his shoulders. "Who knows? The next one could be the lackey for the First Minister of Scotland, saying Shaykh Abrahim is heavily involved in buying a golf course, so don't put him off."

He looked at Catrin. "They never say anything that could come back as obstructing the investigation. It's always a quiet word, as Doug said. And you must handle it without compromising the investigation or being seen to be in open rebellion."

Catrin shook her head. "They came all this way... I suppose they wanted nothing on record?"

He nodded. "Let's see how we should deal with this little wrinkle."

Clearly, the Chief Constable had his own ideas about that.

When she left the inner sanctum, she had her orders. Do nothing to demotivate the investigation team. Discuss the path forward with Hicks only. No-one else, including Wastle and Kendrick, was to be in the loop – other than the specific people she needed. Sayer would be the point person and could choose how to achieve the objective.

Jessop had said, "Pursue all lines, but don't have anything concerning the Shaykh on record until it needs to be. If a politically sensitive figure is behind this, I want him blissfully unaware, and for Nathan Atkins to focus on other things."

"And if he is involved?"

Jessop looked at Billings, then back at Sayer. "Then we will make a call at the time how to deal with it."

She began to see why people like Karen Moore and Aiden Jessop were paid the big salaries.

18 FINGERPRINTS

As much as DS Lough made unexpected progress with the bikers, the interviews with Dalia and Nabil Jaber in Exeter on Wednesday produced nothing of value.

In the interviews in Kensington Police Station yesterday, Dalia seemed frozen with fear. She did not deny renting the car. She would not confirm she let her brother use it. Even the explanation that a driver not listed on the rental agreement was an insurance issue rather than a crime made no impact.

In another interview room, Nabil had sat quietly, showing neither anger nor fear. He did not respond at all, seeming lost within himself. Wastle shared with his team that Jaber might be in some sort of trauma arising from the crime rather than the arrest.

With the silences, they had no way to find out.

Today, after a night in the cells and no intercommunication, they were similarly unresponsive. During the morning interview, each person's attitude was more stoic. They were in a foreign country, with foreign police officers. The siblings acted more like prisoners of war, showing a contained anger.

By the afternoon session, forensic results were damning. No wonder they were in fear.

One of the swabs taken from Nabil's right wrist area showed traces of gunpowder residue. Two of his fingerprints matched those in the blood on Ashley's leg. They also matched his fingerprints on file, supplied by Immigration that morning. It was irrefutable evidence of Nabil's presence at the crime.

A flake of gold paint found in the boot of the Skoda, missed during its valeting at Budget, was consistent with the frame on the Alfred Wallis painting.

There was no trace of Dalia Jaber at Victory House and her alibi remained solid.

When confronted by the evidence, Nabil held to the line of non-cooperation. Even his solicitor could not engage him in discussion.

Eventually, Hicks sent DC Sally Lymes, probably the most empathetic officer on the team, to interview the sister. Lymes carefully explained the spectrum of realities that Dalia now faced.

At best, she would be released without charges. To do that, she must say she had no knowledge of the events and explain her own actions. Currently, it was more likely she would be charged with aiding and abetting her brother. If she continued to be uncooperative, that was the likely outcome. Nabil would shortly be charged with the murder of two people.

At worst, if they found evidence of Dalia's complicity, even though she was not at the crime scene, she could also be charged with the same crime.

Sally finished with, "So much, Dalia, is in your hands to help us decide. Talk to us. Help us to help you."

Dalia Jaber looked down at the table, shook her head and said nothing.

When Catrin entered Michael Hicks' office, he was talking to DI Wastle and DI Kendrick. Sayer's expression asked the question.

"Nothing from them, ma'm." Michael said. "Erica made a good point. We have no idea about their lives. Nor how they regard the police and our interviews. No one is shouting or threatening them. They are allowed breaks and meals. They have legal council. Yet they seem to be in a state of dread, waiting for worse treatment."

Catrin's face showed she understood. "Still, we aren't waiting. Michael, you and I talk with CPS now. The DCC agrees. We feel we have sufficient evidence to charge Nabil Jaber. I also want an extension to the detention order for his sister. Lough's work with Baines swung the DCC, as we now have a route into the weapons used.

"We have the fingerprints, the powder residues, the car route history, and a probable access to firearms. As such, CPS should agree to charge him."

Hicks seemed pleased, as did Wastle. Kendrick looked a little uncertain.

The evening briefing of the team was led by DI Kendrick and was short. Continue what they were doing. DCI Hicks and DI Wastle were currently charging Nabil Jaber with the murders of William and Ashley Harding.

The Super and the boss would be leaving immediately after that for the Wansbury home, to talk with them and Adam, to prepare them. A press release would go out later this evening with the news of an arrest. A press conference tomorrow morning would follow that. There was still a lot more work to do. Keep at it.

As for any briefing, one or more officers on shift were absent, busy with other activities. Given PC Reimer had gone to London and back, her absence now was not a surprise. And DC Peart was away, also.

Reimer and Peart found themselves in Peart's car following Hicks and Sayer in their own vehicles, traveling to the Wansbury home. Jan wasn't catching up on her grocery shopping yet and wasn't sure why.

~~

When they entered the family home, Reimer saw Sayer focus immediately on the boy. He was sitting between his aunt and uncle as everyone seated themselves. DC Samesh Ray gave Reimer and Peart a look of acknowledgement, with a question in his eyes. He wasn't sure what they were doing here. Reimer couldn't enlighten him; neither did she.

Sayer reached out and took the boy's hand, giving it a small squeeze again before she spoke.

"I promised I would keep you informed, Adam. I can tell you some things now. There are other things we now know which I can't talk to you or your aunt and uncle about, and much more we don't know. DCI Hicks has over twenty members of his team working on the investigation, and they will continue to do so. This is PC Reimer and DC Peart, part of the team."

Adam looked at Catrin, his face serious and expectant. His eyes moved to Reimer, now in her uniform, and Peart in his dress casuals. Younger people, like Samesh. Eve Wansbury put her hand on Adam's arm, and he grabbed it, holding her.

Catrin continued, "We arrested a man yesterday. This evening, we charged him with the murder of your father and sister. As present, we don't know the identity of the second person who was with him."

Adam burst out loudly with, "Why? Did he say why?"

She shook her head. "The man isn't talking to us yet, and I am not going to speculate too much. It may relate to the ring stolen from the safe, but we aren't sure. The information your aunt and uncle gave us helped a lot."

"How long will he go to jail for?"

The uncle started to say something, but a look from Sayer stopped him.

She said, "For a very long time, I expect. It is our job to give the evidence to the courts and they will decide. But I hope the people who did this terrible thing pay the full price under the law for their crime. But that won't fix anything for you or your family, I know."

He nodded. "It helps, though, that you caught one of them so soon."

Catrin refocused on the aunt and uncle.

"There will be a press release later this evening and a media briefing tomorrow. It will be confusing for you. We will charge one person with your father and sister's deaths, and release that another person is in custody. We won't be giving much else away, but the media are bound to speculate. The public responded well to our request for information, and we will be repeating our messages to them, identifying a specific vehicle involved."

The aunt asked, "Do you need us there?"

"No. Believe me, if we thought it would add anything, we would ask. But you don't need to. Reporters can be great on occasion, but more often they are after you for their own needs and deadlines."

She glanced quickly at Adam and then back at his aunt and uncle. "It is best if you continue to protect your privacy."

She stood. "Any burning questions, Adam?" Her voice was now firm, more upbeat and collegial.

He shook his head. "No, unless you tell me how to become a police officer quickly and help. I'd like to do that."

His face showed he was only partly joking. His sudden attempt at humour surprised his aunt, Catrin saw. But Sayer took him seriously.

"Oh, you help, Adam, I assure you. As to you becoming a police officer, there is no reason why not, in time. Talk to Sam here, ask him about it, how he became one. And one day, not too far off, we will have you visit us. You can meet these two officers again and other people involved in the investigation, if you would like that?"

He nodded. "Yes, I would. But not now, though. When I am happy again."

Adam said it so casually. The expectations that go along with innocence, Jan Reimer thought. She turned her head away sharply as her eyes filled with tears.

Sayer's voice was warm. "Whenever you and your aunt and uncle are ready. There is no rush."

Outside, as the three officers regrouped, Sayer was all business. "We are off the record here. Michael?"

Hicks looked at Reimer and Peart. "The person who is truly responsible for this crime is the one who wanted the ring back. We think the gemologist is probably right. That person is someone from Yemen with power and money within the tribal structure. The ring could well be back in Middle East now, with Jaber's partner."

Jan had wondered whether her boss had given her report much credence. It hadn't exactly been a top priority item. Clearly, DCI Hicks had, but it surprised her that it was being raised off the record.

Hicks explained. "There are two ways to play this. One is to be transparent with everyone. That will create a lot of documentation of evidence and make some political noise. We would try to support arrest warrants, involve the Foreign Office and so on. But we decided not to do that.

"We will build this part of the case quietly, bit by bit, and wait it out. We want to arrest the ringleader, preferably on British soil. If not, do so at a location with an extradition treaty. Then we make it visible.

"Tomorrow, both of you will be assigned at the briefing to background checks on the Jabers. You will be instructed to clarify any Yemeni links. Everyone else will breathe a sigh of relief that they don't have to flesh out the background detail. Only you will have the full context of your role."

Peart gave a confirmatory nod, clearly buying in.

Hicks continued, "Nothing speculative is to be recorded in print, or in your notebooks. Also, neither of you are to talk about this line of enquiry with others. Ma'am?"

Catrin looked at the younger officers. "You came this evening, hard as it was, to give you something to keep in mind. That boy. When you next meet Farida Al Araqi and she looks concerned about sharing too much, think of that. We need answers; we need insight, we need detail. I want any elements of evidence that link to the person behind this crime. Al Araqi needs to see it from our perspective. You will work on that."

"Yes, ma'am." There was both understanding and resolve in their brief responses.

Sayer continued, "It will appear that DCI Hicks and others are taking little notice of your work. On the contrary, it will have a lot of attention."

Hicks went on. "We have also tracked down the man

who may have been with Harding when he bought the ring. He works in Birmingham. You will interview him there and then go to London to re-interview Al Araqi. Whatever you find, you first bring it to me. Understood?"

Peart said quickly, "We do, sir. And thank you for the explanation. And bringing us tonight."

Sayer, Reimer noticed, seemed satisfied. The superintendent said, "I'm off home."

Peart assumed he would drive Reimer back to the station or drop her off, but Sayer addressed her. "You studied art, you said? Come back with me."

In the silence as they set off, after ascertaining where Reimer needed to go, Catrin said, "Did you get the feedback through Clarry? My thanks for bringing my daughter's present from London. In the past, Melanie used to give me the job of carrying pottery to customers if I called into the shop."

"Oh, yes. Clarry responded promptly. And it was no trouble." Jan added. "I was being nosey. I had read up on your art."

Catrin smiled. "I gathered. Thank you. I take it as a compliment. Jean said you described yourself as an art lover rather than an artist. Is that fair?"

Reimer smiled. "Hard, but fair. I seem to sponge it up rather than turn it out."

As they drove north-east along the A38 back to Exeter, they talked about art. Nearer home, Jan commented, "You have been very productive over the years, as well as being a police officer."

As Sayer turned at a junction, she said, "I'm a bit divided, but not too much. Early in my teens and already passionate about art, I found myself in a bad situation. I was angry at the world and utterly exhausted by family problems going on around me. At one point, I was left in the care of a police officer for a few hours. What we talked about, what she said, made me want to be exactly like her."

She added. "I iconised her, I suppose, but she inspired me to become a police officer. I still want to be one. And I have learned to live with that duality about the job and the art."

Within five minutes, they arrived at the drop-off point for Reimer.

As Jan opened the door she said, "Thanks for the lift. And the opportunity to work on the art aspects with DC Peart."

"Right. The next step for the whole team is to find Jaber's accomplice, whoever he or she may be. What I want, though, is the person behind it all. That is going to be more difficult. You and John are central to that."

As the Mercedes drove off, Jan Reimer watched it leave before heading up to her flat. She was struck by Sayer's personal revelation.

One person charged; one or more still to get. She wondered if Nabil or Dalia Jaber would reveal the names of the others involved.

19 ASSAD

A day later, Thursday, during the media attention about an early arrest in the Harding murders, the search for the stolen paintings came to a crashing halt.

A young boy using a garbage bin at a service station just off the M3 cut his hand. He had pushed the bag his mother had given him too far into the mouth of the bin. After dealing with the cut inside, an attendant on duty went to change out the bag. On removing the metal bin cover, he found pieces of wood, roughly broken, sticking up into the mouth area. Sharp splinters were partly supported by pieces of crumpled, stiff canvas.

An estimated current value of £30,000 of art had been broken up and discarded.

Given that the search for three paintings had been part of the request to the public in both media statements, the attendant reported the find.

It led to a busy day for the Serious Crimes Team in Exeter.

Late evening, the SOCOs found the cheap utility knife

used to cut the canvas out of the frames in a neighbouring waste bin. A plastic bag and receipt also in there showed it to be a cash purchase from a Tesco Express in Basingstoke. The evidence was transferred to Exeter, for forensic analysis.

The Hampshire police worked fast. By midday Friday, they found CCTV coverage of the purchase and sent it to Exeter.

The vehicle was the Budget rental Skoda. Fingerprints on the plastic bag belonged to one person, presumably the customer shown on the video recording. That image was of an Arabic male in his fifties.

They even found the spot on a broken section of the Wallis frame matching the flake of paint found in the Skoda boot earlier.

As Hicks pressed his teams for more information on the man, an interview team went to Exeter prison, now holding Nabil Jaber. A second team drove to HMP Eastwood Park, where Dalia Jaber was being held.

Silent until now, the days in custody had changed Dalia Jaber. CPS had supported a charge of perversion of the course of justice. With no compliance in prior interviews, DS Tydman and DC Lymes went into this one with a plan to hit her hard.

Sally Lymes opened with, "We now have identified the second person involved in the death of the Harding father and daughter."

She positioned a copy of the mug shot of Nabil and a photo of William Harding side by side facing her. She then placed the images of Ashley Harding in school uniform with the older man, as a pair, alongside.

"Forensic evidence indicates that Ashley Harding was shot first, then her father. Both men will be tried for their murders. As you know, Nabil has already been charged."

Dalia stared at the images. She fell apart, crying, to the extent that they had to pause the interview.

Ten minutes later, on resumption, Dalia finally talked to them.

"The man is called Bital Assad, I think. He came into the restaurant Nabil works at, Nabil said. I only know that because when he asked me to rent the car, he said he was showing Mr. Assad possible locations for a restaurant investment. Nabil was to become a minor partner and the head chef. I have never met the man. I assume this picture is of Assad."

Surprised at the turn around in cooperation, the two detectives took a short break, to inform Hicks. They returned with the instruction to go through a whole set of questions. Most of these Dalia had heard before. But she talked first about Nabil and herself, as if the burden had to be released after days of silence.

"We were living the dream of every young person in our village, you see? With help and hard work, and our studies, we had made it. Nabil, a chef in London. Me, a technologist. For kids back home, mothers and fathers said our names with pride and encouragement for their family's future."

The misery showed on her face, immovable. "And now… everyone will already know or hear the rumours of our failure.

"When Nabil came home and I returned the car, he was angry, sad and wouldn't speak about the trip. I thought he and Assad had argued and disagreed, that the hope of a business together had fallen through. The following day, he had gone to the restaurant by the time I got home from work. He was lost within himself, in despair and disappointment, I thought. He would hardly speak to me, or even look at me."

"But it was worse than that, I found out from you. Far worse. Our lives are ruined, as are those of a family in Devon. There is no way back from this. No way."

They let her talk until she ran dry. Fifteen minutes into their follow-up questions, it emerged that her decision to cooperate had been made yesterday, Thursday morning. Lost in a prison environment, she had told her original solicitor she wanted to talk to the police.

DS Tydman gave the solicitor with her now, a woman called Tremont, an enquiring look. She avoided his eyes, looking at her client.

It was half an hour later, during the next break, that Tydman spoke to the solicitor alone. He had met Anne Tremont before.

She told him, "I wasn't informed. Our firm took this case last night, seeing as Dalia is now in remand. Rahman, from Dalton & Rahman in London, was with her during your earlier interviews, as you know. She telephoned him."

"At what time? We will ask her when we resume, for the record, anyway."

"Yesterday morning, nine twentyish. Someone here helped her to do that. Dalia is lost in this place, like any first timer."

"Anne, let me get this right. Early morning yesterday, your client wanted to talk to us, and we were not informed?"

"I don't think Geoffrey was informed when he was contacted yesterday. He took the call from Doulton & Rahman to engage us. You know Geoffrey; he would never have missed on that."

Tydman knew both solicitors.

Anne said, "Do what you need to do, but let's not forget that Dalia Jaber has cooperated now. And she would have spoken to you before this new evidence appeared. Dalia is a woman without a criminal record, in a foreign country and culture. Her tough shell has cracked, and there is a lot of pain inside."

Tydman nodded, "Noted. I'll call it in. Then we will get back. There is still time for her cooperation to have an impact on the charges against her."

~~

Hicks was waiting for Catrin as she emerged from yet another long Task Force meeting. She looked tired. Seeing him there she asked, "What's up?"

As they walked away, for privacy, he said, "I asked Clarry to let me know when you were finishing. A lot is happening. We have identified the other assailant."

"Go on."

"The trashed paintings found yesterday have led us to the buyer of the knife used. I sent Owen and Lymes to re-interview Dalia. She's talking now and gave us a name; a Bital Assad.

"She's talking, that's great. What next?"

Whatever it was, it wasn't positive, she saw.

Michael said, "We learned that Dalia wanted to speak to us yesterday morning. She called her lawyer then. I wish now that we had been able to keep her at the station, not send her off to remand."

Sayer stopped dead in her tracks. Two people coming up behind had to make their way around, doing the social distancing dance.

"Do we know why? Didn't you say her lawyer was

subbing in locals for the remand phase?"

"Yes. It was Owen's question to the new solicitor. Neither her nor her senior partner who took the call were told that. Anne Tremont found out in the pre-meeting with her client. I had my team barrel in heavy with the new information, so Tremont had no chance to raise it. Dalia fell apart. By the time it got going again, the fact came out."

Catrin said, "That's what; at least a day?"

"Twenty-seven hours. We could have known about this Assad then. It seems he is the older man and may be the lead, if Dali's story holds up. Nabil could be the accomplice. It doesn't affect the charge, of course. We are tracking down Assad now, he is based in France, Dahlia said. The request has gone into the French police. Billings authorised it, as you were tied up."

Catrin said, "But it changes things. A day lost. Are Owen and Lymes still with Dalia Jaber?"

"No, they broke. They will start again tomorrow morning, even if it is Saturday."

"Does the team know?"

"Yes, I decided to tell them at the briefing. They are angry. Most are still around."

"Let's go to see them."

She looked around and saw Clarry was waiting. Catrin said, "I'll be along shortly. Anything critical?"

She passed over her Task Force file folder to her assistant.

"Not desperate, but some things we need to do before the weekend."

"I'll be there a soon as I can."

When Catrin walked into the operations room, about half the team were present, some in the throes of preparing to leave.

It must have been her face, as she stood there. As officers on the phones closed their calls, she said, "I apologise for missing the evening brief, but hear that you have made major progress. Congratulations. I also hear that, for whatever reason, we missed an earlier opportunity to make some of that progress. That was due to a process failure beyond our control."

"You are working hard and setbacks like this are particularly galling. Let it go. Leave it to me. We will establish the reasons for this omission and deal with it."

Lough nodded. "Not easy ma'am, with London solicitors."

It must have been the tone of her response which got to them. "I don't give a damn if it was an Old Bailey judge or a London brief. If there has been negligence, legal malpractice, or conspiracy to pervert the course of justice, I will deal with it. You have my word on that. Now, if you are working, keep this progress rolling. If you are off, enjoy your weekend."

With that and "I'll call you," to Michael Hicks, she was out the door.

In the subsequent buzz, Hicks heard DC Palmer's comment. "She had it all laid out, the various possibilities, from negligence onwards. She is going after the lawyer."

Luffy said, "I wouldn't be surprised if one or more of us get sent to London for a serious chat with our Mr. Rahman."

~~

Catrin spent the weekend with her family in Falmouth, at her sister-in-law's home. Jenifer Treneer owned a small handmade paper business in the town, with Chris as a silent partner. Jen's partner, Mason Carrington, was an internationally established watercolour artist.

Catrin and Chris loved it there, and so did Mair. At one point, Catrin broke away for a work-related call but returned in good spirits. When Mason asked her if she wanted to paint for a while, though, she declined.

He joked, "People pay good money to paint alongside me."

Which was true. Mason couldn't travel around the world giving watercolour classes in these times of Covid. Since the pandemic hit, his local classes and on-line sessions had blossomed. He was still busy.

She relented impulsively. "If we go to Pralla, to the cove, I'll paint. Nessa will bring us out a pot of tea and put you in your place."

Pralla, Porthallow Cove, about twenty miles away, was a scenic spot. She and Mason had painted together there several times. Nessa, a local cottage owner, was a friend of Mason's mother and thought the world of the painter. She also gave him a hard time about his fame and the implied airs and graces.

Jenifer's face gave it away. They hadn't told her and Chris, with Mair present. Mason took Catrin into the garden to apologise. She had only met the Pralla resident a couple of times.

No-one could see Nessa. She was in ICU, sedated. The doctors hoped things might improve, but the prognosis was that she would not make it.

Catrin then took some time alone to call her former colleague, Isabelle Kerswell again, in Paris. Morley was holding his own still, and slowly improving. Which was good news.

Isabelle said, "It seems so slow, though, the improvement. I worry all the time about a relapse."

Catrin could relate. "I felt the same way. But when he comes out of ICU, it will be a milestone for you. It was for me. Hold on to the small steps forward."

Isabelle said after a moment, "Funny peculiar, isn't it? Those years where we talked about art all the time. Now our common ground is ICU and Covid. And I don't have to call you 'Ma'am' anymore."

"It means we are still in touch. Give Morely a virtual hug from me."

As she put her phone away and saw across the garden that Jen and Chris were happily talking, she gave a small prayer of thanks. There were days when the Task Force was a real burden, and now she had another setback on the Harding investigation. But to see her husband happy, with energy... she could handle it.

20 CLARITY

The following Monday, in the lobby of the Royal Courts of Justice in London, two plainclothes police officers approached a cluster of people. It was 9.45 a.m. Two solicitors and two barristers were finalising their plans for the Appeal Court hearing about to start at ten o'clock.

The officers took one solicitor aside and spoke to him briefly. He gave a sentence or two in response and walked away to rejoin his colleagues.

The police officers then took the lawyer, Mohamed Rahman, into custody. They led him out of the building as the remaining trio, flustered by the development, entered the Court of Appeal.

On the pavement outside, DI Kendrick told Rahman that they had some questions. Rahman had refused to see them yesterday evening. They could wait no longer. It was related to the ongoing inquiries into the deaths of William and Ashley Harding.

Kendrick cautioned Rahman, then DC Palmer placed him in the back seat of a waiting car with two uniformed officers in the front. He was on his way to Exeter.

At eleven forty, Catrin took a call from London.

"Commander Moore, ma'am," said Clarry, transferring the call.

"You probably know what this is about, Catrin. We are getting calls. Well, Tom Slieman is."

Assistant Commissioner Slieman was Moore's boss.

"Mohamed Rahman."

"Correct. You arrested a senior solicitor of a law firm in public in Central London as he was going into the Court of Appeal. Our patch. And you did that without informing us in advance. A courtesy, but an important one."

"Technically, Ma'am, it was –."

"The City of London, yes, not our patch. You told the appropriate person with the City police, I'm sure. Where is Rahman? Just so I know?"

"Probably near Bristol now, heading here. We have twenty-four hours, and we will keep him for that."

"Would it be too impolite of me to ask what you have on him? If you feel I can be trusted, of course."

The sarcasm was layered thick.

"Of course. Rahman represents Dalia Jaber, now in custody for hiring the car and abetting her brother Nabil Jaber, now charged with murder. They are both Yemeni citizens. Rahman and his partner do a lot of work for Arab clients including the Embassy of Yemen.

"Neither Nabil nor Dalia cooperated with us in the initial interviews. After remand, Dalia told Rahman that she wanted to talk to us. That was Thursday morning. It took twenty-seven hours before the local solicitor engaged in his stead heard that. It didn't come from Rahman, but from her client as we interviewed her again.

"At that interview, we received from her a name of the possible second killer, a man called Assad. Coincidently, we had turned up evidence, including a CCTV image, of the man. My team working this weekend tracked Assad's movements to Paris. He then took a flight to Aden, arriving there four hours before the French police tracked him down."

There was a pause.

Moore said, "There was a possibility, given an earlier timeframe, that you might have got him – or the French would?"

"A possibility, yes. I want to know why, having spent two days with his client and understanding the serious nature of the charges, he did not act on her request. My officers were sent to London and tried to speak to him on Sunday evening at his home. He refused. He had guests, he claimed, and told them he would talk to them during business hours. On Monday, they went to his office first thing, to learn that he was at the courts. When they spoke to him there, he gave them the brush-off again, so they acted on my direct instruction."

Moore responded, "Well, the news is out there, that Devon and Cornwall Police have arrested a solicitor in London. The media will be on it and the noise says it is to do with the Harding murders. You are front and centre on that. Assistant Commissioner Slieman is hearing complaints that a former Met officer is rattling our cage. Tom doesn't believe a word of it but wanted to check. I'll fill him in."

Moore paused, then asked. "What's your gut feel about Rahman?"

"Not sure yet. He may be the sort who places everyone second to his own priorities; clients, police, you name it. But he could be bent. We have two people in remand on

151

serious charges who are first time offenders. That places a lot of focus on the quality of advice of their counsel.

"In the lost twenty-seven-hour period, we could have had a more useful interview with Dalia. A foreign national who killed two people, we believe, has absconded to a country where we can't arrest him. Either we have a case for referral of Rahman to the Solicitors Regulation Authority, or he is complicit in Assad's escape. If the former, we will push hard with the SRA. If the latter, we will charge him. Either way, a lot of mud is going to stick. We aren't making any press statement until we have interviewed him and made our call, with CPS input."

"Sounds good. Well, good luck. But a lawyer won't be behind all this. I take it someone is in your sights who is?"

Karen Moore heard the slight hesitation.

Catrin said, "We are working on that. I have my own ideas, but we have no proof, nor any solid leads. As far as I am concerned, this investigation remains open until all persons involved in the deaths of William and Ashley Harding are in custody."

Karen Moore got the impression that Sayer knew exactly who she was going after.

"You are going after someone in Yemen or Saudi, aren't you? If so, and that person has influence, FCO will show their teeth. No more cosseting by your friend Turner-Jones."

Madaleine Turner-Jones was a mid-level Foreign Office bureaucrat, a friend of Catrin's.

Catrin responded with, "We've already had that warning, from a Nathan Atkins."

"Ah, Nathan. Yes, we know him. Is Jessop shaking in his shoes?"

"Not that I saw. No. He was distinctly unimpressed, I would say."

There was a long moment of silence, then Moore said, "Well, I think from now on, you had better call me Karen, one-on-one. Not ma'am. Tom Slieman said you are more like me than I am. I must be mellowing in my old age. Let me know how it goes."

"Yes, m– Karen, I will. Thank you."

As she put the phone down, Clarry entered, seeing the line clear. "I have both Ursula Otley and DCI Hicks wanting to talk to you urgently, Catrin. Which one first?"

"Michael."

When Hicks connected, his first words were, "We have some issues to resolve with CPS. They want a meeting as soon as possible, online. With both Jackson and Berry."

Ewen Jackson was their assigned CPS case officer. Sean Berry was his boss, the senior crown prosecutor for Devon and Cornwall.

Catrin sighed. "OK, set it up as soon as you can. I have another call to make first, but after that, I'll be free. Say in fifteen minutes at earliest."

~~

Ewen Jackson opened the call with, "We are going for a full committal hearing for Nabil Jaber."

A pre-trial procedure, at the level of the Magistrate's Court. It would assess whether the body of evidence was sufficient to take to the Crown Court for the full trial.

It did not surprise either Catrin or Michael. The failure to find the weapons was one element. They had discussed already that a committal hearing was a possible CPS strategy.

But there was more, they could both tell.

Berry was an older, experienced prosecutor. "With the news that the other person accused is abroad, unlikely to be available to stand trial, it weakens the case against Jaber. We are going to get into the defense teams fighting each other about relative guilt.

"Jaber's barrister could argue the powder residues were from Assad's gun, that he never shot anyone. He was there, yes, but he tried to stop the bleeding in Ashley Harding's leg. It opens a considerable element of doubt, and that's all the jury needs."

Hicks was looking angry now. "No. We can't be thinking of offering a manslaughter plea, surely? My team would be gutted by that. They have –."

Catrin cut him off. "What do you need?"

Berry said, "Clarity. We need to know as a priority who shot William Harding, from a legal perspective. The head shot was premeditated murder. It is our strongest case."

"We will try to get that – and quickly."

Berry nodded. She added, "And, you have heard we have brought in the solicitor, Rahman."

The older prosecutor was curious. "Yes, we heard. It is a news item in legal circles."

She said firmly, her Welsh accent coming out more noticeably, "If we find any trace that he sabotaged the arrest of this man Assad, I want him charged. Not a pussyfoot hearing by a disciplinary committee, but a criminal charge."

Ewen Jackson was looking concerned. He wasn't used to someone dictating terms to his boss. But Berry appeared unperturbed.

He replied, "If you find any evidence that Rahman deliberately – note the word – interfered with the investigation, I will support it. You can include him with Jaber and Assad, for aiding and abetting after the fact."

Two minutes later, alone, Michael asked Catrin how she thought they were going to achieve either objective.

He didn't think it should rest on the shoulders of the current interview teams.

Hicks added, "Erica is reviewing the forensics again, to reassess the shooter positions now we have the heights of Assad and Jaber."

Catrin nodded. They sat silently for a few seconds. She said, "We'll do it. I'll do Nabil Jaber, you do the solicitor. And talk to Jackson again. See if CPS will go along with dropping all charges against Dalia Jaber."

Hicks gave her a sharp look, its meaning clear. She was getting to be hands-on and that was not her role.

She ignored it.

Catrin said simply, "If it goes belly up with Jaber, I will take the hit. You just say you did as you were told. I have no future here; you do."

~~

It was four-thirty p.m. when the Serious Crimes team assembled in the operations room. Michael Hicks brought everyone up to date. They had heard already that Jaber was being brought over from HMP Exeter.

"I will lead the interview with Mohamed Rahman, with DS Tydman. DI Wastle will interview Nabil Jaber, but Superintendent Sayer will lead off with him. Lymes, be prepared to replace her, when she leaves."

He saw the reaction on some of the faces. Some showed surprise as Sayer's name was mentioned. Others grimaced and DC Neil scowled openly. Lough pursed his lips in a small smile. DS Tydman nodded thoughtfully.

Michael was glad Sayer had decided to miss the briefing. She expected this mix of responses, too.

DC Neil asked, "Who will supervise the interview feedback if you and the Super are doing our jobs?"

That was normally Hicks' job.

"DI Kendrick will."

Neil's face made it clear she disagreed with the path forward, but she stayed silent.

In the buzz afterwards, DC Rollins wondered how effective Sayer would be in an interview. "Senior officers get to be – well, you know, administrators, really."

Jackie Neil said, with certainty, "She will balls it up. It should be one of us, not her, an officer –."

She stopped herself as Lough gave her a hard look. He said quietly, "She ran a team at least as big as this one in Organized Crime at the Met. Let's put it this way; if I was on the wrong side of the table, she would be the last one I would want to be poking away at my story."

Jackie retorted, "Not Hicksey?"

They knew his capabilities. Jackie was irritated by the sudden show of support for the Reaper. Lough didn't respond, just looked at her.

"A pint on it," she said.

"You're on," Lough replied.

Angry, Jackie said, "These interviews will either get CPS off their arses or screw up the investigation. It shouldn't be a desk jockey sticking pins in our names doing it for old times' sake."

With that she stormed off.

21 NABIL

"Mr. Jaber, I am Superintendent Sayer. I'd like you to call me Catrin. It is a Welsh name. And I ask your permission to call you Nabil, if I may? Is that agreeable?"

Nabil gave a slight nod of the head. This informal opening had surprised him. And the uniform. And the soft tone of voice. She was obviously a more senior officer from the lapel insignia. Her voice was musical, an accent he had heard from time to time in his restaurant. From Wales, as she said.

He focused on the scar, the white line on her tanned cheek, reminding him of home, of similar lines on people injured at work or in conflict, lines that never darkened. He wondered where her battle had been. Her eyes engaged him, pulling him out of his effort to stay unfocused, to stay within himself.

In the days he had been in custody, he had aged, he knew. There were dark rings under his eyes. He looked exhausted, beaten by life. She sees that, he thought. But she is another one who wants to get inside my head.

In the operations room, Lough was standing behind Starr's monitor. She was charged with making the video-recording to compliment the official audiorecord. She and several other officers heard him say to himself, "Well, well, well."

Starr looked at him and murmured, "He's paying attention."

Jackie Neil's face showed her view of Sayer's cosy start.

Sayer was studying Nabil carefully, glancing occasionally at his legal representative.

"I will take that as yes, your nod. Nabil, with the agreement of the Crown Prosecution Service, I have now taken the decision to drop all charges against your sister Dalia. She will be released as soon as we can schedule a court hearing, as they set bail for her, not us. We will ask that the court set conditions to ensure her appearance as a witness at your trial. Otherwise, she will go home to London. She will live a normal life."

Nabil couldn't contain the smile at the news. He said nothing, but his face reacted, as hard as he tried to stay impassive. It was his first bright spot since Assad came into Taquil's Restaurant.

Sayer leaned forward a fraction and continued in the same collegial tone, "When you kill someone with a gun at close quarters, people like you and me, not psycho-paths, it changes us, doesn't it? We are normal people in abnormal circumstances. We see the bullet or bullets enter the body, the terrible damage we have inflicted.

"You coped better than I did. That is clear. I went into shock. You kept on going. You were, for a period, a soldier, whereas I wasn't. You grew up in a different world than I did. Perhaps differences like that are the reason.

"But we carry the same burden afterwards, don't we? I know where you are, I think. In your cell you are back in time, tracing the exact point you could have done something different. You revisit it over and over – and it gets you nowhere.

"With me, the young man I killed, a teenager really, had just badly wounded a colleague and was preparing to fire at me. I had no choice. But still I went over it in my mind again and again."

Nabil had now forgotten his effort to maintain his detachment. He was hit full force by the realisation that this woman knew what really happened and, from her eyes, she even understood his situation.

In the operations room, among the little group gathered, it had been quiet. Someone said, "She shot someone?"

Another said, "Look at his face." Jaber's impassive stonewalling expression had turned into a look of fear.

Sayer's voice kept the same soft cadence. "In my case, it was in front of a crowd. I had support, I went into shock, I got treatment, I came through it. Still, sometimes at three in the morning..."

Sayer didn't finish the sentence. She sat there, moving her elbows on to the table, her face resting on her thumbs with the fingers meshed. She never took her eyes off Jaber's face.

Nabil could only look back at her, drawn by the fact that since the moment the weapon fired, that thought of what he could have done differently had never moved far from the front of his mind.

As the silence went on, DI Wastle looked at the lawyer, willing him by his expression to sit there, not interrupt.

A minute is a long time in an interview room.

Then Nabil Jaber took a deep breath and looked away, at the wall.

Sayer's voice resumed, a little stronger, more forceful. "We know about Bital Assad, Nabil. I'll tell you now, he is back in Yemen, not Paris. But we identified him as the second person. And we know his height. We have reworked the trajectory calculations and have figured it out. You killed Ashley, not William, as we first thought, didn't you?"

She waited a moment, seeing his expression change.

"Assad shot William Ashley afterwards. But you shot Ashley in the leg, with a gun you had never used before, brought to you by bikers. You had no prior practice with the weapon, Nabil, did you? No real feel for its trigger pressure, the age of the weapon or its wear and tear. You had never stripped it, checked it. You were holding a firearm that had been through the hands of a dozen bikers. The weapon probably hadn't seen a competent armourer since its manufacture."

Behind Starr, the unofficial commentator added another pearl of wisdom. "She seems to know a lot about firearms."

Luffy told him to shut-the-fuck-up.

"A gun like that is worse than any other. It was an accident, wasn't it? You had no intention to kill her or even injure her. You – no, I correct that; Assad wanted the ring. It was far more valuable than anyone knew, and you were his accomplice."

On cue, DI Wastle added, "Nabil, when you shot Ashley, both you and her father went to help her. You tried to stop the bleeding. Assad took two steps forward and shot William Harding in the back of the head."

For Nabil, the description of what happened was so accurate, so vivid, it was as if they had a video of the event. Or Assad had talked. But that was impossible.

His pent-up frustration, remorse, self-loathing, and guilt released in an angry response; he jumped to his feet.

They had hoped for, expected a reaction at some point. The uniformed officer moved quickly as Jaber stood. Nabil's hands were now on the table, his fingers spread as he leaned forward.

He shouted, "I can say nothing! How can you know all this? How? Who told you? I can say nothing! Understand?"

The officer reached him, a hand on his shoulder as his solicitor spoke up, trying to calm him into retaking his seat.

Catrin responded, "Do you deny it, Nabil?"

Jaber looked frightened now, eyes wide. Without realising it, he shook his head as he muttered, "No. But I can say nothing."

He sat down.

As he did so, Catrin Sayer stood. Her expression showed that his last response told them a lot. The video would be enough. It would meet CPS needs.

She looked at DI Wastle, raised her eyebrows momentarily. She turned away as he said, "Superintendent Sayer is leaving the room."

As Nabil refocused, he found one of his regular police interviewers facing him as DC Lymes announced her presence.

Oliver Wastle asked, "Nabil, will you confirm the following statement from your sister? 'I knew nothing about the route of this vehicle. I rented it for Nabil to take a man called Assad to look at potential locations for a new restaurant'."

He waited a moment, then added, "Did you tell her that was the reason for the car rental from Budget?"

Jaber looked beaten.

Nabil thought only for a second. "Yes, I told her that. I can support my sister, at least. That is all I can do. You do not know Yemen and our ways. I have other family."

And everyone is at risk in a world where our shaykh has the final say, he thought.

Oliver could not stop himself. "Adam Harding, ten years old, had family, too."

As the guilt hit him afresh, Nabil heard the accusation and condemnation in the tone of voice of this detective. He was back on familiar ground. He could handle that much easier than the Welsh woman reading his mind. No-one could condemn him more than he did himself.

Wastle saw the now familiar stonewall expression return to Nabil Jaber's face.

~~

Michael Hicks had watched the outburst from Jaber by videolink while in DCC Billings office. He looked at Billings, standing with him.

"She got what Berry needed."

Billings' response was, "Now, let's find out if this solicitor enabled Assad to escape. Your turn. Did you know Sayer had shot and killed someone?"

Hicks shook his head. "No. I haven't kept track of her since the time she was a DS."

The senior officer said, "It was in Malaysia, some visit or other. An attack on a car with her and some Malaysian police officer. Still, let's not distract you. Rahman won't be leaping out of his seat."

Billings heard Michael Hicks mutter, as he left the room, "If he does, I'll throw him back into it."

He pretended he never heard it.

DCI Hicks sat down and DS Tydman switched on the recorder. Hicks took them through the identification step and followed with a rhetorical question.

"Lawyers and policeman never begin anything with a question they don't already know the answer to, do they?"

He was watching Rahman carefully. An experienced lawyer, he wouldn't be one for tantrums or wild outbursts. His eyes and body language showed he was angry. As Hicks opened the file, the email received from France was visible and he made no attempt to hide it.

"This telephone number, Mr. Rahman. Do you know it? Will we find it in your phone records, do you think?"

He reversed the page, pointing at the number.

Rahman hardly glanced at the document. "I don't keep track of numbers; my phone list is names, not numbers, to me."

Then, as an afterthought, he added, "Not that you have any right to access my phone list, anyway."

He must be seething, thought Michael, to throw in gratuitous comments, on record.

"The number is the mobile number of a Mr. Bital Assad, based in Paris. Do you know a Bital Assad?"

"Mr. Assad is an assistant to a gentleman called Majid Fayed. My firm does some work for Mr. Fayed's company, in the areas of contract law. We also handle some import and export regulatory filings. But I am a criminal lawyer, so I have had no significant contact with Assad, no.

"You smile, Chief Inspector. Do I amuse you?"

"No sir, you do not. It is simply the vagaries of the English language. I am trying to ascertain if you are a criminal as well as lawyer. Can you identify the man in this CCTV image, please?"

He passed over the photograph.

Rahman peered at the printout of the CCTV image, from a petrol station. The person filling the tank, the driver it appeared, was facing away from the camera. The face of the person in the front passenger seat was visible.

"This looks to be Mr. Assad."

"Mr. Bital Assad?"

"Yes."

Hicks swept the print back into the folder and closed it.

"Mr. Rahman, I am asking you to allow us to see your mobile phone, the call log, please?"

"I haven't spoken to Mr. Assad on my phone, as I recall."

Hicks countered with, "We are looking for confirmation you received a call from Dalia Jaber, from prison."

The solicitor suddenly looked worried. "I did, yes. I will confirm that. Is that why I am dragged here?"

Hicks responded, "No sir, you are here because you wouldn't answer these questions from my officers either Sunday evening or this morning. Dalia Jaber confirmed the name Assad to us in our last interview with her. She is co-operating with us. Based on her information, we are withdrawing the charges against her."

He could see that surprised the solicitor.

"The French police have informed us they missed taking Assad into custody by only hours. He left Paris for Aden, arriving there four hours before they arrived at his apartment. His clothes and some items are gone, indicating he isn't away on a short trip. And Mr. Fayed, the man you say you do know, is claiming it is a surprise to him as well.

"The person you identified as Mr. Assad in the vehicle is a suspect in the murders. The person filling the petrol tank is Nabil Jaber, as you may have guessed.

"You are here about two events linked to the obstruction of a police investigation. First, your client wanted to speak to us with time-critical information. You did not report that. Second, you have had contact with others linked to the crime without reporting that to us also. Once we go through your phone, we will see how much contact there was, won't we?"

He opened the file again. "This is a search warrant for your phone. It extends to other phone records - your home phone and business phones. I am going to give you some time to think it through. My advice, sir, is that you ask for a solicitor to represent you."

With that he stood, as Tydman stated that they were taking a break. The two police officers left the interview room.

They gave him only ten minutes. On resumption, DS Tydman asked him if he wanted legal representation.

"I would like to make a statement. Based on that and your decision on charges, I reserve the right to legal representation at that time."

"I practised law, criminal defense law, for nearly eight years in Leeds. I have another further nine years in that role so far in London. There has never been anything to suggest corruption of any sort. You can check that. Indeed, you will be checking that with the relevant authorities.

"There have been three complaints against me to the Solicitors Regulation Authority, the SRA, or its predecessor. All came from clients or their relatives. None resulted in penalties to me. For a lawyer in criminal defense, that is well within the low end of the complaint spectrum.

"I refute entirely the suggestion that I aided the flight

of a suspect. Your statement was the first time I heard of any involvement of Assad in this case."

Hicks interjected. "Not from your client?"

Rahman glowered at him. "Communication between my client and myself is privileged, yes? But I chose my words carefully. The mention of Assad in connection with this investigation was first made known to me by you. Listen first, please?"

"Mr. Fayed paid my firm's fees to defend Dalia Jaber. I suspect, but do not know, that Nabil Jaber's defense is similarly contracted. The mews home that the Jaber's share is leased by Mr. Fayed's company. I know that Mr. Fayed paid for the chef training course for Nabil. He was also instrumental in securing the job for Dalia Jaber. Fayed also helped financially a cousin of theirs living here now, a doctor in Manchester. Call it paternalism if you wish, a fairy godfather, whatever. In the world they come from – indeed, that my father came from – it is the culture. Favours granted; favours owed. A heirarchy. A structure.

"My phone will show that I spoke to Mr. Fayed twice since the engagement. Once, after his office contacted me, simply to thank him for the work. The second occasion was after your decision to charge and remand her. He wanted to know how she was. I told him that she was traumatized, as much by the process as by the charge. She was not communicating with me or the police.

"My principal reason for that call was to advise him, given the charges, that the costs would go up considerably. I needed his perspective on how that sat with him. His answer was, 'whatever it takes'. He would support Dalia and Nabil's defense.

"Your comment on my delay in advising you of my client's wish to talk is correct. That is my failing. I was in the middle of the final preparations for the Appeal Court hearing, the one from which your officers removed me. It is a complex case and had a time-sensitive element. We went straight into the final briefing of the barrister. Then I went home late, to a private event. Whether you charge me or not, I will be self-reporting my failure to act to the SRA.

"Finally, if the hearing into the appeal was impaired in any way by my absence, I will seek redress. We will wait on the Lord Justices' decision on the appeal first, of course."

"Now, I would like a break. I want to confer with colleagues about their perspective on the hearing I missed. I will use one of your phones, if mine is being examined."

He was back to being a lawyer in combat, eyeing them, waiting for the questions.

In her office, Sayer looked across at the Crown prosecutor, wondering what he was thinking.

Ewen Jackson's mouth turned down as he spoke. "He blusters well. I'd like to know the time he spoke to Anne Tremont's partner, engaging them, how that fits in. The sequence of his calls to different people had better support his claim."

Catrin nodded. Jackson added, "And we need to know if this man Fayed is anything more than a squeaky-clean benefactor. It still stings, that we could have got Assad in Paris."

Catrin said nothing. It was more than a sting. She did not trust her abilities to stay calm and professional about it.

~~

In the pub afterwards, Jackie Neil said, "What'll it be?"

She was even upbeat about it, pulling out her credit card.

Jan Reimer had joined them simply to see the reaction.

When they sat down and talked about the day, Jackie said, "I was wrong about her. You were right. She must have a lot of interview experience to know how to get straight into his head. That was nowhere near interview guideline standards."

Luffy sipped his pint. "True."

She waited for his wisdom. He said nothing.

Rollins spoke up. "It could have fallen flat on its face. All Jaber had to do was hold to his 'strong and silent' stance.

"True," repeated Lough.

Again, he went silent. After a minute or so, Jackie could not take it any longer. "So, what do you think? Your money was on her all along."

Lough sighed and glanced around the table. "I think she's our superintendent on this case and you should give up the 'scowl at the Reaper' bullshit."

Jan resisted the urge to add to that, given the instructions from Sayer and Hicks outside the Wansbury home. She thought Sayer was doing the job well.

Rollins looked at Reimer. "Are you alright with her and Hicksey pushing you into the background detail stuff, missing out?"

Jan sipped her half of lager. Ecstatic, she thought. "I'm OK with it; yes." She looked at Lough. "For now."

Lough raised his glass. "We have one charged with murder and the other identified. Let's drink to that."

22 FLOOZIE

One bright spot was Catrin's reception at the briefing on Tuesday morning. The glances of mistrust had gone. Some said 'Ma'am' in passing with a new respect. People seemed relaxed around her. She felt welcome.

There was nothing too overt, but after months of feeling out in the desert, she had found an oasis.

By then, Peart and Reimer were on their way to Birmingham by train. From there, they would travel on to London. For background work, said Hicks, during his summary of assigned tasks. The pair would interview a former embassy staffer, William Alistair Allingham, who may have known Harding and may know something about the ring.

Relatively minor items, it seemed.

"A lot of 'mays' there," whispered DC Neil, rolling her eyes. Probably a waste of time and money, she conveyed. Steve Rollins gave her a shrug.

They were assigned to interview Rahman's contacts, to see if his story held up. He had been released.

Bill Allingham told DC John Peart that he would prefer to meet outside if they insisted on an in-person interview. They were in the middle of a pandemic, do you know? Which made it easier for Peart and Reimer; they took the train to the centre of Birmingham.

They met up in Victoria Square, outside the city offices where he now worked. Nearby was a large stone statue of a nude bather officially called 'The River'.

Allingham was in his forties, shaven headed, with the stubble indicating he was mostly bald on top. He didn't seem nervous, just resigned. His first words after introductions were, "You'll want to record this, I suppose; so, let's go over there."

He pointed.

They hadn't planned on doing that, as it was an informal interview, not one under caution. They didn't look a gift horse in the mouth, either.

Jan was taking in the sculpture, the reclining female figure surrounded by a flower bed awaiting new plants and warmer weather. She said, "So that's the Floozie?"

Allingham smiled. "Yes. The original set-up was a fountain, known to all as 'The Floozie in the Jacuzzi'. It used to have a pool around it, but it kept leaking. They are planning to change it back again, I hear. It is about Bill Harding, you said. Fire away."

The voice had a timbre suggesting that Allingham usually led a discussion.

Peart asked, "You were with the British Embassy in Riyadh at the time William Harding was with the Board of Trade. Can you tell us about your relationship with him?"

Reimer had already pulled out her phone and switched on the recorder, showing it to Allingham.

"I was a member of the embassy staff responsible for

visitors. We supported the various government and business delegations from the UK. Everything from organising local arrangements to keeping them out of trouble. When needed, I arranged to get them home."

Peart asked, "To sober up? That sort of getting home?"

"No. The bodies. People die of natural causes abroad, as anywhere else. There, it was heart attacks sometimes, brought on by a lack of understanding of the need for acclimatisation. Mad dogs and Englishmen..."

He paused. "William Harding was a member of one of the trade delegations. We knew each other in a professional contact sense and a few times we went out for the evening. That's it, really."

Peart came back with, "What do you mean by 'went out'; dinners, night clubs, casinos?"

Allingham smiled. "No. To give him local experience; some authentic food and the traditional markets there, called souqs."

They waited him out then.

"Delegations of civil servants or businessmen mostly want good hotels and safety. They are there to achieve an objective then get the hell out, home. Some want a wilder time, but we discouraged it, and occasionally got them out of trouble. Bill wanted to understand the culture a bit, see things. He had no Arabic, no local knowledge, and was sensible enough to take advice. He and I got on well and he always paid the restaurant bills."

"Did you go to Yemen with him?"

It surprised Allingham. "Yemen. No. Neither did he go there, as far as I know."

Seeing their expressions, he said, "Check the travel advisories, back then and now. They say, 'Do not go there. If you are there, shelter in place until rescued', or something like that. There is a war on. The UN needs millions of dollars every year in aid to stave off famine."

He paused. "Even in our time there, the embassy in Saudi didn't take his delegation anywhere near the border with Yemen. Why do you ask?"

Reimer responded, "A piece of jewelry was stolen during the crime. We believe it to be of Yemeni origin and his family said he bought it on a delegation trip."

Allingham stared into the distance, thinking. "A ring, perhaps?"

"Yes."

"He bought one in the market at Souq Al Thumairi, in Riyadh, during a visit in 2009. Their delegation had two visits that year. I think it was the second, so that would be in October. It had a jewel in it."

Peart glanced at Jan. She pulled out the photo of the ring. "This one?"

Allingham looked at it intently.

"It seems similar, but I thought it was silver, not gold. In fact, I am sure it was silver. So, this isn't it."

Reimer responded. "What more can you tell us about that ring and its acquisition?"

Allingham collected his thoughts before speaking. "I went out with Harding because he had a sense of place about him. He didn't try to frame everything in the 'Brit abroad' mentality. He liked to buy small items, not too expensive but not dirt cheap trash either. Bill wanted the context for them, whether a handmade leather belt or a piece of jewelry.

"He was a natural negotiator. It went with his professional role, but the man had also developed the art of 'graceful bargaining' in the souqs. We were walking in the Al Thurmairi souq looking at the stalls when we were approached by a local woman. She was accompanied by a younger man, and they glued on to Bill like a magnet. The woman was selling a ring, a silver ring, explaining it had a valuable sapphire.

"She used a word to describe it, but I don't recall it. I remember looking it up on my phone because the young man with her had already pulled up a web reference. He was helping her to push the sale. But the stone wasn't blue, it was a pink colour. Harding seemed to pick up on it. He was, what's the word? 'Well-rounded', that's it. Knew a lot of things.

"I was telling her we were only looking when she showed him the ring. She had phrases of English but was by no means fluent. Bill seemed to like the ring; a fatal error, showing that."

He grimaced. "There was a desperation about her and her voice. Her plight got to him; I suspect. To me, it wasn't the standard pleading of the marketplace. She was well-dressed conservatively, as well.

"Whatever, Bill examined the ring and asked how much. She said two thousand, I recall. Saudi Riyal, I mean.

"He looked at me and said, 'I'm going to buy it,' then he did something which surprised me. He told her he would pay in pounds. I know he had some local currency, but sterling was an acceptable alternative. They like US dollars and sterling. He gave her eight fifty-pound notes and I could see her calculating, so I told her in Arabic that after exchange fees, it gave her about 1900 Riyal, a fair offer.

"Then Bill gave her another fifty-pound note. She seemed surprised and asked me in Arabic how to give change. Bill picked up the intent and just said, 'no change' and I translated."

Peart interjected, "Why did he do that? Did he say later?"

Allingham shook his head. "No. He saw the value of the stone and didn't want to be cheapskate about it, would be my read of the situation – and him. She said 'thank you' in accentuated English then asked me in Arabic to tell him she was very grateful. She just looked at him intently, as if a weight was off her shoulders, and he smiled. Then she was gone."

Allingham looked at each of the officers. "The thing is, you see, it shows how well Bill had picked up being in that environment. If I had his wealth and understood the value of the ring, I would have done the same, sensing her need. She must have been desperate to sell dowry jewelry."

"Did you tell him that?"

Allingham shook his head. "He was talking about how his wife would love it. The last thing he needed was to give him a guilt trip to go with the present. As it was, I wondered if the sapphire was a fake, just well-cut glass. I had no idea whether he had a bargain or had wasted his money. Anything else?"

Jan Reimer asked, "The word she used to describe the ring. Can you recall it at all?

He paused. "No. As I said, Bill picked up on it."

"Was it padparadscha?"

Allingham's face changed. "It could be. It has the right length and sound to it. But I really can't remember. But it was to do with the jewel, not the ring design."

Peart asked, "Would his work while you knew him have given him enemies over there?"

"Who would kill him now? And his daughter? No. His field was pretty dry stuff. I don't know that side of it. You would need to talk to people in Trade about that. I'm simply basing it on his own description."

'How many trips did he make?"

"About a dozen over the years I was there. With others. It was a team visit each time, with generally two or three people representing the department."

Reimer asked, "The woman; did you get a name, or see her around after that?"

"Riyadh is not like that. No. Once only, then she left."

He looked at his watch. "I have another few minutes, then I have a meeting."

Peart said, "One final question. Did you see Harding in the UK at all?"

"No. We weren't friends, in that sense. He was a client, another civil servant. One week it would be a trade delegation, next a group to talk about some international convention or other. If he mixed with anyone, it would be someone up the ladder. An embassy is like the military, a rank and authority structure. You don't become a deputy lieutenant of a county in England by mixing socially with frontline grunts. But there wasn't anyone I was aware of he was friends with there."

He stood, reminding them of his time constraint. "Harding just made the effort to explore the place a bit, not hide away in the hotel bars."

As the two officers stood also, Jan commented, "From Arabia to Birmingham; that is quite change for you."

He smiled ruefully. "Global to local, yes. Embassy and diplomatic jobs have their own lifespan. At my level, you stay long term or get out before you find you can't, you are hooked to an expatriate life. The overseas assignments were fascinating, and I enjoyed a lot of it. But you need to be constantly aware of your surroundings and safety."

He shook hands with them. "I have a wife and a young son now. I can go to work without watching my back or following a range of customs that I understand but don't agree with.

"Above all, I am glad I no longer need to play minder to visiting wallies groaning out loud about lack of pubs. It never occurred to them how crass that sounds to locals. They were in a country where the consumption of alcohol could have people severely punished."

As he disappeared back to City Hall offices, Peart said, "Well, the mystery behind the ring is partly explained. We won't be finding a sales receipt for it."

Their next stop was London, by train, to see Farida Al Araqi. This time, they wanted more answers, as Superintendent Sayer had said.

~~

In Exeter, Rollins and Neil sat opposite Oliver Wastle, across his desk. Their conclusion was that Mohamed Rahman was telling the truth. The barrister engaged for the Court of Appeal had been persuasive during his interview.

"Mo and his junior were totally focused on the preparations for the appeal when I met with them. We had several new elements to deal with at short notice, so we were all absorbed."

Wastle printed out a document and passed it to Jackie. "Rahman has already self-reported to the Solicitors Regulation Agency, even sending us a copy. You put together the documents on our complaint and prepare a briefing note for the superintendent and CPS. She will prepare the cover letter to SRA herself."

He looked at Rollins. "You are with DS Lough for the next while. We still have those weapons to track down."

23 AL ARAQI

John Peart set the tone with Farida Al Araqui as soon as they sat down. They met in a small meeting room she had reserved at the Museum of Natural History.

"I have it booked only for another half hour. You said three-thirty."

They were half an hour later than planned, due to a delay outside Paddington station.

Peart said, "That's fine. We are investigating the deaths of two people, including a twelve-year-old girl. We will all go to Kensington Police Station if we need to."

Reimer watched the Yemeni stiffen. In their preparations for the follow-up, Reimer was uneasy with Peart. Sayer's instruction was to get Al Araqi outside her comfort zone. Jan thought that pressure was not the tactic, but he went straight into it.

Al Araqi responded carefully, "I am not involved. You have no basis for that action. And if you want to take me to a police station, do it now. I will insist on legal representation."

Before Peart could escalate the problem, Reimer said,

"We want to understand more about the background to the ring we discussed. Your input last time was helpful to us, but restrained, I thought."

Al Araqui said, "It was more than helpful, I felt. I went beyond my area of expertise."

Peart was unrelenting. "You held back information that could assist us. And we, not you, determine its relevance. We want to know more about both the ring and this Shaykh Yusuf Abrahim you mentioned."

He remained calm but his voice was firm and impassive, not persuasive.

Al Araqui showed no emotion, just stared at him, taking his measure. Jan was at a loss how to move this forward.

The gemologist said firmly, "Frank mentioned that Inspector Catrin Sayer, formerly with Art and Antiques, put you on to him. That she now works with you. I will speak to her."

Reimer said, "Yes, she is Superintendent Sayer."

"Whatever. Call her. I will speak to her or to no-one. You must do as you wish."

Reimer glanced at Peart. He was deciding how to respond, to take her to a police station or accept her ultimatum. From her face, Farida Al Araqui did not seem to be at all flexible. Jan gave him a grimace, a quick show of her concern about how this was developing.

Peart reached into his bag and pulled out a tablet computer. As he opened it, he said, "We will call her, see if she is available. If she is, fine; if not, you will answer our questions at the police station."

He passed it to Reimer to set up a Zoom link as he called Exeter on his mobile. He wasn't happy, she could see that. But none of them were. It had got off to the wrong start.

"Superintendent Sayer, good afternoon."

Reimer watched the two women assessing each other over the videolink.

"Yes, Dr. Al Iraqui, good afternoon to you. You told my colleagues you wished to speak with me."

"Yes. It appears to me that you are the one whom I must satisfy. Some days ago, I gave Constable Reimer all the help I could, under the circumstances. Now you or someone else sent officers back to see me. Clearly, you or they think I know more than I do."

Sayer said, "PC Reimer got that impression, yes. So do you?"

"I have no more facts. In giving you the names of the jewellers, I was doing my job, using my expertise. In giving you the name Shaykh Yusuf, I was exceeding that."

Reimer wondered how to respond, but Sayer said without hesitation, "I don't buy that. You are a British citizen now. We checked. Unless you have something to hide, I expect you to help us as much as possible. A Yemeni man has, we believe, murdered a young girl and her father. Your insight could move forward our investigation. The public has been extremely helpful so far, so I ask you to reflect on why you would not do all you could to assist us?"

That's more like it, thought Reimer.

It seemed to resonate with Al Araqui. "Tell me, if you wish; the ring came into the possession of the murdered man somewhere in the Middle East, did it not?"

Sayer responded, "Yes. He had not sought out that ring. It just happened."

Farida nodded. "Probably sold to him by someone wanting cash, a woman, probably."

She sighed.

"I know nothing of this ring or the event. I have no

more facts, only fears. Fears for this woman based on my own life, years ago, and the experiences of other women.

"If I were to fly back to that part of the world with PC Reimer here, she would feel the hours of flight, the sense of distance. She would see modern airports and richly appointed public plazas. I would feel that I was going back a thousand years. I would be in a country without the rights that matter to me now. It is not necessary, Superintendent, for you to remind me of my citizenship. I give thanks for it daily.

"A married woman there generally sees the world through a different lens. A woman selling dowry jewelry to a stranger is in a desperate situation. Such women feel abandoned, shamed, or are in financial difficulty.

"I have seen rings and necklaces surfacing for reasons of desperation over the years. I have heard their stories in women's groups. One thing I will say is that you probably won't locate the seller. She is either back in the domestic situation she tried to escape, dead, or living in another part of the world, where she has probably changed her name. Also, going to the Yemeni authorities won't help you."

Catrin said, "Thank you for that explanation. Why will we not receive help from the authorities?"

Farida bridled a little at the question. "To ask a man in authority there about such shameful events; you, an outsider, a westerner? Something that may involve an authority figure. No, that would not happen. There would be great politeness, but no information.

"One thing. Look for any efforts by a jeweller or another person to try to buy the ring from the victim. The first solution would always be money. And it would not be in writing. Someone will have contacted the owner in person."

She reached into a purse on her desk, taking out a wallet and unfolding a piece of paper inside. She showed it to the camera on the tablet.

"This is a photocopy of my British passport. I, more than most people born here, value this and the rights it gives me. I will not be pressured by the police. Nor will I tolerate an accusation of failing to help you in an inquiry into the death of a child. But I am not foolish enough to make accusations I cannot substantiate. People like Shaykh Yusuf Abrahim are powerful men, at home and abroad."

Sayer nodded slowly. "Why would someone wait so long, though? It is years since Mr. Harding bought the ring."

Al Araqi thought for a moment. "Sometimes these items are family heirlooms, passed down over generations. It would take little, a family reminiscence, or a reminder of the loss such as an anniversary, to reinvigorate a search.

"How would you feel, Superintendent, if you found out that something precious, say a family bible, had been vandalised? Mounting the sapphire in gold is not as distasteful, perhaps, as turning a hollowed-out family bible into a resin covered objet d'art. Yes, I have seen that in my museum work. But it would invoke the same repugnance, a desire to retrieve and restore it, care for it within the family."

Her voice lightened. "You are the ceramic artist, Sayer, correct?"

Catrin responded evenly, "Yes, I work with a friend on ceramics."

"I thought so. You will understand then. To transform a hand-worked object into something modern can be a desecration. No matter how fine the new work appears."

She pursed her lips then gave a small smile. "Do we understand each other, Superintendent Sayer?"

Catrin responded, "We do, and your input ties in with much of my own thoughts in this case. I thank you again for your insight."

Peart and Reimer were on the train home. John had reported back to Michael Hicks, to close the loop.

His mobile rang and, as he answered it, Reimer's phone rang also. Hicks had brought them into a conference call with him and Oliver Wastle.

"Oliver and I were talking. He had the idea that if Wilkinson's in Plymouth made the ring, did they show it off? The shop has a web site with images of pieces they have for sale or recently sold. Anyone keeping an eye out for a 'pink sapphire' on the internet may have seen it. Tomorrow, call in on the owner, check it out."

Reimer added, "And whether he had any enquiries in person or over the phone, as Al Araqi said."

"Exactly."

~~

The following morning, they caught Roland Wilkinson at his home, about to leave for work.

He asked if they could talk outside. "My wife is quite nervous about visitors. Her mother is eighty-four and lives with us. You have more questions about the ring, you said?"

Jan asked, "Yes. You examined it. There is a suggestion that the stone could be a padparadscha sapphire. Is that a possibility?

They saw him flush, embarrassed, or annoyed.

"It was a good stone, that's what I recall. I am not a

sapphire specialist, and this is a local business. You are talking about expert gemologists?"

Jan nodded. "Yes. One in Hatton Garden. But he isn't one hundred percent, he is going by your photographs."

Wilkinson let out a long sigh. "If it is, my valuation would be meaningless. But a stone of that quality on a silver ring is unlikely. I must admit, the original mounting swayed me a lot, so I didn't consider it to be that valuable. He could be right and, if so, I am rather embarrassed. After all these years, though, I can't say one way or the other."

He looked as if he wanted to escape, uncomfortable now.

Peart asked, "Did you display the ring you made on your web site at all?"

"Yes, we did. I was quite proud of the work we had done. We never listed it for sale, only as an example of a bespoke piece completed for a discerning customer."

Peart added. "And were there any enquiries about it?"

The jeweller thought for a moment. "Not to me. But there were a couple to my assistant at the time, Beverley. I remember her telling me that she had explained the ring was not for sale. She told the callers it had been a commission for a VIP, a royal appointment to the county."

John Peart continued, "And would she have commented on the caller at all? Local, distant, or what?"

He shook his head. "No. That didn't come up, or if it did, it slipped by me."

Jan asked, "You said, 'at the time'. Is she no longer with you?"

"No. She left about two years ago. She met an Australian and they live in Melbourne. She works now for an opal jeweller there, I think."

"We would like her name and contact information, if

you could."

It was later that Oliver Wastle approached Jan Reimer. "The interview with the gemologist; how did that go from your perspective?"

Jan thought for a second. "It turned out to be productive. She described a background story that tied in with Allingham's recollection. Her insight provided a lot more general background."

From his face, it wasn't the reason for the question, but her answer hadn't surprised him.

"I'm moving John Peart to work with Lough, to do more on the drug tracing. How do you feel about continuing to build the background file on your own?"

"I can do that."

He nodded. "DCI Hicks wants you to work on that and put more time into preparations for the NI exam. Get it under your belt sooner."

Her qualification as a detective under the new National Investigator Examination scheme. She was one of six uniformed officers in the constabulary entered. It was the reason for her assignment to Serious Crimes.

She smiled. "I can do that, too."

She thought that Sayer hadn't missed the looks that Al Araqi had given her and John Peart, after all.

PART 2

DIASPORA

24 FAYED

The small cluster of police officers met in Sayer's office a week after Nabil Jaber's interview: Sayer, Hicks, Wastle, Kendrick, Tydman and Reimer. On her whiteboard, Sayer had written four names in a column.

Nabil Jaber
Bital Assad
Majid Fayed
???
[Yusuf Abrahim]

She began with the comment, "No notes, please. Just listen.

"We have evidence that Jaber and Assad committed the crime, but Assad is in Yemen, untouchable at present. Both assailants were acting for another person and, from what we know, the Yemeni tribal structure may well be a factor.

"Majid Fayed is a benefactor to both Dalia and Nabil. They owe him a lot. Is he involved? We will shortly arrange to interview Fayed in Paris, as part of the investigation.

"Ultimately, that line of investigation leads to this man Yusuf Abrahim. Whether he has any involvement, we cannot say at present, and it will be difficult to find out. We are limited in our ability to probe into that, as well; there are political sensitivities."

"Michael and I want your actions from this point forward to cover two aspects. The first is the logical investigation route by the team, evidence-based; the guns, the drug payment, who Assad works for. Fayed is the next step there."

She paused. "The second area to work on is less linear, less documentable. Jan Reimer and John Peart have already done some of that background work. There is also a cousin of Nabil's in Manchester, a doctor. He, too, has been supported by Fayed. How does he see these developments? How will others in the tribal heirarchy living abroad – the diaspora – feel about this crime? Will they see it as a betrayal, and if so, by whom? Jaber? Assad? The person who made them do it? The Shaykh?"

She took the board eraser and wiped out the name Yusuf Abrahim.

"But we don't follow up on him directly. We remember his name, though. The first issue now is to see where Fayed stands."

She looked at Michael Hicks. "Who should do the interview with Fayed?"

Before he replied, Kendrick said immediately, "I should, if it is in Paris. And I want DC Henley there."

That surprised both Sayer and Hicks, but not, it appeared, Oliver Wastle.

Erica continued, "My French is good, and Adara Henley's is fluent. Fayed is a businessman and probably speaks English. But if he is not involved, and wants to be helpful at all, perhaps a discussion in French will set the right tone."

Sayer paused for a moment, then looked at Hicks. He nodded approvingly.

She said, "Work on it, and I will set up the authorisations."

DS Tydman spoke up. "The doctor in Manchester, the man that the lawyer mentioned. His cousin Nabil has participated in a terrible act, leading to the death of two people. He may not know anything useful to us about the crime, but he will have family and friends here and abroad. What do they gossip about or know? We should talk to him."

Sayer glanced at Michael; the meaning was obvious. They had already discussed that possibility. "You are on the same wavelength as us; we should. But first we clarify, if we can, whether their common benefactor is clean, or is in some way involved."

It was later the same day that DC Adara Henley met with Hicks and Kendrick. It surprised Henley that Superintendent Sayer was also present. Adara was told she would join Kendrick on a trip to Paris.

Henley had been second seat on one session of the interviews of Dalia, with DI Kendrick. One of the newer members of Serious Crimes, it had been a big step for her to be on the interview team. But Dalia had not spoken during that interview and Erica Kendrick posed the questions. Adara thought she really added nothing.

When they were all seated at the table, Sayer addressed her. "Your file says your French is excellent and you are of the Muslim faith. How good is your French, really?"

Adara looked surprised. "Fluent, ma'am. My mum and

I lived there until I was thirteen, then she met my dad. My new dad, I suppose. I probably have an English accent overlaid now."

She looked at DI Kendrick. "DI Kendrick has talked with me. She has good French also."

Kendrick said, "Passable. Yours sounds fluent to me."

Sayer gave Hicks a nod. Clearly that was a significant point for her.

DCI Hicks said, "This man Fayed in Paris. At the last team briefing we said he may be involved, or not. He could also be someone who has an employee, and two other people he has helped, let him down."

"Understood, sir."

"We want you to interview him with DI Kendrick. In French. And you may carry a lot of the load. Can you do that?"

Adara looked at them. "I'd like to give it a go."

Sayer responded, "Not a 'go'. There is probably only one kick at this can. I'll take it that means you will."

She looked at Michael Hicks, passing it back to him.

Hicks added, "DI Kendrick and you will prep this interview until you are sick of it. Between you both, while doing it, you need to leak out that Nabil Jaber is suffering, racked with guilt. He is carrying the burden alone and is feeling guilty about killing Ashley. Let it slip out. And you will close that out with a phrase from the Quran, in fluent French."

It was Sayer who passed over a piece of paper. "This one. What does it mean to you; not the phrase, but how it would go down with Fayed?"

Adara looked at the page and read it out loud. *And whosoever is conscious of Allah, He will make for them a way out.*

She recited the verse in classical Arabic, then again in French. "French, ma'am?"

"You speak Arabic?"

"Yes, some. We know the Quran in Arabic."

Catrin said, "Then in French or Arabic, as you see fit. How will he take it?"

Adara saw they were watching her, waiting. "If Mr. Fayed is angry at whoever used Jaber, he will take it that prayer will guide him. If he hears that Jaber is remorseful, he will probably feel that others involved should also be in custody, to share the responsibility and the punishment."

Sayer responded. "Part of it will be how you convey the message. If he sees you as police officer, but with more insight as a member of the same faith, it may resonate with him. Possibly it will motivate him to assist us in some way. Good luck. Make it work."

She stood. The meeting was over. As the team trouped out the door, they saw two of the consultants from the Task Force sitting there waiting.

~~

Majid Fayed was a wealthy man. If they had no other information, simply arriving at his home revealed it. It was a detached, older house, comprised of a two-storey gable-roofed main unit with, on the south side, a three-storey, square, flat-topped tower. It was the most prominent home on the quiet street in Rue des Tennerolles, close to Bolougne-Billancourt, on the west side of Paris.

Both sections of the home were old and restored. A newer metal fence and double gate between two solid gateposts protected its privacy. Before pressing the buzzer to announce their arrival, Adara said, "I wonder if the flat roof reminds him of homes in Yemen? This place cost a packet."

Majid Fayed spoke French fluently, and Arabic. He had good German and English. On entering, they had started out in French, as planned. He welcomed them, offered juices and a small dish of dates, a traditional welcome to guests.

When the interview proper started, he switched to English. Fayed smiled at Kendrick. "Despite DC Henley's and your own excellent French, I would rather ensure there is no room for misunderstanding through interpretation."

Fine, thought Erica. After all that planning. Let's get to it then. "Mr. Fayed, what is your relationship with Nabil Jaber?"

He paused, giving a flinty expression. "A fellow villager. He is from a poorer family. I am a benefactor to his family and several other families from my village."

Adara said softly, "The third pillar?"

Of Islam, almsgiving. Part of one's wealth to be shared with the community, particularly its poorer members.

He nodded. "Yes. That is all. I have no knowledge of this event, no involvement with this crime."

Kendrick led him to talk about the history of that contact and his assistance to the Jaber family and several other poorer families from his village. Fayed did so in short phrases, with pleasure in his voice at times, but not, she thought, pride or arrogance. If anything, it was a duty for him.

She focused again on Jaber. "Your contact was limited, one of occasional interest in his development, in his education and career?"

"Yes; to him, to his sister, and to his cousin Daud, now Dr. Zaid, in Manchester. A fine man who has done so well. With him, at least, God has blessed my service to his purpose. And Dalia, I think. Nabil duped her, but she was not otherwise involved, I heard."

Erica asked, "Did it surprise you to find that we arrested Nabil for the crime?"

He gave her a shrewd look. "I am nearer seventy than sixty, Inspector. There is little that surprises me in life these days. Gives pain, or pleasure, yes. Surprise, no. Not to a Yemeni."

He sighed. "But to answer your question directly, Nabil can be easily led, for better or worse. He has a warm personality and is a talented cook, but he has always been too impulsive, his father told me once."

Adara flashed a look at her boss. She was supposed to speak, also. She asked, "Would he be led by Bital Assad, your employee, perhaps?"

Fayed said nothing for a moment. "Assad has a stronger, harder personality. Yes. But I cannot see Nabil Jaber killing a child or a man in cold blood."

Adara saw the opportunity. "He won't speak. Our colleagues see both guilt and remorse; it is eating away at him."

She glanced at Erica, who gave her a brief, imperceptible nod to continue.

"Assad is from your village, also?"

He shook his head. "No. He is a Tawban man, from the coastal area." He looked Adara in the eyes and said, "I took him on to my staff at the request of another, a businessman now living in Germany."

"I see. His name, please?"

"An Omani. A Mr. Sultan Khan, living in Koblenz."

"Where is Bital Assad now?"

"Precisely? I do not know. He left Paris suddenly, as I told the detective from the Prefecture. I tried to contact him by phone and text, naturally. I had one email, which I am sure they sent on to you. A sentence. That came from Yemen, from his brother's computer."

His voice took on a sad, mocking tone. "Mr. Bital Assad expresses his regrets, but he must resign his position immediately, due to urgent family matters."

Erica Kendrick asked, "And how do you feel about that?"

Fayed moved his gaze from Henley to Kendrick. "How would you feel? Having the French police, then you, appear with your news and selective questions? I am disappointed and betrayed by two men I helped. I am angry at the implications that I am in some way involved or was aware of this crime. I was not. Nor would I ever be involved in such activity."

They paused, to allow him to regain his composure after the flash of anger.

Erica changed the subject. "There were items stolen during the incident. Some English art, which they later destroyed, and a ring of Yemeni origin. The art taken was an attempt to throw the investigation off course. The focus seems to have been the ring, a sapphire originally set in a silver band and later reset in gold by the victim. What do you make of that?"

Fayed looked away for a moment, reflecting on what he had heard.

"My first thought is that someone with power and control over both Assad and Jaber sent them to steal the ring. You may draw your own conclusions."

Erica responded with steel in her voice, pressing him. "We would rather hear yours. That is why we are here."

He huffed. Dalia understood the expression but had never experienced it so clearly. The man's cheeks puffed and released air.

"I will not speculate and point fingers at others. But I will give you two suggestions. Find out more about the tribal structure and the ring. Talk with Dr. Zaid. He is deeply affected by the news of his cousin's arrest."

Tydman was right, Erica thought.

"And, through him, talk to someone who knows more about the ring. Tell him you want to talk to the Sufi, that I said so."

He paused. "He will check with me, of course. But that is all I will say."

Adara asked, "A Sufi? A man or a woman? A name perhaps?"

He gave her a penetrating glance. "No more from me."

The two detectives could sense he was going no further on that point. Adara took the opportunity to act on her instruction from Sayer.

She said in French, "As I said earlier, we see that Nabil is overwhelmed by events, by remorse, it seems, even though he says nothing. Whoever the person is who organized this crime, it could be hard for us pursue charges. We will see. If not, he or she still must face God."

She switched briefly to Arabic. "*And whosoever is conscious of Allah, He will make for them a way out.*"

Fayed gave her a shrewd look and said a few words in the same language.

Adara looked at her boss, the expression clear. They were finished here.

Outside, Adara checked that no-one else was behind them.

"Fayed's last response was, 'that man's judgement will come sooner than you think, perhaps'. I'm thinking now that the diaspora knows who instigated the robbery, but they won't speak about it to us. That is what I took him to mean. Other than perhaps this Dr. Zaid and the Sufi he mentioned."

Erica mused on it. "Sooner than you think, he said. Will someone in the diaspora act, in revenge? Or is the person ill, dying perhaps?"

Adara thought about it and shook her head. "I can't see revenge as a motive. There are no blood ties to the victims in Devon. There would be anger that Jaber was arrested, his freedom sacrificed for a jewel. That alone would not result in reprisals."

They were silent, thinking it through. Adara said suddenly, "A Sufi, a mystic. First, we should follow up with this Dr. Zaid."

Kendrick nodded in agreement, as she checked her phone. "The direct flight to Exeter tomorrow morning is now cancelled. We are on a connection through Heathrow."

Still, thought Adara, it gives us a night in Paris.

The following day, they were in Heathrow when a text came into Kendrick from Wastle. The bail renewal hearing that morning for Nabil Jaber had been far from routine. He had used the occasion to plead guilty to the charge of killing Ashley Harding.

25 BAIL

For Oliver Wastle, attending the bail hearing at the Exeter Crown and County Courthouse was no more than a formality. Continued remand would be automatic. They had sufficient evidence for the charge and Nabil Jaber, being a foreign national, posed a flight risk. In the unlikely event of questions arising, he simply wanted to show his presence as a senior police officer.

At the point the defense barrister was asked by the magistrate for his reasons against continuation of remand, Nabil Jaber found his voice. He cut across his own barrister's response.

"I plead guilty to the charge of killing the girl, Ashley Harding. I plead not guilty to the charge of killing William Harding."

It was so surprising, for a second there was total silence in the courtroom.

Nabil had focused only on the presiding magistrate. Oliver saw that the man was taken aback, startled, but only for a second.

It had taken Nabil days to resolve this path forward. His solicitor was competent, he thought, and had mainly stayed silent during the long interview sessions where Nabil remained unresponsive. His litany of 'it is up to the police to prove their case' was meant be supportive, but Nabil could not relate to the man. The woman Sayer had got to him more than his solicitor.

This way, he decided, closes the process a lot faster. He wasn't hiding now. The truth of his awful actions was out there, and he was saying, 'yes, I killed the girl'. God help me, he thought. But yes, I did that.

The magistrate, a seasoned judge in his fifties, responded directly to the prisoner's box. "This is simply a bail hearing, Mr. Jaber."

He refocused on the defense barrister.

"Mr. Firth?"

The barrister had turned to speak to Jaber's solicitor. He looked shocked and concerned. The magistrate wanted confirmation now that the barrister would not oppose remand, given the outburst by his client.

Firth looked back at him. "A moment to consult, if I may?"

Nabil Jaber spoke out again, loudly. "It is a court. I make my plea on record."

He looked obdurate, defiant. The magistrate refocused on him.

"You have, Mr. Jaber. Bail is denied. These charges are forwarded to the Crown Court."

He addressed the CPS barrister. "Mr. Kent, will you be separating the charges?"

"I must take counsel, Your Honour."

"Quite."

The magistrate spoke to Jaber again. "Mr. Jaber, if the

charges are separated, you will be sentenced by your own confession for the crime of unlawfully killing Ashley Harding. You will still go to trial, perhaps with others, for the unlawful killing of William Harding. Those steps will take place at the senior court of law, the Crown Court. This hearing is adjourned."

He stood, for a second staring at Jaber as the court rose. Then the magistrate left the room.

Ewen Jackson looked at their barrister, Kent. A junior, he raised his eyebrows but said nothing. Johnston said to Wastle, "Jaber may need a psychiatric evaluation of his fitness to plead."

Wastle was already pulling out his phone to call Hicks. As he walked off, he said, "Nabil Jaber sounded to me as if he knew exactly what he was doing."

They would be back at the prison soon, interviewing Nabil. Intuitively, he felt the man might give up more about the gun, given the plea that he fired it.

As the news made its way up the chain of command in the Devon and Cornwall Police, Catrin found people congratulating her. Some of them, she didn't know at all.

Her first task was to call the Wansbury household. She let them know that despite the admission by Jaber, the investigation was still active. Two people had been present. Both needed to face justice.

She gave the press briefing alone, mid-afternoon, without taking any questions. She stated that Nabil Jaber, a Yemeni citizen, had used his bail hearing to confess to the killing of Ashley Harding. The investigation to apprehend others involved in the crime was ongoing.

The press spoke over each other, throwing questions as she turned away and left the room.

Over the next few days, as the run up to the Christmas and New Year holiday loomed, the Serious Crimes team refocused. The plea by Jaber now meant that they needed to consolidate the evidence against him ready for trial; prisoners had been known to withdraw their confessions for a host of reasons.

Once that was completed, a smaller team was assigned to the investigation. Erica Kendrick led the effort to extradite and arrest Bital Assad. She still reported to Hicks, but he and Oliver Wastle were given a new investigation into a murder in North Devon, near Ilfracombe. The body of a local pub owner had been found at the base of the cliffs near Bull Point Lighthouse. That investigation had Michael Hicks as the SIO, but the case was under Superintendent Kettle's purview.

Erica's first success came within days, the formal proof of Assad's presence at the crime scene. Previous efforts to secure DNA samples from personal toiletries in Assad's apartment in Paris had met legal blocks there. They needed that information to compare with the DNA traces found on the Harding safe keypad. A smooth-talking Devon woman speaking good French had persuaded the Sûreté to do the comparison in their own labs. It was a match.

While the use of that evidence in a British courtroom may be challenged by Assad's defense counsel, science was science. It made a more compelling argument in the laborious effort to extradite the man.

Catrin complimented Kendrick, telling her she would take it as an early Christmas present. Erica's response was that she wished it was an extradition order, gift-wrapped.

~~

Hicks made the request for Catrin's direct involvement in the contact with Dr. Zaid. Part of her role was to be the visible face of the Harding investigation, so if Dr. Zaid had picked up any of the media coverage, she would be known to him. Clarry made the contact through Dr. Zaid's office. Their meeting was set for seven p.m., a Zoom call.

When the link activated, the man at the Manchester end was still in medical scrubs, obviously still at the hospital, in a small room.

Michael was sitting with Catrin, both in camera view as she spoke. "Thank you for agreeing to talk with us, Dr. Zaid. I am Superintendent Sayer, this is DCI Hicks, who is leading the investigation."

Zaid nodded. "I saw you on television, Superintendent. I only emerged from the operating theatre a short time ago."

She said, "Your cousin's involvement in the Harding crime must be very upsetting for you, I realise. My reason for calling is to ask if you will meet with members of DCI Hick's team, to help our investigation. We spoke some days ago with Majid Fayed in Paris, and he suggested it."

"It is a tragedy for the Harding family and my own extended family. Majid called me, yes. As to meeting with your team, I am not sure how I can help, but I will do so, but virtually. At present, I have completed the second day of three operating theatre slots. I cannot risk meeting with anyone new, in person."

Catrin said, "I well understand that infection concern. My husband was recently in ICU with Covid. We will arrange a videoconference to fit your schedule. I am sure you are tired now, if you have just come out of surgery, so we won't prolong this call. We will be in touch."

Before she could close the call, Zaid said, "What did

Majid say to you, can I ask?"

Hicks responded. "Our officers got the impression that Mr. Fayed was not involved in this crime. He simply employed Bital Assad, the man we suspect was with your cousin at the Harding home. Fayed told us to talk to you, and to 'the Sufi'. Who is that person?"

"Majid Fayed is a good man, an honest and faithful man. As to your question, the Sufi he mentioned is a woman living in Belgium, and I understand his meaning. But you are right, I am tired. Could we do this tomorrow morning early, say 8.30 a.m.? I am back in surgery tomorrow, late morning."

"Of course."

He paused. "There is a boy, I understand, a son."

Hicks responded, "Yes, Adam Harding, age ten. He has held up well, considering, but he is in therapy. It has been a tremendous blow."

Zaid looked anguished, losing his professional composure. "Of course. I will pray for his healing. And help you all I can. Good evening, Superintendent, and to you also, Mr. Hicks."

He cut the call.

Hicks looked at Sayer. "Nabil's confession must have hit him hard. His cousin, killing a girl."

She nodded. "Agreed. And we will have an opportunity to find out more from him and this mysterious Sufi. Who will do the interview with Zaid?"

"Owen Tydman, and we will include Henley again. Erica and I will monitor it. We think Owen should continue the contact with Dr. Zaid."

Catrin stood, ready to leave, head for home. As Hicks picked up his file and did the same, she said, "I will be going up to London in the next few days. While I am there, I plan to talk to people at FCO. Are you OK with that?"

He caught the drift. "The Foreign Office? We have made all the right contacts and requests, but Erica has nothing substantive back from them, as you know."

She nodded. "I will talk with other contacts I have. But not the person who tried to warn us off. I'll find someone who knows what is really going on."

26 LAURIE

When Catrin made the booking for lunch at the rest-aurant in Old Church Street, in the Royal Borough of Kensington and Chelsea, she found it was full. Space was only available by reservation in the pre-holiday madness of celebratory lunches. She said quickly, as the apology began, "Mrs. Turner-Jones recommended you; in fact, she is one of my guests."

The polite refusal turned into a question of how many people, and would twelve forty-five be suitable, albeit a little later than usual for her guest? They had a nice table for four, very quiet and confidential normally. The restaurant may be a little noisier now, unfortunately.

Looking at the menu, Catrin hoped that the information gained would merit the cost; she had said she would pick up the bill.

Catrin and Madeleine Turner-Jones, of the Malaysian desk at the Foreign and Commonwealth Office, had become friends over the years. That was an unlikely development considering their early interactions. Turner-

Jones was upper class, could be officious, and had come across as the ultimate bureaucrat. All that changed the day in Kuala Lumpur when Catrin shot their assailant. One of the accompanying Malaysian police officers had been badly wounded in front of them. From that point on, Turner-Jones was Catrin's ally. Nearing retirement now, she was her 'go to' person at the Foreign and Commonwealth Office.

Mid-morning, she called Catrin. "Sorry, but we can't do it. You are off-limits at present; that came down this morning from the Minister's office. No-one from the Gulf States team can attend. I have been pulled without explanation into a meeting that doesn't concern me, so we must cancel. But go there anyway, please, and enjoy the lunch. They are giving you a table for two now."

It was the last sentence that made Catrin turn up.

The man who did arrive was compact, short and trim, with grey hair and a suntan. He wore a dark suit and, less usual these days, he wore a tie.

"Superintendent Sayer, I'm Laurence Parker. Call me Laurie."

As he sat down, she asked, "You are with FCO?"

"No, no. Used to be with MOD. Now I am sort of a consultant."

Ministry of Defence? Sort of? What did that mean, thought Catrin, her antennae up. Her eyes briefly swept the room, to see if others had arrived. He caught the gesture and smiled.

"I used to work in the Gulf States, with a special focus on Yemen. Madeleine and I know each other. She called and explained her problem, but I was looking forward to meeting you, so I came anyway. You know my brother-in-law, John. Sir John Vale, the sculptor."

Catrin's face lit up. "Well! Yes, I do. How is he?"

"Grouchy, at all the closures. 'The demise of the arts', he calls this last year. Galleries closed. Theatres closed. Shops closed. Not too happy at all. But while he is groaning a lot, he is staying well."

"Please give him my best."

"I will. Although he was not too happy when you left Art and Antiques, I recall. Still, you want to know about other things now."

Down to business.

Catrin said, "I was hoping to meet someone know-ledgeable about a man called Shaykh Yusuf Abrahim, but I am off limits, Madeleine said a couple of hours ago."

After his fulsome start, Laurie just nodded, and said nothing for a moment. "I don't work for the department. I have no current departmental knowledge. What do you want to know?"

"Would you be able to talk about tribal structure in general, and the ability for authority figures like Abrahim to persuade lesser mortals to do their bidding, say a robbery? In general, of course, to give the cultural back-drop, that sort of thing."

As they worked through their starter course and into the arrival of the main dish, Laurence Parker gave Catrin a detailed analysis of the current politics of Yemen, the Shayk's political role and his assessment of the man.

"Abrahim is a very effective power player and stays at the right level; not too high, not too low. He is respected by some and feared by others, but his followers are devoted to him."

During the remainder of the main course, Catrin told him a few details about the issue of the ring.

He paused. "The other side of the Shayk. Abrahim gives the impression of being a frail old man now. His health is not so good, but he is still cold-blooded and ruthless, a control freak, who would not think twice of sending people to steal a possession of personal importance, particularly if a generous financial offer had previously been turned down. Does that help?"

"It does. Unfortunately, he is beyond our reach, as is Bital Assad."

Parker spoke up. "Of course, we have no extradition treaty. But in that part of the world, a little like anywhere else if truth be told, it is not what you do, it is what the world believes you have done. Sometimes, I have noted, public revelations about people there can be as personally damaging to them as a prison sentence. But, of course, that is not a matter of law and formal investigation, is it?"

Catrin said nothing in response. She was surprised that the man was on the same wavelength so quickly. He was a lot like his brother-in-law, it seemed; forthright when he chose, silent otherwise.

He watched as Catrin suddenly examined a piece of the seabass on her plate. Parker said softly, "Perhaps I am not the first to think of that idea."

As Catrin looked up, his eyes were steely bright. "My brother-in-law, as you know, is not a man to prance around the tulips. He would say, based on what you told me, there is a boy and other relatives out there who deserve some justice. Damn well give it to them."

He cocked his head to one side. "John is like that, isn't he?"

Catrin nodded, thinking through the message. "Sir John? Yes, he says it as he sees it. That's my experience. A little like you, perhaps?" She was absorbing the message. She doubted Parker would say that unless he was sure Turner-Jones was on board. For her to be so disobedient to the Minister's instruction was a surprise.

Parker feigned denial. "Oh, no, I am required to be a lot more diplomatic in my life. Like Madeleine."

He looked at Catrin, then glanced at the clock on the wall. It was clear that, whatever he did these days, and for whom, Parker needed to leave soon. She looked for their waiter as Laurie said, "No need. Madeleine picked this one up on her account as her apology for cancelling. I was to tell you that earlier."

On her return to Devon, Catrin's last planned meeting before the holiday break was a two-day session of the Task Force, a stage called Keystone Three. Several of the participants had hotel reservations overnight.

Half-way through the first morning, a DCI Jane Roberts from Central Services Division suddenly felt unwell, with a rapid rise in her temperature and a sore throat. An antigen test showed she was Covid positive. In accordance with protocol, as they had been in the same closed room together, albeit wearing masks, the meeting was cancelled, and all members asked to quarantine at home.

By the evening, Catrin still tested negative. She slept in the spare room and ate dinner separately. While she and Chris were a little apprehensive, Mair was focused on it, talking about school friends who had bragged about their parents having Covid and insisting that she wore her nurse's hat. Chris had to constantly keep her away from Catrin, reminding her.

By the following afternoon, Catrin had a dry cough and a pale red line on the antigen test strip. She had Covid, too.

27 COVID

As she felt increasingly worse physically, as if she had a severe head cold and flu, her thoughts were of Chris and Mair. Would they become infected? Had they already been exposed through her? What would happen to them?

Fortunately, being a superintendent had its privileges, particularly when the news of the Task Force meeting interruption was circulating in the Middlemoor building. The police doctor took her call immediately. He sounded more reassuring than concerned.

"The current variants are proving less severe that the initial virus, in general. Do you have a family doctor here?"

"No. We got my daughter Mair on to a paediatrician's practice but have not found one for us. Chris still talks to his specialist in London regarding his long Covid symptoms."

"With luck, he has good antibody protection. If Mair gets it, you may not even know, other than by testing. It could present in her with symptoms all schoolchildren pick up with bugs. And you could be over this in a few days, or at least coming out the other side. Rest, keep your fluid levels up; you know the drill. If you worsen, call me. You sound stressed, as well as having a sore throat and cough."

She admitted it. "I am. We had a milestone meeting in the Task Force this week which never really got off the ground. Postponing it will be a problem. I'm late on my Christmas planning and shopping. It all comes together, with the memories of the first time our family caught Covid, with Chris so ill."

There was a pause.

"You are a superintendent. Delegate and trust people. Ask for help, get back to bed and rest. That's my best advice to you now."

Ten minutes later, after the call finished and she reflected on his advice, she made two calls – one to Clarry, about work issues, the other to Jenifer Treneer. Then she took two paracetamol and climbed into bed.

Their family solution arrived in convoy; a Range Rover, Mason Carrington's car, followed by Jenifer Treneer in her small Ford.

Within minutes, Chris and Mair, masked, climbed into the Range Rover and were whisked off. They were on the way to Falmouth, to quarantine there at Mason's home. Jenifer was staying with Catrin.

As Jenifer stood in her bedroom doorway, Catrin said croakily, "Thank you. But I asked you just to collect them and take them home with you, not stay behind. It's against the rules."

Her sister-in-law responded with, "Arrest me when you get over it. When was your last dose of paracetamol?"

Catrin told her.

"I'll make some hot Lem-Sip. Or would you like an

herbal tea?"

Later, as she surfaced briefly, she heard noises in the kitchen. After sleeping again, in the early evening she was woken by a sudden burst of sunlight through what had been a cloudy day so far. Not that Catrin had paid much attention to the weather, or anything else.

Jenifer must have heard her visit the bathroom. Her sister-in-law's first comments were, "Chris and Mair are still clear. How are you doing now?"

The delay in her response was answer enough. More paracetamol More liquids. More sleep. And her phone switched off.

The following day, Catrin finally surfaced late morning, feeling a little better but exhausted. Not great, still congested, but the headache had gone. She wanted a shower, and then to get dressed. When she returned from the bathroom, she found the bed stripped and the sound of the washing machine running downstairs.

Her self-appointed Cornish nurse checked her out. The antigen test strip still showed a strong red line. Catrin said, "As the doctor told me, I am starting to feel a little better. Not great. Still tired."

"Would you like some lentil soup for an early lunch? I just made a batch. You should eat a little."

By the evening, Catrin was feeling more her usual self. Energyless, but at least her mind was clearer. The antigen test was now a paler red line.

The house was immaculate, she finally realised; cleaner than she would have made it. In the lounge, the bare, artifical Christmas tree was standing in the corner.

Jenifer said, "The Christmas tree box was out, but not unpacked, so I did that, put it together to let it settle. I assume you want to decorate it all together, with Mair?"

Catrin nodded, smiling. "I'd hug you if I could. Thank you for everything. It's like you read my mind, getting the place ready."

She paused. "I panicked a bit, I think. I put you and Mason to too much trouble."

Jenifer smiled. "Nice to know you panic like a human being. All I hear from Chris is how on top of things you always are. And it's no trouble. Mason is having a great time with them at his place."

Mason and Jenifer had a strange arrangement, Catrin thought. They each had small homes in Falmouth within walking distance of each other, despite being in a long-term relationship. They could be found at either home at times, but each kept their independence. Jenifer claimed that Mason's home was more a studio than a domestic dwelling.

The following morning, day three, Jenifer and Catrin tested themselves. Jenifer was still clear. Catrin had a very faint line on the test strip.

"You will be clear by tomorrow, I predict. And I am on my way home. You have food in. You can call. When you are ready, Mason will bring them back; they are keen to see you."

As she picked up her backpack, masked, at a distance, she said, "If I am pulled over on the way home, I'm going to threaten the cop with your name. Give me a ticket and I will say the Reaper will fire him – or her."

They had been talking earlier. Catrin had shared her anxieties more openly, including her sense of isolation tied to the Task Force project.

When Catrin checked in with Clarry, she found the Keystone Three meeting had been rescheduled to the first full week of the New Year. Only one other Task Force member had gone down with Covid after the original set. None were badly affected.

"There is also news of Nabil Jaber. DCI Hicks wants to talk about it when you are up to it."

The news came from Exeter Prison. Nabil Jaber had been attacked and beaten the day Catrin went ill. He had a broken nose, extensive bruising, and a broken finger.

The attacker was not known for any gang association or racial issues. He claimed he had simply lost it; affected by depression brought on by the prison Covid measures and Christmas looming. Also, it was his sister's birthday. She was about the same age as Ashley.

Jaber had been treated at hospital and returned to the prison. He refused special category status, objecting particularly to being housed with paedophiles. Any more threats or problems, and they would probably transfer him to another prison, perhaps in northern England.

Hicks concluded with, "After sentencing, he will be transferred anyway, they say. If he gets a long sentence, he needs a prison set up for lifers."

It had better be a long sentence, Catrin thought.

"Any other developments?"

"Lots on the Ifracombe investigation. On this one, we have the arrangements sorted with the Belgians for the visit to the Sufi in the New Year. Kendrick and Henley again."

Dr. Zaid had told them, before Catrin's trip to London, "Her name is Nawra Ghulam, and you will have to talk to her in person, in Arabic. She does not use the internet. Nawra lives in Brussels and is nearly eighty-five. She is a Sufi. Do you understand the term Sufi? She will tell the truth with impunity. Her focus is God, her garden, and a life of prayer. In a way, she is like the monks and nuns in monasteries, but without the building. Material things are less relevant to her."

When asked why he and Majid Fayed had mentioned her, Zaid said, "She is from the family who made the original ring and has many connections. She knows what happened to it, we are told."

Hicks finished with, "By the time you are cleared to come back, it will be the holidays. I'll let you know of any developments."

"I'm not off to any work Christmas parties. I have neither the energy nor the invitations."

It was a light-hearted remark to finish off.

"You'd be invited to ours, the team bash. Even Jackie Neil thought you should be there."

The rumour had spread in Exeter headquarters that Sayer and four of the Task Force members had caught Covid. In the Serious Crimes team briefing, Hicks confirmed it.

"Superintendent Sayer is not badly hit, she says. Her family seem to have missed it. She will be back after the statutory period."

"Perhaps they will see the bunch of them catching Covid as an omen," suggested Jackie Neil to others, after the briefing, "and cancel the Task Force, give it up as a failure. Still, I'm glad the super wasn't hit hard."

Jackie was working now on a set of interviews in the investigation into the death of the pub owner. She was a bit envious of Adara Henley, she admitted to herself. Henley and DCI Kendrick were, as of this morning, making plans for a visit to Brussels in the New Year, on the Harding case. These days, her own horizons stretched as far as Ilfracombe.

28 SUFI

Sitting next to Erica Kendrick on the second leg of their trip from Exeter, Adara mused that she had not flown as much as this before; two trips to Europe in a little over a month. They had been delayed with icing conditions on the Exeter to London leg and their connecting flight to Brussels shifted to a flight two hours later. Brussels was reportedly unseasonably warm, at ten degrees today.

Adara was thinking of the line of people in Heathrow with suntans and light clothes, in transit home from Spain and elsewhere, now scowling at the weather outside the terminal. They were heading back to work and the winter realities of the New Year. A year ago, the airport would have been nearly empty.

She felt her nose was turning into a pin cushion for Covid test swabs. Still, there were benefits. In Brussels, perhaps she would have time to see the famous central square, Grand-Place. Not while interviewing the Sufi, though. That meeting would be in a garden in the suburbs.

The two detectives were met at Brussels Airport by two officers of the Federal Belgian Police, one a driver, the other an Arabic-speaking female officer who would interpret as needed. Her name was Nadeem. The driver, Jerome, was efficient but taciturn, and clearly would stay with the vehicle.

Nadeem had confirmed in a text message exchange that the delay in arrival would be no problem for Ghulam. They had spoken with her son, to be sure.

The sight of the red-tiled roof of the small home, the side wall covered in ivy, was the first surprise for Erica Kendrick. From what they had been told, they assumed the home would be large, if Ghulam lived in a sort of 'granny annex' in the garden. It wasn't that big.

As the son met them at the house, he was polite but a little distant. He did not invite them in but led them to a double wrought-iron gate at the side through which they entered the garden. In the early afternoon sun it was pleasant, and felt warmer than the forecast temperature.

The Sufi was a small woman in ordinary casual clothes and a headscarf, rake thin, with tendons on her lower arms that were visible. There was not an ounce of spare fat on her body, it seemed. Nawra Ghulam smiled and welcomed them, offering tea and fruit, a contrast with the son's reserve.

From their background check, Ghulam had apparently become a refugee in her youth. From a marriage that lasted ten years, she had a son and daughter. What happened to the husband wasn't clear, but he wasn't in Belgium.

From a market stall business, she had saved the funds to establish a small convenience store. Once her son was married, she gave him the business and worked in the background, supporting the shop and helping raise her grandchildren.

At age seventy-one, she had arranged for an old outbuilding in the garden of the family home to be refitted as a small bedsit-cum-kitchen. Other than the garden and the mosque, she went nowhere, even rarely into the family home she had once owned. For over fourteen years she had lived a life of gardening, contemplation, and prayer.

Her first comment, in French, was that she didn't buy much, and had no milk or sugar. A stacking set of plastic garden chairs had been set out on the small patio in front of her home; to Erica's eye, no more than shed-sized summer house.

Around them was a wide array of flower and vegetable beds, some plants familiar to her, many not. Police detectives were not reliable gardeners; their work hours disrupted hobbies too much.

After a brief exchange with Nadeem, Mrs. Ghulam announced in Arabic that they were welcome and, as the weather was pleasant, would they be happy outside rather than the lounge?

Adara's suspicious look at the summer house made Ghulam smile. "In the main house, I meant. Do you speak Arabic?"

Adara replied, "Only a little."

Erica chose for them to stay outside; it was clearly the Sufi's preference. She then did the introductions via the Belgian officer, confirming the Sufi's wish to be interviewed in Arabic, not French. Ghulam's quick nod confirmed that, as she scurried into the summer house returning in a minute or so with a tray containing cups and a clear pyrex teapot with mint tea. Once she had served them, she announced her readiness to continue.

"How can I help you?"

Erica reprised in translatable portions the backdrop to the visit and their interest in the ring, at which the Sufi nodded vigorously, interrupting her.

"Please show me the picture of the ring. Others showed it to me, but I would like to see it again."

Adara drew the photographs from her file and passed them over. The old woman studied them intently and smiled.

"It is the sapphire I remember, yes. My uncle, Emile Ratzon, made the original ring in silver in the year 1963. He and another man, a seller of precious stones, visited Shaykh Abrahim – the current Shaykh Yusuf's father – and helped him select the jewel and approve the ring design. It was a big sale for Emile, with a lot of esteem, to sell to the Shaykh."

She grimaced. "The recipient of the ring died during delivery of her third child, five years later."

"In 2001, November, my nephew, the maker's grandson, became very angry because of this ring. Shaykh Yusuf had given the ring away as a bridal gift to secure the marriage of two families, men he valued."

Ghulam looked wistful. "Yusuf is not like his father, who found balance in his life. He is entirely about the things I have no interest in, power and politics. My nephew was angry that the ring was leaving the house of Ibrahim, where it should have stayed, to be passed down to future generations."

She paused, reminiscing. "I think the current Shaykh saw it as expedient, and would find a way, a marriage of someone else, to get it back into the family. He plays people like pawns."

She gave a big sigh as she passed back the photograph. "And the smallest pawn turned out to be something else. Not a knight or rook, but someone of metal, of resolve. Seven years into her marriage, the last known owner, still childless, found her husband had pronounced *talaq*, a unilateral divorce. She left him and the ring disappeared with her."

Kendrick asked in English where this was, as the woman waited for the translation. "In Saudi, in Riyadh. I should have said."

She waited for any more questions, but Kendrick gave a small smile and a hand sign; please continue.

"The wife left the home, sold items she owned and left Saudi, supposedly to visit her sister in Europe. Germany, I think. But she never returned. The ring went with her or was sold by her. Now, having seen the photograph and heard of the sad events in your country, I can only assume she sold the ring before she left. Her name is Hanan, and I do not know where she is or if she is even still alive."

She looked at Kendrick. "And if I did know, and she still living, I would not tell you. But I do not."

"That Shaykh Yusuf wanted the ring back is common knowledge within our community. He made that known at the time she disappeared. Which is not correct. The ring was a gift on marriage to the bride. It belonged to Hanan alone. She had the right to sell it. I know no more than that."

She sat still, waiting, assessing Kendrick, who asked, "Why, do you think, a man like Nabil Jaber would help someone retrieve the ring, if the Shaykh or another person had located it?"

Ghulam thought about it a little. "Again, I have no knowledge. Like many others of any faith or none, they forget to observe God's will. Rather, they follow man's direction. A powerful man has those who serve him. They pressure or entice others. If a man is prepared to kill for a crust of bread, he will take smaller risks for a bigger prize."

Kendrick nodded her understanding, the allusion to the Shaykh as a powerful man.

"Your comment earlier. You would not tell us the location of this woman Hanan because you fear reprisal? Against her, or you?"

"Possibly against her, yes. From her ex-husband or her father. Or even the Shayk. I fear that for all Yemeni women in her situation. Too many disappear, here and everywhere. Some are killed."

It was the interpreter, Nadeem who spoke. "Mrs. Ghulam is known in our communities in Belgium to be outspoken on the subject of so-called honour killings."

"In what way?" asked Henley, her interest aroused.

Nadeem translated her own interjection and Adara's question for the Sufi. Ghulam spoke softly and firmly in response.

Nadeem translated. "They are a crime, yes. There is no mention in the Quran or Hadith of honor killing. They are contrary to the spirit of Islam. I say they are against God's purpose for us, his children on earth. To support honor killing is a blasphemy. Men argue the Quran with me on that word, but I will not be moved on this point."

Erica Kendrick smiled. "Constable Henley and I agree entirely. I begin to see why you are less worried about any reprisal from the Shaykh for talking to us."

Ghulam gave her a penetrating look. "I think I have more friends than enemies, I am glad to say."

She returned to the original question. "Also, if Hanan is alive, she has a new life, for better or worse. She does not need her past to descend on her. She has had enough judgement from men."

Her expression became one of distaste. "A reprisal against me, for simply telling the truth to you. I doubt it. I am known to more Yemeni than the tribe of Shaykh Abraham. He would not dare."

Ghulam's tone of response made it clear to Kendrick that she was finished.

"Thank you for the information. It is very helpful. Is there anything else; not knowledge, but suggestions to help us, perhaps?"

The old woman thought for a moment. "The ring that was stolen has not turned up yet?"

"No."

"If Shaykh Yusuf now has it, he will not leave the stone set in this British gold. He will remake it in Yemeni silver. Not with my family, though. We have no more jewellers. Our last died in Yemen four years ago, in the fighting. Look for the sapphire set in silver."

She paused, looking again at the photograph of the gold band, with its hallmarks. "But without our mark. No Yemeni jeweller would reproduce that. It would be seen as theft to them."

Kendrick moved on. "You have been very helpful, Mrs. Ghulam. What I would like to do now is have DC Henley make some brief notes of the history of the ring you have provided, in French. Then have Nadeem translate them into Arabic. If you would read through and change or clarify anything you wish, then sign and date the document. We will use this document as a formal statement, as evidence. Is that agreeable?"

As Nadeem translated, the Sufi gave a brief nod and said, "That will be acceptable."

Kendrick smiled. "While they are doing that, perhaps

you could tell me about your garden."

Once the formal documents were put away and Erica Kendrick thanked Ghulam again, the older woman focused on Adara and said in Arabic, "You are observant, my child?"

Adara looked wary as she responded in Arabic, "Not as much as I should, Mrs. Ghulam. No."

"When you suffer enough, we are here. Remember that. And you have always been uncovered?"

"Except at the mosque. Yes."

"Do not totally reject the hijab. There may be a time it is appropriate for you. You are part of change in the world for women, which is a good thing. But do not forget God."

She looked back at Kendrick, impishly. Erica was eyeing Nadeem, awaiting interpretation. Once made, Ghulam smiled at her. "You did ask for suggestions, earlier."

Impulsively, Adara asked, "Would you like a photograph of the ring, so other family members may see it? I have copies. Ma'am?" The last question was to her boss, to check that to do so would be appropriate.

The old woman replied, "Thank you. But no. I have it here now. And I will not share it with others."

She touched her forehead.

"It is best this way. The sapphire is from Nigeria, I just recalled. My uncle said it was very valuable. But that depends on what you value in life, does it not?"

As Nadeem interpreted, Ghulam stood up, Adara saw, with an ease that belied her age. Her life in this garden and small home kept her supple. Looking around, Adara tried to think what it would be like to live so confined. It made her feel claustrophobic.

She felt the touch on her arm, a surprise in the new

world of social distancing. Ghulam was smiling at her. "It is not so small as you think when God is around you, close by."

Adara smiled. "You would make a good detective, Mrs. Ghulam."

The old woman shook her head. "No, assuredly not. Not now."

29 PROPOSAL

The following day in Exeter, Kendrick was briefing Hicks and Sayer.

"We need her formal statement officially translated into English. She spoke on record about the ring history only."

Catrin nodded. "Is she not worried about some reaction from the Shaykh? Seeing as she already thinks he could be vindictive against the ring seller, this woman Hanan."

Kendrick shook her head. "No. She dismissed it. It turns out she is outspoken on issues like honour killings and is well regarded. Henley was impressed by her."

Hicks refocused on the facts. "We have the link Jaber to Assad, Assad to someone in Germany, perhaps this Sultan Khan that Fayed mentioned. Presumably that person is linked to Shaykh Yusuf Abrahim, but we have little to move on against any of them.

He stopped, looking at Sayer. "Catrin?"

She was lost in thought, looking down at the desk. "Sorry. You are right. I was thinking about something I

223

heard in London. Abrahim may have power, but he also has visibility and a standing to protect."

There was a knock at the door. Clarry entered. "Sorry. But as you are together, Trevor Wansbury called, about Adam's visit. Could next Wednesday work; they will take him out of school for the day? He's holding."

Catrin looked at Hicks, who nodded. "Clarry, confirm it and sort out the timing. Thank you."

"A bright spot," she said. "I think he will enjoy the visit."

~~

Aiden Jessop listened in silence as Catrin laid out the situation.

She said, "I'm bothered by the fact we will never charge this man Yusuf Abrahim. He manipulates others loyal to him and they can pressure people like Jaber. Abrahim is ruthless. I wonder if Harding's execution was to remove a witness, or a result of the outrage around the 'desecration' of the original ring? We will never know."

Laurie Parker's words came to her.

"Abrahim works through cut-outs, by phone calls. Probably the man in Germany, Khan, who foisted Assad on to Fayed, is part of that. The Shaykh is untouchable, but I have a proposal."

Jessop gave Billings a glance before returning his gaze to Sayer.

"Go on."

She took a deep breath. "Bring Abrahim in for questioning if he enters our jurisdiction. Hold him for as long as we can and make sure the world knows about it. Then when FCO make us turn him loose, we face the consequences."

Jessop responded, "Would anyone care? Not us, I mean; we do. I mean, will he shrug it off simply as bad treatment by the Brits?"

Catrin responded, "Not according to my information. It has less to do with the magnitude of the crime than his decision to execute it for a piece of jewelry. It would undermine his status and place in question his decision-making capability, which could cause a loss of credibility. But it wouldn't see formal justice done."

Jessop gave her a long look, in silence. "They didn't teach you that at the Cambridge course, I take it?"

"No sir. Nothing like that. Certainly not."

"If I gave you the go ahead, would you do that? Carry the can? And if so, why?"

She gave him a hard stare. "I wouldn't have brought it to you and DCC Billings if I wasn't prepared to see it through. So, yes, I would. Why? I want to be able to tell the family this is the man we believe to be behind it all. We can't bring him to trial, but the world will know he did it."

She paused, then added, "And, he treats people like pawns. If we do this right, perhaps he will trade Assad for his own freedom, send him back to face trial."

Jessop's bottom lip stuck out as he pondered the proposal.

He said gently, "Mr. Atkins would throw a fit. Probably he would arrive in a helicopter next time."

There was a silence for a long thirty seconds. Then he said, "Doug, I see a problem with this. And your face says you do too. What's yours, fear of Nathan's wrath?"

Billings smiled dismissively. "We are supposed to be sending Catrin back to the Met with experience. 'Stretch her,' I was told. Not by the neck until dead, though."

He focused on Sayer. "Frankly, I am more afraid of the

Ulster woman, Barrington, than our friend working for the minister. In any event, whether you carry this one or not, you would return to London with a target on your back. The Foreign Office will throw darts at it."

Jessop smiled at Catrin. "Doug and I have worked together for too long. That's my concern also. But it is a fair idea, a trade of the Shaykh for Assad. I'll think on it carefully. Meanwhile, explore every legitimate approach for the return of Assad, futile as that may be."

He stopped.

"This was your first murder case, I know. It's bitten you, hasn't it?"

Catrin nodded. "The first I have supervised, but not the first to hit me hard, I must admit."

She was thinking of a Malaysian police officer, a young woman killed in London some years ago.

After a moment, she whispered huskily, "I owe it to the boy, Adam." She put a hand to her mouth as she cleared her throat.

Jessop said, "Let's talk about the Task Force now. Just to cheer us both up."

Aiden Jessop liked black humour, Catrin concluded. He had probably heard rumours that the Task Force was entering rougher waters now. There were two camps of thought, and it was all about money.

She said, "We have just completed Keystone Three. Out of that we are heading towards a strategy that meets the objectives... and considering a second one which almost meets them. We have a challenge or two in moving forward. But I'm working on it; so is Ursula Otley."

Jessop nodded. "Still on the timeline, are we? Are we likely to have any delays? Sounds like it could get bogged down."

Catrin shook her head firmly. "We hold to timeline. They know that. It's not negotiable. Are you getting complaints about me?"

"Too right, it isn't. And no, not complaints, as such. You are from the Welsh valleys, I recall."

"Pontypridd, yes."

"Someone wondered if you were from Cardiff, some-one old enough to recall that Cardiff Bay used to be called Tiger Bay. They say you bite."

She said nothing in response, just watched him. Perhaps Jessop was seeing her as a bit of a tiger now, with the proposal about the Shaykh.

Jessop closed the meeting. "Thank you Catrin, that will be all. Doug, hang behind for a moment, will you."

As she left, she had the thought that Cardiff Bay was now a multi-ethnic community in the city, including a lot of Yemenis. She wondered what Aiden and his friend Doug were now plotting.

30 VIP

Adam Harding had asked for several things; a ride in a police car with lights flashing and 'just a little bit of siren'; a visit to a cell, to see what one is like; a meeting with a police dog and handler; and to talk to 'forensics' in their lab.

While it wasn't a visit of a dignitary or a politician, the Serious Crimes Team treated the preparations as if he were a visiting VIP.

It was one of the SOCOs who came up with the present; a 'forensic kit' in a case with a UV light, fingerprint detection, a magnifier, and specimen sets. And a child's police cap with a small Devon & Cornwall Constabulary badge, one from some team event or other. The latter was a bit 'iffy', as the rules said official badges were reserved only for employees, but the Deputy Chief Constable made an exception. "If he uses it later in life to rob the Bank of England, I'll take the hit."

DC Samesh Ray, his liaison officer for the weeks after the incident, was his tour guide. When Adam was taken to the Serious Crimes operations room, every team member who could make it, on or off duty, was there.

He looked around at the crowd of faces. "There are so many of you. Thank you. I never realised how many people there were."

The DCC had just presented him with the cap and badge and, wearing it, seeing him, one or two had to cover their emotional responses.

With a typical boy's sense of bald diplomacy, Adam asked, "Who made the big breakthrough? There was one, I suppose?"

DCC Billings said gently, "The entire team worked very hard. All of them. It was a team effort."

Seeing as that didn't quite satisfy the VIP visitor, Lough called out, "Starr and Brenda did. They found the car that was used and everything else followed from that."

Starr and Brenda were ushered forward and, within seconds, were talking away with Adam about CCTV cameras as the DCC focused on the aunt and uncle.

It was later, as Adam went to meet the police dog and handler that Catrin corralled the Wansburys in her office and they talked.

"I wanted to let you know – and please keep this to yourselves, at present – it will be announced in the next month or so that I will be leaving the Devon and Cornwall Police to return to London, to the Met. That won't happen for another couple of months after the announcement. The timing is not finalised."

She wasn't going to say that some of that timing was related to careful checks on the travels and activities of a Yemeni shaykh.

"But if word got out and you misunderstood the reason, I wanted to take this opportunity to tell you myself."

She watched Eve Wansbury's face change, so she added, "It was planned. I was transferred here for another job and that will finish by the Spring.

"I tell you this because it has been a special privilege as a police officer to work with the team you met today and to have met you both and Adam. He is a very impressive boy, the way he has handled these tragic setbacks. I wanted to thank you for your understanding, particularly through the frustrating periods when we had no news for you."

Trevor Wansbury said, "We heard you were leading a reorganisation team. That's what has finished, I take it?"

"Not finished yet, but the timeline is clearer now. The other thing I want to emphasise is that the investigation continues. Less may be said now, but it remains an open investigation and is not dormant, I assure you. DI Hicks is still assigned and as you have found out, he knows his job."

Eve Wansbury said, "We'll be sorry to see you go. As will Adam. From the beginning, you treated him honestly and didn't talk down to him. I think he idolizes you a bit. The talk about becoming a police officer, I mean."

Catrin's mind went back to her conversation in the car with Jan Reimer near the beginning of the investigation.

She said, "I'll do everything I can not to let him down. So will my team. Can I ask, what is going to happen to him now? There is no reason for me to know, but..." She tailed off.

Eve said, "It looks very likely we will be able to keep him, and he wants to stay with us. It has been quite bureaucratic, as you can imagine, but one of the social workers is strongly in support. So is Adam's therapist."

Trevor said, "I think it will be fine. We wait and pray on it. We have a solicitor handling the court side of it and there are no others claiming custody. It is mainly now the wait for background checks. Not having children of our own is not helping our case, I gather. They are assessing if Eve and I are suitable people to raise Adam long-term, until he reaches legal age. We –."

He stopped as Catrin's expression changed from interest to incredulity. Despite being masked, her reaction was obvious.

"Forgive me," she said. "It is the irony of it all. I know the reason for the checks, of course. It is simply... I mustn't say more. I'm glad it is going that way for you and Adam. I wish you speedy resolution of the matter."

As the Wansbury's stood, knowing that they needed to get on, meet up with Adam, Eve asked. "Who will replace you as superintendent – for the investigation, I mean?"

"That will be up to senior management to decide. I don't know that yet. But with Deputy Chief Constable Billings in command, it won't take long to resolve when it is needed."

As she saw them to the office door and into the care of Clarry, she mused that it was a necessary lie. It was best that way. No-one would be appointed above Michael Hicks on this case immediately after her departure. Jessop had accepted her plan but kicked her off it.

The Chief Constable had called her back in to see him, alone, the day after she made her proposal. Jessop began with the possible outcomes.

"It becomes entirely political; you realise that?"

Catrin said, too quickly for his liking, it seemed, "Yes, I understand."

"I'm not sure you do. What I mean is that it becomes a battleground where the outcome cannot be predicted. And there will be a loser, I guarantee it; if not the shaykh, then us. Perhaps both."

He sounded sombre. "Consequences that could have any of us – including you – out on our ear. With Doug and I, we are at the end of our careers, anyway. But you…"

He let it hang, waiting.

Catrin said carefully, "It is still the right thing to do. Abrahim can't get away scot-free, and I want Assad back. I am prepared to take that risk, if you and the DCC will push the Foreign Office to make sure that happens."

It was only a second or so, but she saw his resolve. "They will be pushed – hard – I guarantee it. And not only by me."

He paused, not clarifying his comment.

"You won't get off scot-free, I expect. But we organise this with you out of the way, back in London. We will make the closure of your contract fit this approach, some time after Keystone Five."

And then he told her that the less Catrin knew about the next steps, the better.

31 ZAID

It was late-January before Catrin was informed of the visit of Dr. Daud Zaid, Nabil's cousin.

Hicks told her, "Tydman has been keeping in contact with him. Zaid is coming down next week, first to see Jaber. After that, he has requested a meeting with us. I have agreed, of course. He has already said that anything he learns from his cousin will not be discussed with us. It was a condition of Jaber's agreement to see him."

Nabil was still in HMP Exeter. No further problems with his fellow inmates had surfaced.

"Do we know why he wants to meet with us? If he talks to Nabil, there is not really anything more we can give him."

Hicks responded, "He was quite open about the reason. He wants to talk to us about Fayed, and to understand the progress to bring Assad to justice. We are interested in what he may have to say."

As she nodded, he asked, "Do you want to be part of the meeting?"

Catrin shook her head. "No. You and Erica do that.

Involve Henley, I suggest; she met Fayed. No. What I want is for you to bring him along to me for a wrap-up meeting, just me and him. And I want Reimer available, on standby, to join us at a moment's notice."

Michael gave her a suspicious look as she said, "And no offense, but it really is best if you aren't there."

"None taken. Are you sure, though?"

She looked at him. "Absolutely sure. Yes. Not a word to anyone else."

~~

When Michael Hicks showed Dr. Zaid into Sayer's office and said goodbye, his final words were to Sayer. "Reimer is outside, ma'am."

He left, closing the door.

She began with, "You have had an unusual and probably quite hard day, Dr. Zaid."

"Unusual, yes. Your staff have been very professional. I was a little concerned about the visit, particularly after seeing my cousin, but they didn't question me at all about that."

She gave him a brief smile. "Nor will I." She waited on his response.

He looked out the window. "It is a change to be away from the snow up north; you have had a few nice days together, it seems."

A deflection. "True, but we can get some powerful rainstorms, I assure you."

Again, she waited.

Zaid looked back from the window to her.

"My cousin mentioned your insight when you inter-viewed him. It will sound strange, but that helped Nabil, I feel. He is still traumatised by his own actions, and guilt."

"I am glad you see it that way. DCI Hicks told you his sentencing hearing will be in two weeks?"

"Yes, as did his solicitor. She said public pressure was a factor in the scheduling, given the visibility of the case. I don't think I can be there. Operating theatre availability drives everything for me. But I talked to my wife. She will attend."

"And will Dalia?"

His face clouded over. "No. She has cut him out of her life completely. We cannot even mention his name to her. She says her employer may move her overseas soon; she has put in a request for a relocation, at least, once she has met any court obligations here. She feels tainted, living in England now. But we are helping her, as best as we can."

Catrin grimaced. "Your wife will attend, to show support for Nabil, or what?"

He examined her carefully. "To support him in his resolve to take responsibility for his actions. And, as I understand it, there is negligible likelihood of this man Assad being tried here, to see that the crime is properly recorded as having two perpetrators. We find that hard."

Catrin sighed deliberately and sat back before responding. "We are on the same page on that, I assure you. I gather you informed my colleagues that Mr Fayed was a good man, would never be involved in this matter? We had reached that conclusion also, but why was that important to you?"

"Majid Fayed paid my first-year fees through university. My family had no means to do so. He has done similar acts for other members of our community, too. My own view is that he is as angry about this as I am; in his case about being betrayed by his employee's actions. It is a small repayment of his support to me to speak for him now."

She asked, "Is there much discussion of this news within the broader family? In Yemen and in the diaspora, I think you would term it?"

He nodded. "It is discussed. Contentious with some, a great sadness with most. There is everything from calls for harsher punishment than British law would allow, to a conspiracy theory that the British police forced a confession from an innocent man. It runs the gamut."

She pressed him a little. "Would you agree that someone other than your cousin and Assad – not Mr. Fayed, I mean – is equally or more responsible for this tragedy?"

"We have drawn that conclusion. Yes. And you have spoken to Ghulam, I heard."

She stood. "Dr. Zaid, I am going to take a risk with you, more than I have permitted my team to do, mostly because you are a doctor. You understand professional ethics and are a healer. I will be at the borderline of my own ethical standards, but I am going to trust you with some information. One moment."

She opened the door and beckoned Reimer in, pointing her to the chair adjacent to her.

"This is Constable Jan Reimer, a member of the investigation team. She had specific responsibilities to follow up on the art stolen during the crime. That focused down very quickly to one item, a ring. Jan, tell Dr. Zaid what we know about the ring. Give no names of people here but include the dates for its possible transfer to Mr. Harding and the background given to you in Birmingham."

Reimer looked at her superintendent, then the stranger. "Yes ma'am. If you say so."

Catrin added, before Reimer started, "You have family; they have contacts, you said. We need help."

"What sort of help?"

"Communication."

"It is not likely that our people will readily provide information to the British police. Nor other police, for that matter."

"I'm not asking for input, but communication out-wards. Details you will be provided with now, inform-ation we shouldn't be releasing, really, will be important."

She proffered a small notepad to the visitor, but he shook his head while pulling out his own leatherbound notebook. He pulled two business cards from it. "My contact information. And if I can have yours, please?"

Reimer gave Catrin a look to check, then gave him her card, as did her superintendent. Catrin looked at his, with the string of qualifications after his name. "Is it Dow-ood, Dr. Zaid? How do you say it?"

"It is simpler to call me David, the English equivalent, if you contact me. It is what my team at the hospital uses."

32 SENTENCE

The Crown Court judge spoke calmly throughout. Any emotion expressed was in the carefully written text of her sentencing report rather than its pronunciation. The judge was a small woman of Indian ethnicity, dressed in a red robe and white horsehair wig that would appear ludicrous outside a Crown courtroom.

"Nabil Usamah Jaber, you are guilty by your own admission of unlawfully killing Ashley Harding. The pre-meditated criminal act was theft, you stated. You have pleaded guilty to constructive manslaughter, the death of an innocent child during the execution of that crime. In accepting that plea, the court has recognized that it was not your intent to kill her.

"You have assisted the court and relatives of the deceased by sparing them a drawn-out trial. Also, you have no prior record of criminal acts or violence.

"I note, however, your constant failure to assist the police in their investigation. You have refused repeatedly to identify the person or persons instigating the crime. Similarly, you refuse to identify the other party or parties present during the crime. As a result, a suspect named as Bital Assad has evaded capture. And by your own admission, there are now two illegal firearms, one of which you claim is defective, out in the community. I have considered all these elements, and the recommendations on sentencing by the prosecution and the defense.

"I must also bear in mind that this crime does not stand alone. You will return to this court in due course to stand trial for your role in the death of William Harding.

"Ashley was only twelve years old at the time of her death. She was a young, innocent girl with her whole life and promise ahead of her. It was a heinous crime, callously planned and cruelly, ineptly executed. Those factors led directly to Ashley's death."

She stopped reading her written notes and looked directly at the man in the dock. Nabil Jaber had bowed his head, looking at the floor at the point the judge talked about Ashley. He did not look up as the sentence was revealed. He felt numb, focusing on the fact that the trial for the death that he did cause was finally over.

"I sentence you to imprisonment for life, with a tariff of nineteen years before you are eligible for parole. Appropriate deduction for time already served in custody will be applied administratively, as will the relevent sentencing surcharge for the victim support fund. Parole is not automatic and will depend on your ability to demonstrate to the Parole Board that you no longer pose a threat to society."

That statement resulted in Jaber looking at the judge briefly, a bemused look, as if it was self-evident that he would never do anything like this again. His eyes returned to focus on the floor. He would return to prison, to a lost life, to the new world of incarceration. There was justice, he felt, that his real life and dreams were gone, as dead as

Ashley Harding. He had no idea what was left.

Catrin Sayer, in dress uniform, sat with Michael Hicks. During her course in Cambridge, she had spent a week on a module dealing with the evolution of sentencing in manslaughter and murder convictions. In Nabil's case, the defense had successfully argued the lesser charge of constructive manslaughter with CPS. Yet the sentence decided by the judge was more applicable to a murder conviction. The defense was not going to appeal, she thought. Jaber had wanted to plead guilty to murder at the outset.

The judge waited only a moment.

"Take the prisoner away."

Catrin remained seated as the proceeding closed. In a couple of minutes, she would give a brief statement for the media outside the court, particularly thanking the public for their support. As they broke, she saw Eve Wansbury, now looking ashen, sitting with her solicitor. Hicks had moved forward, talking to Ewen Jackson. He glanced at Catrin, but she shook her head, and walked over to Wansbury.

Eve said, "Trevor stayed home with Adam."

"And you?"

"Holding up. I was thinking that Jaber will be in his fifties when he is released. If he is released. Our family bereft. An absolute waste of lives."

Catrin agreed. Eve paused. "You have met Mr. Driscoll previously, I think?"

Her solicitor. He obviously recognised Sayer as they shook hands.

Catrin looked at Eve and said, "There is someone I want you to meet, if you will agree to do so. Over there. The Arabic looking woman."

"Who is she?"

"The wife of the cousin of Jaber. Her husband is a surgeon in Manchester. They see it the same way. Are you up to it? Not the best time, but…"

She left the question hanging. Wansbury looked at her solicitor first. He said, "It is entirely up to you, Eve. Is she likely to be angry, superintendent? If so…"

Catrin shook her head. "I doubt it. Not at you, Eve, no. Not ideal timing, as I said, but I hope it might help a little."

Eve looked at her. "You do the talking."

"Mrs. Zaid? I'm Superintendent Sayer."

The surgeon's wife looked apprehensive. Not at Catrin, but in seeing Eve Wansbury with another person accompanying her. Catrin ploughed on.

"Can I introduce Mrs. Wansbury? She is –."

"I know who you both are, Superintendent. I can only offer my profound condolences to you, Mrs. Wansbury, and to your family."

Eve murmured her automatic response of appreciation, assessing the woman carefully. Mrs. Zaid sounded cultured and professional.

Catrin said, "I am in a strange position here, limited in what I can say, of course. I have had several discussions with you and your husband, Eve. I also spoke with Dr. Zaid. I suspect you have more common ground than you could possibly imagine."

She looked at Eve. "I am particularly thinking of Adam. When I met him and he told me what happened from his perspective, it struck me that he wouldn't have seen Nabil, only the eyes through the balaclava he wore. Eyes that reminded me of Dr Zaid's."

She switched her gaze to Mrs. Zaid. "It would be a

terrible legacy of this tragedy if Adam grew up fearful of faces like yours, of eyes like your husband's, a doctor who saves lives. Now is not the time, but perhaps you should consider staying in touch? It is just a suggestion."

Hicks appeared at her shoulder. "Ma'am, the interview. Mrs. Wansbury, Mr. Driscoll. Are you also speaking to the press?"

Eve shook her head as Driscoll answered. "No. Not with another perpetrator out there. We do not see this as closure."

He flashed a look at Sayer, then at Zaid.

Hicks continued addressing Eve Wansbury. "We can make sure you avoid the reporters when you are ready to leave, if you wish?"

As Catrin moved away, she said, "Why not have some-one do that for both Mrs. Wansbury and Mrs. Zaid? Give it a few moments, though, if they wish."

She moved out of the emptying courtroom to face the cameras. Hicks beckoned two uniformed officers over, gave them instructions and followed his boss.

Moments later, in the foyer of the court building, Catrin looked at the array of cameras and the faces of reporters, with Michael Hicks at her side. The cluster went silent, knowing she would speak. Soon they would be talking across each other, forcing questions.

She spoke carefully. "Our thoughts and prayers today are with the Harding family and their relatives. The sentencing of Nabil Jaber for his criminal act against Ashley Harding closes one part of our investigation. The Devon and Cornwall Police continue our efforts to arrest the second assailant. We believe that person to be a man called Bital Assad, now in Yemen, and are seeking his return to the UK to face charges.

"We thank again the public for their early and many responses to our requests for information. Their assistance was crucial in the early stages of the investigation. Thank you."

She turned away quickly, not prepared to answer questions. That was the decision of the communications director; there was to be no speculation or chance of forced errors.

Hicks said nothing also as they walked away. The communications staffer with them gave Sayer a slight nod, signifying it went as expected. There are no sidebar comments in the vicinity of a press scrum. One never knows who is taking camera shots or carrying concealed recorders.

~~

That evening Mair suddenly stopped playing and looked glum. Catrin smiled at her; something was coming, she knew. A confession, or a problem.

"Henrietta's mum saw you on television."

Catrin smiled. "Yes, I did an interview, so I am not surprised. We talked about those, remember?"

The glum face persisted. "She said you locked away a bad man forever; until he dies."

Quite a burden, it seemed, thought Catrin. She picked up Mair and sat her on her lap.

"No. First, it is our job to find the person who does something wrong. It is not our job to decide whether they did it or say how they are punished. The courts do that. Other people listen to what we say, and what the person who we accuse says, then they decide."

Mair nodded seriously. The daughter of two people working for the police, the role of the courts had come up before.

She clearly wasn't finished. "But forever? What if he says he is sorry?"

Catrin gave her daughter a hug. "Well, it is not forever; Henrietta has not heard the whole story. The man will be in prison for a long time because what he did was very, very bad. But he can show he is sorry, and some day can be let out. OK?"

Mair sighed. "He must be really sorry, though, not pretend, right?"

"Yes. Do you want a story?"

Catrin wanted to take her daughter's mind into something more uplifting. Mair talked on as they searched through the current favorite books.

Catrin thought of William Harding and his death. She would be happy with a whole life tariff for Assad.

33 BENETEAU 43

Over the next month, there was no progress in the Harding investigation; no breakthrough by the Foreign and Commonwealth Office to extradite Butil Assad.

Hicks and Kendrick accompanied FCO staff to a meeting at the Embassy of Yemen in London, where they provided a summary of the core evidence against Assad. The discussion moved from evidence to protocol and international law. They were now waiting on deliberations within Yemen's justice system, without a clear indication of when those would take place, and what the possible outcomes might be.

By mid-April, the work of the Task Force was as complete as it could possibly be. While still on schedule for its final report delivery, it had, as intimated weeks earlier to the Chief Constable, ended up with two out-comes. For the last month, Ursula Otley, Les Henry and Catrin had worked with both the finance sub-group and the full Task Force to try to reach an accommodation that would allow a single report. Each time, it fell through.

Finally, Catrin took a decision and organised a conference call with Otley and Henry.

"No more meetings now. We go to Keystone Five with the two agreed reports. The executive can make the decision."

Henry was crestfallen. "We were so close at the last meeting."

Otley grimaced. "Close, but immovable. Particularly Thompson and Felworth. I agree with Catrin. Les, if we re-open it again, we will have something else shift. This was the third attempt."

Henry gave a big sigh. "Not as neat as we would wish. K-Five is ten days away."

The consultancy's framework called for two of the key decision meetings with the Chief Constable and the Police Service Executive, Keystones Two and Five.

"Well, don't dwell on it, in the interim," he said.

Clearly, they saw, he would, contrary to his own advice. This was the last major assignment of his police career. He had postponed his retirement to be the 'inside' support vice-chair for the 'outside' Task Force chair.

"I won't," replied Catrin. She didn't say that she would not even be around. She had a holiday booked.

~~

Catrin sat in a seat at the transom, smiling, the wind in her hair, watching Li at the helm and Chris standing at the prow. The Beneteau Oceanis yacht was turning slowly, aligning to enter its slip stern-first. Inside the cabin she could hear the children talking excitedly, looking through the porthole in a ritual established over the last few days.

A forty-three-foot sailboat under power needs care and expertise to dock smoothly.

Catrin recalled her first encounter with Jian Li Yeung, in Bangor, on her first case as a detective constable. At the end of that investigation, she and Li had sailed on the Menai, the waterway between the mainland and the Isle of Anglesey. They went to lay flowers at the point where Han, Li's brother, had been dumped after his murder. The perpetrators had by then been arrested. Soon Catrin and Li were parting ways.

Detective Inspector Dafydd Powis, the officer in charge of the investigation, took them on that trip in his own yacht, another Beneteau, a smaller boat. He had let Li sail back, including docking it at the marina in the village of Y Felinheli.

Catrin could see the same concentration in Li now. They were in St. Helier, Jersey, at its main marina, busy with the spring influx of boats and sailors.

Jian Li and her husband, James Hoi, had rented the boat. They lived in Hong Kong and were keen sailors. Chris Treneer had sailed in his youth and was more skilled with sailboats than he admitted. They made up the sailing crew.

Catrin, Jean and Melanie were the landlubbers and galley hands. And the children, Lili, Mair and Daniel, James and Jian Li's son, were having a good time.

All but one day this week they had sailed as a group. That day, Li, James, and Chris took the yacht out in fair winds to put it through its paces, the type of day that racing sailors enjoy. Catrin was anxious about Chris, despite the promises by James to keep him from the heavy work. She realised he needed to go; it was part of his progress.

On other days, they sailed more sedately but with enough movement to excite the children. Even then, the speed over the water surprised Jean. Chris had responded,

"We could sail faster in this wind, but it would be less comfortable."

Jean had retorted. "It's fast enough, thank you."

The time ashore, the beaches, the meals together, all added to the pleasure of Catrin's first big holiday since moving to Exeter. With Jean, Melanie, and Li, she was with her closest friends and their families.

Li had been the instigator of the holiday.

"We want to try an Oceanis out; we are thinking of buying one, or one in this class. There are some for rental in Jersey and we haven't been able to travel abroad for a while now. We will still come over and rent one, even if it doesn't work for everyone."

They planned well to ensure it did work out.

At first, Jean was concerned about three families on a 'small boat'. Li squashed that concern. "It has three bedrooms with double beds, and lots of bunk space for the kids to have an adventure."

Some meals were in the marina restaurants, others onboard, the adults dining after the children were asleep.

It was a dinner on board at sunset when the topic of Hong Kong and James and Li's decision came up. Li was a maritime lawyer who had moved into business management. Now she was a mid-level executive in a Hong Kong shipping company. James worked in finance in Hong Kong.

"We stay, through thick and thin, we decided," said Li. They had been wondering over the last year or so about the future, with the return of Hong Kong to China and the increasing control by Beijing.

James Hoi was a quiet man, but he became more vocal now. "My family history is there. We were there before the British arrived, even. If families like ours move, there is no voice for a different future than one dictated by the mainland."

James reached out and took Li's hand. "We stay, we work hard, we live our values and see what happens."

Melanie broke the increasingly serious mood with the comment, "And if it goes belly up, you've got us. We'll take you in. You can come to the UK. There is this new visa arrangement."

Li smiled. "Back to Bangor, to go sailing there? We are Hong Kongers. We stay. You, Melanie, should be beating up on Jean and Catrin to do more art business visits to us in Hong Kong. You sell well there, as you know, and are missing out on an active market."

Catrin said, "Oh, you stirrer! On holiday, too!"

Years earlier, they had an exhibition of Sayer-Hughes art in Hong Kong. It had sold well. Melanie had been forced reluctantly into the role of its business manager. She still chided her wife and friend for not doing more overseas direct business.

Jian Li caught Catrin alone at one point, as people were changing to go to a restaurant.

"Happy?" she asked.

"Yes. Why ask?"

"I catch an expression of yours every now and again. Somehow, it makes me think of those days before I left England and flew home, after Cheney injured you."

The damage to her cheek, by a gang enforcer, Colin Cheney.

Catrin smiled. "No, the holiday is wonderful. I am enjoying it, honestly."

She paused and took in her friend's expression, her focus on her. "Every now and again I think of the Harding investigation. That this man Assad is still free…that's all. The case has got to me."

Li said softly. "It's another wound, one that won't heal with surgery and time. You may want to consider talking to Dr. Herrington again."

The psychologist in London who helped her years ago to cope with the damage after her face had been injured. And at other times, too.

Catrin hadn't thought about that. Li was right. It was something to consider.

The following evening, during Mair and Lili's playtime before bed, Lili moved away from the toys and approached her mum. Jean was 'mum', Melanie was 'mummy'.

"Who is my daddy? Daniel has his daddy here and Mair has hers."

She stood there looking serious in front of Jean. Her ally, Mair, had crept up and stood behind her. Daniel, the youngest, was already in James and Li's bedroom, the door closed, to let him get to sleep.

Jean smiled. "You have two mummies. We have talked about that. Your mummy and I love each other very much and we had you."

Melanie was silent, watching her daughter's face. She glanced around the adults, now quiet, and asked Lili, "Is this from last week. With Angela?"

Lili nodded. Melanie sighed quietly. "Angel by name but not by behaviour. A school friend."

She looked at Jean. "It's time, love. And perhaps there is no better time, with our friends here."

She dropped to the floor and sat Lili on her lap. Mair went to Catrin and climbed on to hers. She saw a story-time coming.

Melanie began with, "Remember we talked about your mum and I giving blood when you had that bad scrape on your arm? How it bled?"

Lili nodded. "I had lots of blood coming out of me."

"Yes. I said your mum and I give blood to the hospital for when people need it. When they lose a lot of blood, we give them bits of ours. If we ever needed it, there would be bits for us to use there. Remember?"

"Yes, we share."

"Angela is right. To make a baby you need a bit from a woman and a bit from a man. Aunty Catrin loves Uncle Chris, so they had Mair. Aunty Li and Uncle James love each other and they had Daniel. Your mum and I love each other but we needed a bit from a man. The bit to help me make you in my tummy came from Uncle William. He donated it and helped me and your mum."

Catrin looked at Jean, then at Melanie. Jean was intently focused on her daughter and partner. The couple had never revealed previously the donor source for Melanie's pregnancy, and Catrin had never asked. It was a private matter. Somehow, she had assumed they had gone for an anonymous donor provided by a clinic.

William, the husband of Liz Marshall, their gallery owner. Catrin remembered a coffee session in a cafe after a gallery event, with Melanie looking up someone in Debrett's peerage. William had seemed too knowledgeable. She had checked on him also. He turned out to be the Honorable William Lionel Esquith.

"Aunty Liz's William?"

"Yes. He is a very nice man and he helped us. But he is not your daddy in the way that Mair and Daniel have daddies. You have two mummies instead. Is that OK now?"

"Yes! I have my bit from Uncle William."

She smiled at her mummy, then gave her a kiss before running back to the toys. Mair squirmed off Catrin's lap to join her.

Melanie looked up. "Now you know, too. Jean and I asked him together. He is a lovely man with a personality and qualities... we like."

She looked at her wife. Jean said, "And when we go back home, Melanie plans to try for a sister or brother for Lili, from the same donor batch. We waited, given Covid, but we won't wait any longer, we decided."

Across the cabin, Mair piped up. "I'm Lili's sister." She was still listening.

"And if we have another girl, you will have a new sister, too. Or perhaps a brother."

Mair clapped her hands, excited at the news.

Li said quietly, "Thank you for including us in that. We don't know him, only Liz, but I know you must have chosen with great care. I am amazed how you explained it so easily to Lili."

Melanie shook her head. "No. Not easily. We have talked with others in our situation. We have looked on-line for advice and listened to Lili as she learns things. This is a big step for us. I'm glad Lili is happy with the explanation, at this stage. It will help later on."

Jean said, "William took early retirement from a finance career in the City of London when he met Liz, and she started the gallery. We have worked closely with him over the years. It seemed right. And he was very happy to be asked."

She looked at Catrin. "You are crying."

Catrin nodded. "This holiday, with you all. And now this news. Yes, I am. It is too much after... I feel I have been...."

She stopped, sniffed, grabbed a tissue, and wiped her eyes. Then she focused on Chris. "Some time soon, we must go home. To London, to Spitalfields. That home."

"Agreed. Although I could stay on this boat a while longer, I must admit."

In two days, they would be parting, the holiday over.

Li said, in her best mangling of a Bangor accent, "We Welsh have a word for it, you know... hiraeth. You English won't really understand. Homelonging. That's what you have got."

Catrin smiled. "You are right. It's true. I never thought I would say that. And about Spitalfields, not Wales."

Fleetingly, she realised before she could go home, she had to close out on the Task Force. That meant presenting the report, with its implications for the employees of the Devon and Cornwall Police.

She threw the thought out the other side of her mind. She didn't want to spoil this holiday at all.

34 KEYSTONE FIVE

Nathan Atkins didn't traipse all the way to Devon this time, he stayed in Whitehall. Catrin and DCC Billings were together on the Devon end of the videocall.

"We are hearing that the tribal gossip is finger-pointing at Shaykh Yusuf Abrahim for the Harding attack. Some of the facts going around could only have come through your investigation."

'Probably," said Catrin, brightly. "We are still tracking information on Bital Assad and any connection he has to the ring. Obviously, questions must have a factual basis and sometimes those facts become visible."

"We expressly told you not to pursue enquiries against the shaykh unless you had factual information."

"We aren't, Mr. Atkins. We are following all leads to Bital Assad. Diligently. Unless I am directed otherwise, I will continue to do so."

Atkins directed his attention at Billings. "Do you have anything to add, Deputy Chief Constable?"

"Not from me. No."

Atkins suddenly switched gears. "When do you return

to the Met, Superintendent?"

Catrin responded. "I finish here soon and take some relocation leave."

She wasn't going to be more precise.

"Thank you. Goodbye."

The call was cut.

"Rude sod," said Billings. "I think the last bit was a veiled threat. He squinted, trying to look the hard case. Watch out for him."

Catrin said nothing.

"Not the best day for you, is it? This now, and the decision meeting this afternoon."

The critical meeting of the Task Force with the chief constable and others.

She responded, "I'm more worried about that than about Nathan Atkins."

~~

Chief Constable Jessop looked down the meeting room table at the assembled clusters. The representatives of the Office of the Police Commissioner sat at the bottom left. The accountants faced them. Nearer, on his left side, were the territorial commanders or their deputies. On the right sat the Task Force leaders and the consultants.

Jessop opened with, "We have only one reason to meet today, and it is slightly different than we expected for Keystone Five. We are to pick an option from two choices, not receive one report. After that, I receive their work and formally present it to the governing body. I want no major disagreements surfacing at that time among the core participants. Whatever we agree today, we live with and stand by it."

His gaze swept the eyes around the table. He was

making it clear that all sectors represented were to speak up now or stay silent thereafter.

His eyes moved to the agenda. "Dr. Otley, as the consultant lead, Superintendent Sayer has asked you to set the scene. She will then cover the key decision issues."

Otley stood and moved between the bottom of the table and the display screen. The consultancy logo and her name popped up on screen and the room lights were slightly dimmed.

"Thank you, Chief Constable Jessop. It is a personal pleasure to do that. You will recall we provide a framework for organisational development. We went through this at Keystones One and Two. Our approach is tailored to your sector, one in which economic viability and societal role must be balanced. We secured that contract as words like Wuhan and Covid entered our vocabulary. The world has changed.

"The impact of the pandemic has been a learning curve for our organisation, as it has for the Task Force and for every serving staff member in your command. The chair of the Task Force is not bringing you a single report, but two. These reflect the majority and minority positions of its members. It would be trite to say that the group failed to agree on one report and is therefore a failure. I think not. I sincerely believe it has done its job well, with dedication and openness. As open as one can be, peering over a mask at the faces of other masked people.

"With the chair and deputy chair of the Task Force, I agree that the process has run its course. We cannot resolve the path forward without your input. I commend the members for their hard work and team spirit. Likewise, I thank the chair and her deputy for their leadership and dispute resolution skills. And I thank the chair for the decision she made to come back to you now.

It has been a pleasure to work with them."

She smiled at Catrin and Les Henry. "With that, I will turn it over to Superintendent Sayer."

Jessop asked, as Catrin stood, "One moment. Your firm is not advocating either path forward, is that correct?"

"Yes, sir. That is correct."

As she moved away, Catrin took her place. People looked at her, then at the screen, for a new presentation set. It was switched off.

Catrin opened the file she was carrying and produced two printed draft reports. Each was about a half-inch thick. She held one in each hand.

"This is the Keystone Five meeting of the Task Force sequence. I bring to you a strategic plan proposal and an alternate."

She held up her left hand. "The minority report is the same in most areas as the majority report. It meets completely the objectives set for us."

She held up the other hand.

"The majority report meets most of the deliverables. It falls short in the year one financial projection by just under a million pounds. By year five, cumulatively, its shortfall drops to less than three hundred thousand pounds. That sounds a lot of money, but it is between one and two per cent of the total operational budget.

"The differences between the two reports are best characterised by a single concern. The majority believe that we cannot undermine our core objective of service delivery, certainly not to the levels given in the minority report. Shortly, I will take you through these differences at the macro-level and leave you and your staff to review the supporting background material.

"As chair, I support the majority report. I was brought

in partly because of my recent training at Cambridge and partly because I am an experienced police officer without any prior history with this constabulary. Both attributes helped me during the discussions. But I also supervised an operational case in conjunction with these Task Force duties. As you know, it was highly visible, the double murder of a man and his daughter. DCC Billings said it would stretch me. It did. But it also grounded me daily in the realities of my profession."

She put down the reports and focused on Jessop. "I am glad I was part of the Harding case for the team and the family. It was also a constant reminder of the true purpose of this exercise. We cannot measure functional efficiency solely by financial parameters. Nor can we look at the realities of a police officer's job in these uncertain times using solely historic reference points. We had to address some hard fundamental issues and question some cherished assumptions. Some of these we discarded and others, originally seen as obvious cost reductions, we retained."

She picked up the remote and switched on the screen. "Let's start on the issue of near-retirement options and their cost implications."

An hour later, after her presentation and some questions, Jessop led the meeting to its close. The part-icipants would then have only three days to review the detail and respond to him directly.

The head accountant for the Office of the Police Commissioner focused on Ursula Otley. Earlier questions by him showed he was firmly for the minority report, the lower cost option – but he was by then in the minority at the table.

"We haven't discussed this at all. The contract with

your company includes an incentive bonus, one which relates only to financial parameters. The majority report will eliminate much of that. I know your company, by contract, does not make a recommendation on a path forward. I want to know how you feel personally about this situation. You have been through many of these exercises."

Otley glanced at Sayer and then at Jessop. "You are quite correct that we will not make any recommendation, so that question is a bit of a dilemma for me to answer.

"Last week I had a conference call with the other partners in our firm, to make them aware of the situation as we entered Keystone Five. The outcome was that we accept unconditionally the decision you make. There will be no comeback on issues of our company's performance versus that of the Task Force. Nor will we request a review of the incentive clauses of the contract.

"Superintendent Sayer and Chief Superintendent Henry worked tirelessly to achieve the goal set for the team. I have every confidence in them. That is as much an answer as I will give."

35 GUNSMITH

The urgent call to Sayer came two days later from a Superintendent Josten, with the Birmingham Police.

"Your investigation into the Harding murders; do you have a fix yet on the gun, or the calibre of the weapon used?"

"There were two weapons used, one a 9mm, the other a Sig Sauer .32."

"We have a gunsmith here in the Queen Elizabeth Hospital ICU. He isn't going to make it, I understand. Covid. He wants to make a confession to the police, his wife says, and is putting off intubation to do that. His lungs are in a very bad shape, and she is highly stressed. I have a couple of my people who know him setting up to join them by videolink."

Catrin asked, "Right now?"

"Yes. She says, quote, 'He said it is about the girl killed in Devon'. Do you want someone to link in?"

"Yes, I do. I really appreciate this."

"Have your person join a link we will text you in the next couple of minutes. We will be ready to go in about ten, but it is all a bit of a rush. I'm not sure how well it will work. I'll let you go, but fill me in afterwards, if you would?"

"I'll call you. Thanks again."

Clarry transferred the link to DI Kendrick, who brought in the first IT person she found, called Jess, and DS Lough. Michael Hicks was out, having his second vaccine shot at a clinic near his home.

Afterwards, Kendrick called Hicks, who arrived at HQ in time for the evening briefing. Catrin, coming from another meeting, entered in time to join.

It was the first update item.

DI Kendrick explained the background and said, "It was a windfall, but hard. Jess has gone home and will see the psychologist, but she was the hero of the hour. We lost the videofeed twice and sound once, but she fixed the problem each time fast. She broke down afterwards. It was not easy to watch."

She kept her voice level. "Thomasino Guilini, Tommy G in the trade, has been in trouble over the years. He was a legit gunsmith but lost his firearms certificate and dealer's license in his early fifties. Caught in a sting operation, he received a nine-year sentence for supplying weapons. Since his parole five years ago, he apparently did more of the same, selling guns to criminals.

"He caught Covid a few weeks ago and deteriorated. When Birmingham called Superintendent Sayer, he was about to be placed on a ventilator. Guilini had been holding off, his wife said, making the decision about talking to someone or not. Her priest talked with him on-line. With their permission, he called a contact in the Birmingham Police.

"If Guilini is right, the guns are a Beretta 9000 9mm

and, as we know already, a Sig Sauer .32. He supplied the Sig. The Beretta has a trigger flaw, he thought, from a brief inspection of the weapon. They wanted a dozen rounds for the 9mm and a full magazine for the Sig Sauer. That was the deal, Guilini said. He offered to fix the Beretta. They asked the cost and timing and when he told them, the buyer refused flat. Guilini took the money for the Sig. He wanted to know if it was used to kill the girl."

She paused. "The buyers were known to him. He identified Ryan Smith and another patch member of the D-Crew, Christopher Monk, also known as 'Monkey'."

DC Rollins said, "It doesn't matter he confessed. This supplier will get prison for selling the Sig if he pulls through."

Lough said, "I told him it wasn't the gun he sold to them that killed the child. It killed the man."

DC Joan Childs, sitting next to Rollins, said jokingly, "You were too nice to him, Luffy. Should have left him thinking about it."

They both laughed.

Michael Hicks was about to say something when he saw their expressions change. He glanced sideways. Sayer was looking fit to bust, her anger at Child's comment barely contained.

Hicks said, "Childs and Rollins." Then he turned to Kendrick. "Erica, I take it we have the full recording edited together now?"

She nodded, sensing his meaning.

Hicks continued. "You two will review the interview together before leaving tonight, making notes. Identify anything of interest to this team that the soft-hearted DI Kendrick and DS Lough may have overlooked. You will give the feedback at tomorrow morning's brief."

He focused on everyone gathered. "And Guilini won't

be charged. He is on a ventilator now until his wife's sister and brother-in-law arrive to support her as he declines. She will then meet his request to switch everything off."

He looked at Catrin. She nodded slowly, then said, "Michael, talk to Ewen Jackson to get CPS primed, but bring in Monk. Get a warrant and search his home and the D-Crew clubhouse for weapons."

Wastle asked, "And Stuart Baines? What about him?"

She looked at Hicks, questioning his view. He asked Kendrick, "Any mention of him at all?"

"None."

He paused a moment. "Let's send DS Lough to see him and make an evaluation. I will be guided by his insight and experience."

His eyes had moved from Lough to the pair of younger officers as he spoke. Rollins blushed and Childs looked away.

Childs needs talking to by someone, Catrin thought, making a mental note to review her file.

She looked at Lough. "Assuming CPS agree, I suggest you do that after Monk is in the cells and both have been charged. Softly. See if he breaks rank."

Lough nodded in agreement. "Yes, Ma'am."

As they broke up, Joan Childs spoke to her colleague and they both went over to Lough. She said, "I'm sorry, Luffy. I was reacting to Guilini selling the gun, and I thought you should have stuck it to him. I'm surprised at the Super. So angry."

Lough said, "When you watch Tommy G on the recording, you'll see why. Be prepared for that. As to why Sayer was so angry, her husband used to work here, a good bloke. He has been struggling back from Covid, the long Covid symptoms. I heard he was borderline at one point for a ventilator, too."

He stood. It was finishing time and he wanted to get home. "You are detectives. I'll leave you to put the clues together."

He moved past them, then turned. "And Childs, I have seen you twice this week with your mask well below your nose, against regulation. I didn't say anything. This is fair warning; if I see that again, I'll report you. This isn't Ten bloody Downing Street, where anything goes."

Starr and Brenda were leaving together as Lough walked off. Starr said to Rollins, "I've set up the file for you and sent you the link."

She was about to walk on when Brenda gave the pair a look. "Pissing off Luffy, the boss and the Super in one fell swoop. I haven't seen that happen in a long time."

~~

The arrest of Christopher Monk took three police cars and two detectives sent to his home. Given the involvement of guns, they thought about using a tactical unit.

It was Lough who said, "It's a farm. He has an annex to the farmhouse. His parents live in the main house. They are alright. A show of police presence should suffice. He won't have other bikers there. For the clubhouse yes, but for Monkey, we go to the main door as normal, I suggest."

He was right.

When Monk's dad opened the door, seeing DI Kendrick in a tactical vest waving a search warrant, he called, "Chris, get here. They want you, not us."

The search of the property didn't turn up any guns. They found a box of nine-millimetre ammunition, less the number the gunsmith had mentioned they wanted. When asked, the father shrugged, giving the police car now containing their son a cold stare. "Not for here," he said. "We have a shotgun and a licence, but nothing that would use those bullets."

Luffy asked gently, "You won't try to claim your licence covers the box of ammunition we just found?"

The father pursed his lips and shook his head and then looked from Lough to Kendrick. "One time... but not now. I heard one of you say the pack was open?"

Lough didn't reply, just gave a slow nod.

"God knows what Chris is into. But no. I was not involved in their purchase. Nor did I know they were on the farm. We want nothing to do with it."

Oliver Wastle, hearing the feedback from the arrest, re-checked the video. With Guilini's breathing issues, it was hard to follow in places.

He called Hicks. "We thought he supplied ammunition for both guns, but no. The box of nine-millimetre rounds obtained by Monk fit the picture, too."

Monk wasn't going to enlighten them as to where he bought the ammunition, that was clear. He was as aggressively uncooperative as Ryan Smith.

Ewen Jackson said, "We can charge him now with illegal possession under the Firearms Act. If you get a firmer link to the gun used, we have him for a mandatory minimum of five years on that alone."

Catrin responded, "If we can make the link, I want Monk and Smith in the dock with Jaber and Assad."

Jackson shook his head, "That's too far a stretch, with what we have. Accessories, yes, but separate trials."

Catrin said, "We'll see. Perhaps if they are facing life, one of them will stop acting like stereotypical biker hard cases."

Hicks gave Johnston a smile. "And you think I'm too pushy?"

Catrin added, "Let's see what Lough turns up by showing Baines his tender side. How is that for balance?"

The following day, DS Lough and DC Childs arrived at the home of the Baines family. Given his medical needs, the court had given Stuart Baines a home-restricted bail. His barrister had argued for the release. With two broken wrists and skin grafts, the help he needed was best provided by his parents. Now, months later, in better health, Baines was still on bail.

He scowled when Lough and Childs walked in. His mother said, "We'll leave you to it, then."

'No," said Luffy, "Not at present, Mrs. Baines. We'll see in a while. I just have some information first which you may want to hear, too. But how are you doing, Stu?"

Joan Childs thought, we are not here as welfare visitors, Luffy. But she kept her face straight and her mouth shut.

After listening to both Stu and his mother for ten minutes, Lough said, "Monkey is under arrest now, as well as Ryan."

He looked at the parents. "You know Christopher Monk, I take it? He likes to go by the name Monkey."

That led to more discussion with the parents about Stuart's friends.

Lough brought it back on topic. "Ryan and Monkey are now charged as accessories to the murder of William and Ashley Harding."

"No! They weren't there. Honest, I know that. I told you about the package."

"The guns, Stu, the guns. Monkey and Ryan supplied them. We have direct evidence. And worse still, I must say, for your patch Ryan. I'm here because I know you better than anyone else in the investigation team."

Baines was looking scared.

"We had no evidence that you and Ryan knew the purpose of the guns you supplied. That's why we couldn't charge you both with the Harding murders. But now we have the testimony of the gunsmith who sold Ryan and Monkey the Sig Sauer. He offered to fix the trigger of the Beretta, the gun that killed the daughter. Ryan said no."

He watched Baines absorbing the news. Lough's hand moved, finger pointing as he went on. "Prior knowledge of the weapon flaw; Jaber admitting the gun went off unexpectedly. Connect the dots. We have Monkey and Ryan, for sure. The question is, do we include you?"

He looked at the parents. "Your son is at a crossroads now. I'm hoping he is not so deeply involved that he can't get out, or he will go down with the other two. He wants to be as hard as Ryan and the others, I know.

"When I go back to the station, I am required to make a recommendation about charges for Stuart. At issue is whether he should stand as an accessory to the murder of a twelve-year-old girl and her father.

"What DC Childs and I are going to do is this; we won't take you in yet. We will sit in our car outside, give you a chance to talk together. Stu, if you then want to make a full and complete statement, call your solicitor and have him call me on my mobile."

He passed over his card.

"If we don't hear in, say, fifteen minutes, we'll drive off and the uniformed officers in the other car outside will collect you. Either way, Childs and I will interview you on record at the station. It's your chance to show coop-eration. That will go a long way with CPS."

Stu Baines retorted angrily. "If I talk to you more than

I have, they'll go after me."

Lough shook his head. "You don't get it. Forget the brotherly biker love. To the club, Ryan and Monkey are foot soldiers. Expendable. Your half-patch is still new; you are nothing. This isn't about club business. This is a pair of patches doing something for half a bar of heroin and getting two people killed. No one will bother about them or come after you. It wouldn't surprise me if the club takes back their patches for stupidity. And yours."

He stood. "I don't want to see a young person like you spend your best years in prison. When it comes out how callous Ryan was about a defective gun, I don't think any D-Crew member will support that. But it's your call, your fork in the road. You decide.

"Mr. and Mrs. Baines, we will see ourselves out."

He looked at Joan, signalling they should leave.

In the car outside, he said, "Sayer said wait until both patches were in custody. That's what she meant."

Joan Childs and Steve Rollins had reported during the morning briefing on their review of the video. They apologised to Lough and Kendrick. The work moved on. Childs drew the partner role with Lough today without any hidden agenda behind it.

It took six minutes. It was Mr. Baines who called, not the solicitor. Stuart was going to be fully cooperative. He was calling his lawyer now. They appreciated Sergeant Lough being so considerate.

Joan said, "Stu just had one of his broken wrists twisted a bit. Or he will have the beginnings of a black eye when we interview him."

Lough said, "Parental love, Joan. Parental love. They probably told him they would cancel their bail support. I would. See how he likes it inside, as a sampler for a prison existence for most of his adult life."

Within two days, information from Stuart Baines allowed officers questioning Christopher Monk to get him to slip up and rebut facts put to him, rather than stay silent. Baines identified Jaber and Assad as the people they met for the swap. One of those denials tied to Ryan Smith and Monk meeting a guest at their clubhouse, a biker from Koblenz. To throw Smith off, Lough claimed the biker was from Cologne.

By then, Monk had worked out that Baines had been talking.

"I met no-one from Cologne. That week the club had two visitors from Koblenz, not Cologne. I did no more than smile at them and say hello. That was all. Baines will say anything to get you off his back."

He refused to identify the visitors, claiming he had no idea who they were.

It was not lost on the detectives that he admitted having contact with bikers from Koblenz. Sultan Kahn, the businessman who foisted Assad on to Fayed, lived in that town.

36 CEMETERY

It was the end of April when Catrin received a message via Clarry to return a call to Dr. Zaid. He would be available today, but not for the next two days, other than evenings, due to his surgery schedule.

"My wife and I are returning to Exeter, Superintendent, next Tuesday, to meet Adam and his aunt and uncle. I want to thank you for making the contact with Mrs. Wansbury. We have spoken several times. The meeting will be at the cemetery where his family are buried. You attended the funeral, I gather?"

"Quite a few of my officers did also, yes. He is a remarkable young man, I feel, given his experiences."

"I look forward to meeting him. And his aunt and uncle. The tragedy, and Nabil's role in it, has been a constant area of discussion in our extended family. I was wondering if you or DCI Hicks could be there? I would like to return the favour you did us."

"Introducing Mrs. Zaid was a small thing, Doctor Zaid."

"It wasn't, but that is not what I am referring to. I

meant your words when we met, in being open with me about the background to the tragedy. I may have something for you."

"In that case, one or both of us will be there, probably me. I have more control over my schedule than DCI Hicks at present. He has the Harding case continuing, but his team has another big investigation."

"Well, until then, if it works. I have sent the details to your assistant."

~~

It was late afternoon on a blustery and unexpectedly cold day at the beginning of May when the two police officers arrived at the Plymouth Road Cemetery in Tavistock. Two uniformed patrol officers with a car were there also, to ensure privacy.

The boy had chosen the location. It was the site of the new plaques memorialising his sister and father, placed above their cremated remains, next to the grave of his mother.

Dr. Zaid and his wife were formally dressed, her in dark blue, him in dark grey, with a black raincoat. Catrin could see that Trevor Wansbury was tight-lipped. Perhaps he was uneasy about the arrangement, she wondered. Eve Wansbury seemed more at ease.

After introductions, Adam focused on Dr. Zaid, looking serious.

"What sort of doctor are you?"

It was a beginning.

"I am a surgeon. I work in Manchester."

Adam swung his arm around, pointing at the grave. "My mother had surgery. It slowed things, Dad said, but she died. And now my sister and father. They are all here now."

The pain shared by him was evident to all. Zaid dropped to a crouch, his arm across his knee, his back straight with his head slightly below Adam's. His wife bent forward a little. Zaid's raincoat trailed on the grass, picking up drops of water, getting damp.

"May I call you Adam?"

Adam didn't respond, appearing uncertain. Zaid asked, "Or Mr. Harding?"

"Adam."

"Surgeons operate on people to make them better, or to ease their pain. Sometimes we operate to make their life more comfortable, not being able to cure them. It is part of being a doctor. If I could help you in any way, not surgery obviously, I would. But all I can tell you is how sorry we all are that you lost your father and sister and that our family prays for you daily."

"In Manchester?" Adam asked.

"Wherever our family is. Here in the UK, in Yemen, in Saudi Arabia, in the USA. We are spread out now. A member of our extended family has committed a terrible wrong to you. But if our prayers are not helping you now, I hope one day they will."

Catrin saw the man's knee tremble a little. The strain of the position was getting to him, but he wasn't moving. The boy was deciding, Catrin thought, how to respond to this adult.

"You have the same eyes. All I saw was his eyes through the mask. But you sound different. Gentle."

It was Trevor Wansbury who broke the spell. "You'd better stand up, Dr. Zaid, before you fall. Your coat is getting soaked at the back."

As Zaid did so, Adam looked up at his aunt, then held her hand, unsure what else to say for a moment. Then he asked, "Can we pray?"

Eve gave a questioning look at the two Moslem visitors, then turned to Trevor, expecting him to speak. It was Mrs. Zaid who responded.

"May I do that? When I was a nurse, I had a colleague who always said the same prayer before each shift. One to Saint Barbara."

It surprised Eve, but she nodded.

Tahira Zaid said, "O God, teach me to receive the sick in your name. Grant those placed in our care abundant blessings. Strengthen in me whatever may bring joy to the lives of those I serve. Give me grace, for the sake of those sick and suffering."

She stopped, waiting to see what would happen. Trevor Wansbury went straight into the Lord's Prayer, and the others, to varying degrees, joined him.

As they finished, Adam asked Mrs. Zaid, "Who is Saint Barbara?"

"The patron saint of surgeons, Adam. Doctor Zaid and I met through working in the same hospital."

She leaned forward again. "And there are many ways of suffering, aren't there?"

He thought a moment and gave an emphatic nod, then a smile at the two visitors.

A little later, as they turned away from the grave and the memorial stones, the boy focused on Catrin. He spoke about the visit to the police headquarters and his experiments with the forensic kit.

"I do want to be a police officer, you know. It's not just a passing interest."

She smiled at him, pained she would be leaving him soon. The Wansbury's hadn't told him yet, she knew. The two families were having afternoon tea on neutral ground, at a local hotel. She and Michael Hicks were not joining them but heading back to Exeter.

Earlier, the Zaid couple had met with Catrin and Michael alone at the local police station. Daud Zaid provided some very useful information, the name of a contact. He was a relative living in Oman, and the man's niece was a servant to Shaykh Yusuf's household.

Three days later, albeit as third-hand information, they heard the reason why Abrahim wanted the ring back. It was an answer that simply blew Kendrick away, she said.

37 MAID

"Her name was Hanan Al Imani. She stole the ring, Shaykh Yusuf insists. My niece is a servant at his home."

Kendrick had let the older man tell it his own way, rather than conduct a formal interview. The facts had been spilling out without a sense of a chronology. But the first name of the woman was the same as mentioned by the Sufi.

Erica and Adara were facing the same computer, with an Arabic interpreter, linked to the man in Oman. They had heard him speak of the familial link between him and Daud Zaid. He explained it for the recording, but it was complex. In a diaspora, family bonds are important, if complicated.

His information came from his niece, Luhar, still a maid in the Abrahim household. So far, it tied in with the story provided by the Sufi. New insight came when Kendrick asked, "But why now? Do you know?"

"Shaykh Yusuf is seriously ill. He has some form of cancer, but I don't know what. He has been to doctors. His mind is melancholy."

Kendrick grimaced internally while her face showed her encouragement for him to continue. Hopefully he would do so a little more coherently.

"His daughter is... how would you say... obsessed with jewels and fine things. She talks of this sapphire, particularly. She is very knowledgeable about jewelry but is a mean-spirited person. She makes Luhar afraid sometimes, and my niece is ten years older than her. The daughter complained repeatedly about its loss from the family. I think that is the reason."

He blinked, thinking. "Luhar says it is a rare sapphire and the Shayk's daughter wanted it back. He spoils her."

As the interpreter finished speaking, he added, "Perhaps he wanted to make her happy before he dies."

Erica thought fleetingly that perhaps the Shaykh should have died before sending people to kill a man and his daughter for a bauble.

"How did they react, do you know, to the robbery and murder, and the arrest of Nabil?"

"It is not discussed at all, at least in the presence of Luhar. But there was a big event at their home the day after Mr. Assad visited, a celebration, really. And afterwards, another row."

"Why was that?"

"Apparently, the daughter thought she would get the ring. The Shaykh said no, it would be restored. He would keep it but promised it as part of her inheritance."

He stopped.

Adara spoke up. "She wanted it now?"

"Well, yes. But that wasn't the issue. She liked it in its gold setting. To put it back into silver angered her."

Adara looked at Erica Kendrick. Their faces showed the same disbelief. Adara asked, "They are not troubled by the theft, or the deaths, or that Nabil Jaber is in prison?"

"Luhar says she has never heard it discussed. You must understand, that would be seen as a matter between Mr. Assad and Nabil, not one involving the Shayk. And it is their home. A business matter would be unsuitable for discussion there."

It is fantasyland, thought Erica. She asked, "The Shaykh is ill. Is he in hospital, or undergoing treatment?"

"He has been twice to Germany for treatment. And there is a possibility he will go to the USA very soon. They are waiting on some medical results. Either there, or to India or Pakistan, perhaps. Luhar doesn't know which. She will know only when she turns up for work and her boss tells her. There is a daily briefing for servants on family and visitors in residence, about what must be done, when."

As they thanked him for his information, he asked for the second time whether his niece would be at risk.

"No, not at all. As we informed Dr. Zaid, any inform-ation we receive will only be used for background purp-oses. We will hold to that. We thank you and your niece for your help."

~~

In the feedback to the Serious Crimes team at the next briefing, it was Jackie Neil who spoke up. "So, we now have most of the picture linking the deaths to Jaber and Assad through someone in Germany to the Shayk. And not a shred of evidence beyond Jaber and Assad. And no sign of getting Assad. What happens now, boss?"

Before Hicks could answer, she added, "And where is the Super? There's a rumour –."

To be cut off by Hicks forcefully. "One thing at a time;

please!"

He paused, forcing a silence on the assembled team members.

"First, the Harding case. Most of you are already working on different assignments anyway. We will inform you further of any developments as they arise."

He focused directly on DC Neil. "Not all avenues are closed. You will hear more when it is appropriate. After all, I don't want any rumours started, do I?"

She grimaced.

"To my final announcement for the morning. Superintendent Sayer is now on relocation leave for a few days, before returning to the Met."

Rollins interrupted, asking, "Does that mean –?"

To be overridden by an increasingly obdurate Hicks. "Tomorrow, at 9.30 a.m., all officers on duty are to be in their assigned locations. Any absences must be authorised by an inspector level officer or higher. That comes down from DCC Billings. And no, I am not going to speculate. The results of the reorganisation will be communicated, that is all I can say. Get on with your assigned jobs, please. We have work to do."

As they set about their various tasks, it was DC Neil who said, "It's a pity Sayer didn't put in an appearance today."

Rollins looked at DS Tydman, who was impassive. "So that you could grill her on the changes? She wouldn't say anything, you know that."

Jackie shook her head, "No, I didn't mean that. She did alright, in the end. Even I think that. We should have given her a proper send off. Said something nice, you know?"

Tydman pursed his lips. "I don't think Superintendent Sayer would welcome that. Not because of the Task

Force, but because she doesn't see the Harding case as closed. She may be off it now, but I don't see her as accepting plaudits from anyone until it is over. And you have Fran Mowbury to interview in Plymouth, so..."

Get on, was his message.

As Jackie Neil picked up her bag and a file, her final comment was, "Well, there is sod all she can do about it now. She is going back to the Met. It is over for her, isn't it?"

From a distance, Oliver Wastle had watched their exchange silently. As Jackie Neil passed him, she got the impression that Wastle knew something she didn't. It wasn't his expression, just a glance from him. Perhaps she was reading too much into it, she thought, as she found DC Palmer waiting at the door for her, to head off to Plymouth.

~~

"Where to now? Can you say?" Les Henry asked Ursula Otley. He had taken her and Catrin Sayer to lunch at the Exeter Golf and Country Club for a farewell meal. They had formally said their farewells to other Task Force members days earlier.

"Yes, I can; the contract is signed. The North West Ambulance Service. One of my colleagues kicked off with them last week and I take over at the Keystone One meeting. I will be in and out of Bolton, not Exeter, for a while."

She looked at Catrin and smiled. "You will be back in London and Les will be playing golf. A well-earned retirement."

He smiled. "Overdue. I only stayed on the extra year because Aiden pushed me to do so, as Catrin was coming in. Inside and outside experience together, he said."

Catrin looked at Otley. "Does it get to you, not being anchored, always working on a new project, a new location?"

Otley shook her head. "No, not really, these days. I was 'anchored' as you put it to my first job; rose from being a university entrant to CEO. Then came the takeover and restructuring. When I was forced out, I was traumatised, I must admit."

She paused, looking across the dining room, reflecting. "Two people I met in my outplacement support had also been through the 'axe and eliminate' experience. We decided to set up our own consultancy based on our shared experience. When you are dealing with people's livelihoods, you owe it to them to do this process properly and fairly."

She looked at Catrin. "You and Les did well, I have said that. But it is not your high point from being here, is it?"

Catrin responded after a moment's thought. "No. I must admit. I think we did the best we could, and I am satisfied with the Task Force work and product. Nor has the other job, the Harding case, exactly reached a high point, as you put it."

She picked up her glass of sparking water. "But that's not over, yet. Here is to you both, thank you for all your help. To future high points, including some holes-in-one for you, Les."

Chief Superintendent Henry, for one more week and a day, picked up his glass. "Well, I will certainly drink to that."

They revealed the changes in the Devon and Cornwall Police the following day. Many were surprised, mainly because they seemed to have little initial impact. Sure, there were people let go and others who received early retirement packages. There were tears, anger and disappointment. Almost everyone affected was not a real surprise.

There were several unexpected retirements announced, phased over the next year. It was clear that the people involved had already been consulted, or at least made aware, before the general announcement.

One was Michael Hicks, promoted to superintendent (acting). DI Wastle was promoted to Hick's former position. The temporary appointments were fixed length, with the purpose of fostering leadership change.

The more astute picked up that the team mergers and the unit reallocations announced at the same time were significant. They would reduce 'management' numbers in favour of 'operational' personnel. That affected both the civilian staff levels and officers carrying warrant cards.

Overall, it was a two-day wonder. Within a week, people settled down and life returned to the work they needed to do. The person happiest about the changes was the director of finance. He was best placed to understand the cost implications.

When Jan Reimer was given her news, she had nearly finished her studies. She would transition to a detective constable in the team, DS Lough said.

"There is a recommendation here, on the file, from Superintendent Sayer. You should consider a two-week course on cultural and art crime fundamentals. Did she discuss it with you at all? I know you worked closely with her on the Harding case."

Jan chose her words. "She mentioned that there was a course in London, yes. I asked her about gaining expertise in the area, as it is an interest I have."

"I talked with DCI Wastle. We are in support of your doing it. We don't see it as an immediate need, as you should get settled into your new role first. But you can register for it. Say, in about six months. How does that sound?"

Jan nodded, obviously happy with the decision. What she didn't say was that Sayer had told her that her first goal was to become a plainclothes officer. Sayer had paused a moment, then said, "If art crime is your field of interest, you should accept the need to move. Living here, that's not an easy decision to make, trust me. But if you do, contact me or DI Mark Harper, assuming he is still in charge of Art & Antiques. But no guarantees."

Superintendent Sayer had given her a Devon and Cornwall Police business card. On the back were a London number and a personal email address. That had been two days before she left.

Sayer's final meeting while still officially on the books of the Devon and Cornwall Constabulary was with Michael Hicks. He drove to Falmouth, where Sayer and her family were spending a few days after packing and clearing their rental home before returning to London.

They met for a meal in pub. What was discussed there was never recorded, nor did DCI Hicks note the meeting in the system.

The one-year maximum assignment with the Devon and Cornwall Police had lasted ten months. Some there would miss her presence, but the majority were glad she was gone, that the Reaper had finished wielding her scythe.

PART 3

RESOLUTION

38 CITATION

The following week, after landing and taxiing, a white Citation jet with a motif in gold on its tail pulled into its assigned stand. Ronaldsway Airport in the Isle of Man was a convenient refuelling point on its journey. It had set out from Qatar earlier that morning, destined for New York.

As the engine noise died away, the main door opened downwards into its role as the entry stairs. Two people, a man and a woman, approached it from the Executive Centre. Behind them, two uniformed Isle of Man police officers appeared, waiting.

The ground handlers kept their distance rather than start their regular service duties. Prior to refuelling, usually someone would check if any passengers wished to freshen up in the centre.

The man in the lead spoke to the co-pilot now emerging. He, in turn, spoke to the jet captain. A minute or so later, an older passenger in a dark suit and a white keffiyeh headscarf stepped down the jet stairs. A similarly dressed aide came behind him, now talking agitatedly into a mobile phone.

The plainclothes police officers from the IOM Police served an arrest warrant on Shaykh Yusuf Abrahim. He was being transferred to the custody of detectives from the Devon and Cornwall Police. They did not try to handcuff the shaykh, but the uniformed officers now went either side of him. He was in their charge.

Yusuf Abrahim was a diminutive, almost frail, older man. His glasses now darkened with the sunshine, hiding his eyes. The aide became more voluble, aggressively objecting to the act. He moved constantly from Arabic on the phone to English with the police officers. Another aide emerged behind them looking equally upset.

Words like 'illegal' and 'rendition', 'embassy' and 'diplomatic' interspersed an indignant flow from the aide. The IOM officers ignored it; the aide was an irrelevance to their task.

The door of a nearby jet opened. Out of it came a middle-aged plainclothes police officer. Behind him an older officer, white-haired, emerged and stood behind his companion. A younger plainclothes officer, a woman, also stepped out.

Michael Hicks stood to one side, silent. DCI Wastle arrested Shaykh Abrahim on suspicion of involvement in murders committed in Devon. They would fly to Exeter, he told him, and he would be interviewed under caution. He or his colleagues could make any arrangements for legal representation there. Now he must administer the caution.

As Wastle recited the litany, the door of the Executive Centre opened again. A uniformed police officer of more senior rank appeared with a woman in a business suit. Shaykh Yusuf looked at her, sensing her presence was significant. She stared momentarily at the Shaykh, then turned and shook hands with her IOM colleague.

Catrin Sayer had flown to the Isle of Man this morning from London to witness the arrest. She would now return with her former team to Exeter.

As DCI Wastle and DC Reimer led the prisoner over to the waiting jet, Catrin called out, "One moment!"

They stopped as she approached. She gave Hicks a look as her head turned, focusing on the Shaykh's left hand.

As she moved closer, in front of the man, she asked politely for him to raise his arm. As he did so, she focused on the ring on his little finger, a bright silver band with a pale pink stone. It was only for a moment; then the man dropped his arm again, tired of the request.

His first words spoken were quiet, with a slight taunt. "You like it? It's a sapphire. It belonged to my mother."

Catrin stayed impassive as she asked. "Yemeni silver, I take it? Has it always been in the family?"

It is more than I expected, she thought. A real present, in fact. Abrahim seemed less amused now and ignored her question. Instead, he said, "It has great sentimental value for me."

This woman knew something about Yemen, then, or its silver. Perhaps she knew too much.

Catrin looked him in the eye. She had seen photographs of this padparadscha sapphire mounted in gold. Now it was mounted in silver again.

"And for me, too," she said softly. She turned to Wastle, awaiting his next move.

Oliver Wastle was watching the man carefully. As Abrahim understood Sayer's comment, his face went through a range of emotions: fear, then anger and finally revulsion. That a woman, an unbeliever, could respond to him so confrontationally was an insult.

Oliver Wastle said quietly to DC Reimer, "It is evidence. Bag it."

Catrin ignored the changing expression on the Shaykh as she turned to Michael Hicks. He pointed at the jet stairs and said, "Middle seat, port side, across from me," as she nodded and entered.

The Shaykh would find himself on the back row, next to a waiting uniformed officer. That, no doubt, would be perceived as another insult.

"Who is she?" Abrahim asked, a question from a man used to giving commands and getting answers.

Wastle kept his face straight as he responded, "Super-intendent Sayer, sir. Metropolitan Police in London. She was formerly with the Devon and Cornwall Police. The ring, please?"

The newly appointed DC Reimer had produced a clear plastic evidence bag. Shaykh Yusuf saw that she, too, had an interest in the ring. By now he understood its significance, of course.

His staff would call the right people in the UK, he knew. His mind was working on ways and means of getting these irritants off his back, wondering if he would have to give up Assad to do that.

And he would punish severely the fool who chose the refuelling stop here.

As Shaykh Yusuf Abrahim entered the aircraft he was led, for him, past his normal middle seat to the rear. This officer called Sayer was now in his place, looking out the window. She ignored him completely.

It had been Michael's and her decision together that she would join them. It would be appropriate, a proper finish for them both for the Harding case. Catrin requested that they also meet with an eleven-year-old boy and his aunt and uncle. She wanted to be there when Hicks told them about the real culprit for his father's and sister's deaths.

Ewen Jackson in CPS was worried about the weakness of the case against Abrahim. Neither she nor the Chief Constable had the same concerns, it appeared. The overwhelming driver, they claimed, was the retrieval of a fugitive in Yemen, someone with less power than the Shaykh.

In the pub in Falmouth, Hicks had said, "Jessop is ambivalent about you joining in. He understands, but he and Doug Billings think you are taking an unnecessary risk."

She nodded. "I am. Providing I am invited, it is non-negotiable. It's for me this time, not only Adam. I want to see Abrahim under arrest, no matter for how long. It's my closure point."

As their jet climbed steeply after take-off, she closed her eyes and rested for a moment or two. When she opened them again, she watched Reimer, diagonally across from her in the first row, in a rear-facing seat. Jan had taken the sealed evidence bag from her purse to examine it carefully.

It will be hard to see it properly through the plastic; it deadens the reflections, Catrin mused. Suddenly seeing the senior officer looking at her, Jan blushed and returned the bag to the purse.

Catrin gave her a small smile of understanding, she thought. She was wrong. Covered by the background engine noise, Jan leaned across. As tears came to her eyes, she whispered to Catrin, "If it wasn't evidence, I'd flush it down the toilet."

Catrin's face showed she understood completely. The sapphire was beautiful, but as Frank Hamal would say, 'it has a story'. For her and DC Reimer, it was a part of that story which brought only pain, as it did for a family in England and, probably, for an unknown woman from Yemen who could be alive or dead. Someone who hopefully found her way to some sort of freedom, the sort that Farida Al Araqi held so dear.

She would speak to Michael. Reimer should join them again to see Adam Harding, perhaps. It might help.

39 HARINGEY

The arrest of Shaykh Yusuf had its repercussions, as predicted.

He was in custody in a cell overnight. Interviews on arrival in Exeter and during most of the following day were fruitless. He was released early evening. Within an hour, the same jet in which he had intended to fly to the USA flew him direct to Dubai.

By then the media had the story. Not from tight-lipped police officers in Exeter, however. 'Reliable but protected sources in the Yemeni community' were cited. The Daily Mirror named Abrahim 'The Sapphire Shaykh', the potentate allegedly behind the death of the Harding couple.

Images and video clips of him in meetings with other important people resurfaced. All were backdrops to the coverage of the allegations.

Chief Constable Jessop, with DCC Billings, handled all media inquiries with communications staff. Their refusal to comment on media coverage either way protected the constabulary. It also spoke volumes to their own position. The closest Jessop came to support the media stories was a comment. "At the outset, we stated we would pursue all avenues of inquiry into the deaths of William and Ashley Harding. We have done so."

As Shaykh Yusuf transferred to his waiting jet, the media, lawyers, and diplomats left Exeter by road or headed to hastily booked hotels. Collectively, they could have formed a convoy to wave him off as his jet flew overhead. But that night, or by the following morning, they simply dispersed.

Catrin Sayer was already home. She left within hours of arrival in Exeter. Catrin made no attempt to contact anyone there after she left by train. In her mind's eye she could see what was going on, who was doing the interviews and what was likely being said – and not said. She simply went home and got on with preparations for her return to work.

Police officers know how to throw suspects off balance. It is part of their training. Shaykh Yusuf Abrahim was particularly vulnerable, they thought. A man used to giving orders and receiving subservience from others would not take well to a day in the cells and interview rooms; the periods left unattended, the DNA swab, the finger-printing. He would not be mistreated, but he would perceive it as such. Abrahim would be presented with the evidence of Assad's guilt, a man now living in Yemen, where the Shaykh had political influence. They would see-saw between the Shayk's 'suspected involvement' and his country's failure to return Assad for trial.

On the Friday, Catrin had a call from Carlos Martin,

Barrington's assistant. She had expected a call from someone, perhaps Moore or Barrington. Even an instruction to report to Slieman's office was a possibility, but Martin's call was unexpected.

"I want to confirm your meeting with Miss Barrington at 9.30 a.m. on Monday."

"Yes, that's what I have. I'll be there."

"Miss Barrington says there may be some developments to deal with, but the timing is confirmed."

With that, he rang off.

~~

The following Monday, French police arrested Bital Assad at Paris Charles de Gaulle airport. He was supposedly returning from a long holiday in Yemen. Assad then awaited an extradition hearing. By chance, he had a barrel load of lawyers leaping to his defense. In claiming his own innocence, Assad explicitly stated his admiration, love, and loyalty for the great Shaykh Yusuf Abrahim. He claimed he had never spoken to him directly.

'The Second Sapphire Killer', as he was dubbed, probably should not have done that. The denial was enough for several media outlets to use three facial photos of Abrahim, Assad and Jaber together in their on-going coverage.

In New Scotland Yard that morning, Colleen Barrington looked across the meeting table at Catrin.

"You did the plausible deniability bit again, after Commander Moore told you not to do that. FCO are making noises about you. It is part of their investigation into the diplomatic incident around the Shayk."

She sighed. "They and our friends in SIS and MI5 have

been talking to people. Quietly, thank God; they are good at quiet. They even have CCTV coverage of you in Ronaldsway Airport."

"The invitation was a courtesy. It was still my personal time."

Barrington said bluntly, "Personal time or not, you were then on the Met's payroll, carrying a Met warrant card. You were present during a politically sensitive arrest of a foreign national. We have all seen the coverage; he is probably ruined in his world. The Foreign Secretary is feeling the heat from some important people in the Gulf."

Catrin kept her face straight. "What now?"

"Now I get the job of dealing with the problem you present. You won't be heading south of the river today. Instead, you go to Wood Green. That's a direct order from Tom Slieman."

A police station in Haringey, North London.

"As what?"

"Special Assistant to the Area Commander, Chief Superintendent Waddell. You will have area responsibilities for Wood Green station. Also, you get some cross-borough activities, including the North London moped thefts. The teenage wannabee bikers have gone crazy up there."

"Do I get my own police bike to chase them down?"

The truculence was to cover up the sting of the rebuke that the change in role implied. Not a rank demotion, at least, nor a reprimand. They were simply making it obvious that she was side-lined.

Colleen gave her a look which made it clear that she wasn't going to answer that. She said, "You are luckier than you think, having this cobbled up for you. Believe me."

"What did the Commissioner and Karen say?"

Colleen paused. "Moore is seething. I shouldn't tell you what she said, but I will. 'Haringey; put her there. It's Saxon, meaning Haering's Enclosure. It can be Sayer's Enclosure'.

"That is mainly because she didn't know, I suspect. Not that she disapproves of sticking it to a shaykh, but the fact you deliberately joined the arrest. You made it obvious and, in doing so, jeopardised your career. She has supported you to the hilt and has big expectations of you."

Catrin blushed with embarrassment. "I know. I just felt it better for her not to know. Not to get involved. Given her battle royal with John Reed."

Barrington retorted, "And I am not touching that one at present."

"Too hot?"

Barrington nodded, adding, "And the Commissioner said that you should expect a call from someone you know."

Catrin showed her puzzlement. "What does that mean?"

Barrington stood, picking up two folders, making it abundantly clear that the meeting was over with.

"I have no idea. I passed on the message she wanted delivered. Now, I've got another meeting and you must pack your shoebox again."

Catrin shook her head. "I've nothing to pack to take to Wood Green. Since I left Undertow to go to Cambridge, I have felt a bit of a nomad."

It could have been worse, she thought, as she left.

In the following days, it became evident that Devon and Cornwall Police were unrepentant. The media still covered the case, including the surprising decision by Abrahim to move to Pakistan. He would receive ongoing medical treatment in Lahore.

He had been heading to the USA for an important medical consultation, his people claimed. He was an old man. The treatment by the British police had done nothing to help his condition.

~~

In Exeter prison, DI Erica Kendrick held one last meeting with Nabil Jaber and his lawyer, accompanied by DC Henley. Jaber was to be transferred to a prison in Scotland the following week.

The request was simple, the offer clear. If Nabil Jaber would provide more information to incriminate Bital Assad, facts that would strengthen the extradition case, they had agreement from CPS to amend the charge for Nabil in the death of William Harding. He would be tried as an accessory, not a co-defendant.

Showing the judge that he was now assisting the prosecution could lead to a lighter concurrent sentence on that charge and, more importantly, be a powerful element of his prison record during consideration of parole in due course. As far off as it sounded, he needed evidence of rehabilitation to present to the parole board.

Nabil sat through her proposal, listening this time, not switched off. That was a positive, Erica thought.

As she sat back, waiting, Nabil focused on Adara Henley. "Where are you from, originally?"

Adara glanced at Kendrick, who gave a brief nod.

"France. I was born in France. My parents met there. My mother was an immigrant from Egypt, my father a sailor, from Liberia. He didn't stay around."

She left it there. Nabil nodded. "You will understand, I think."

He turned and focused on Erica. "No."

He paused, then added. "You had the real guilty party in your hands for what... hours? He is too powerful. He controls everything dear to me now. To give you Assad, I would be happy to drag the man kicking and screaming back from France to join me. But no."

He suddenly looked lost, bereft. "I would give my life in a heartbeat to have that young girl alive, but now all I can do is give up everything else for my village and my relatives there. It is the only good thing I can do."

~~

In her second day at Wood Green, Catrin took a deep breath and called Commander Moore. Her assistant, Inspector Matta, took the call and told Catrin she wasn't available. She would pass on the message.

Moore didn't return the call.

One other ongoing issue was the sapphire ring. To the Devon and Cornwall Police, it was evidence, the gemstone from the crime. To lawyers acting for Shaykh Yusuf, it wasn't the same stone at all. It was illegally removed from him and was still his property.

The police position was there no way it was being returned to him voluntarily. They took it to Frank Hamal. He confirmed that the stone in the ring was the same as in the valuation photos.

Mark Harper filled Catrin in, over a cup of coffee after a general briefing session at New Scotland Yard. He had just heard that the Shaykh was taking it to court, to retrieve his property. "Given Frank Hamal's expertise, they won't get very far. Frank is a formidable expert witness in court."

Catrin smiled. "He is first class; so polite when he tears the throat out of any opposing barrister's expert, yes."

She heard also that Reimer was keeping her lines of communication with Art and Antiques open, as well.

As the news of the FCO investigation spread, it was clear that Nathan Atkins had concluded that Catrin's role in the arrest of the shaykh was central, not peripheral. Catrin learned that nugget from Madeleine Turner-Jones. The FCO staffer insisted on taking her to lunch in a place favoured by people from the Foreign Office.

"One has to show solidarity, Catrin and, besides, it has been a long time."

She spoke as she gave a small wave to people at another table.

Catrin watched the expressions on the people across the room. "I don't think the Foreign Office has a branch in Wood Green, but you are mixing with an undesirable."

Turner-Jones said contentedly, "I am, aren't I? But I can hold my own ground with people at FCO, I assure you. Including the current minister's lapdog. Laurie sends his best wishes."

"He was very helpful. Thank you for arranging for him to come to lunch when you couldn't."

Turner-Jones smiled. "He spent time in Yemen, I know. I was going to bring someone else from the Gulf Region desk as well, until we got dissuaded. Or high-jacked, forcing us to miss the lunch. Nathan's doing, obviously."

Looking more concerned, Madeleine said quietly, "I hope you can hold your own, too. You have the training and experience. This SIS man assigned to the enquiry for the minister, Cunningham; I don't like him at all."

Catrin responded, "I don't know about him. I only met Atkins once, as he read the Minister's rulebook to senior officers in Devon."

Madeleine mused, "Your people moved you very fast, didn't they? Still, Nathan will never go out to places like Wood Green. He's a Westminster man. You may be lucky."

Catrin stared at her, deciding what to say. "Unfortunately, no. I'm not supposed to tell anyone, but I am called to a meeting with him. He will have a colleague and this man Cunningham with him. It is tomorrow, at Scotland Yard. Commander Moore's explicit instruction is that I must attend. So, I haven't told anyone, have I?"

Madeleine Turner-Jones wrinkled her nose, making her glasses rise on her face. "Nathan's mind is made up, so tell him nothing. He is just fishing for things to support his report damning you, along with the Chief Constable in Exeter. I wish you the best of luck."

40 PUPPETEER

As she entered the meeting room in New Scotland Yard, the first there, Catrin saw it was large, thank goodness, for the few people involved.

That there would be repercussions to her participation at the arrest of the shaykh was a given. She was still not sure of their severity, other than her current exile to Haringey.

Chief Constable Jessop's words when he accepted the proposal from her came back: 'there will be a loser, I guarantee it; if not the shaykh, then us.'

She was now lost in the political minefield. This interview was important, though, and she must make no blunders.

Catrin sat there alone, waiting; she was nervous now, thinking back over the Harding case. At the end, it had been only a few minutes with Adam Harding and the Wansbury couple during her strange day in Devon. That, and the flight with Shaykh Abrahim.

She was glad she got to see the ring more than the man; the source of all the sorrow and effort to arrest the perpetrators.

Michael Hicks, Erica Kendrick, Jan Reimer, DCC Billings and herself had visited the Harding home. Adam had given her a big smile as they walked in. Billings had done the talking, as the senior officer. He explained the arrest and its possible consequences.

Eve Wansbury summarised it neatly. "You have identified the person who was behind it all, but we don't have the evidence to prosecute him here. Now we have a chance to bring this man Assad to trial, but all that will be in the hands of people in London to sort out."

Adam said, "We've got to get him now. He killed my dad."

It was the first time since the funeral that Catrin had seen Adam cry.

Reimer had waited in the background. Afterwards, she asked for the assignment to drive Catrin to the station for her train back to London. Billings, Hicks and Kendrick were on their way back to headquarters. They had interviews to handle and faced the forthcoming mayhem defending their actions.

Reimer's parting words were, "I wish you were still here."

As Catrin shook hands, she responded as lightheartedly as she could. "If the Met kicks me out, I may come back. Be careful what you ask for!"

As the meeting room door opened and the visitors came in led by Nathan Atkins, Catrin sat resolved. To see the shaykh arrested, to be there when Adam was told, it was worth it. Whatever happens now, so be it, she thought.

Taking stock of the room and the table, they settled themselves in chairs on the opposite side from Catrin.

Atkins, she knew by sight. He simply began with, "This is Mr. Cunningham with SIS, and my assistant, Ms. Brigham. We are here now, Superintendent Sayer, due the complications arising from Shaykh Yusuf's arrest."

Atkins focused first on the offending party, the Devon and Cornwall Police. They had been foolhardy to follow enquiries 'beyond their remit'. In doing so, they had created difficulties for 'the government of the day and their allies'.

She found out that Nathan and his team had spent three days in Exeter 'getting some answers'. After the best part of a year working there, she knew how successful that would be, despite his claim. She had seen London bureaucrats with the Chief Constable of Devon and Cornwall. There were no remnants of tar or feathers on Atkin's suit, she thought.

He continued his introductory monologue. The main culprit was Jessop, he claimed. Then he focused on her.

"I want to know; indeed, the minister wants to know about your part in this problem."

He sounded aggrieved. "Given that you at least have had some international experience..."

He emphasised 'some', as if he considered the information to be suspect.

"... and members of the Asian desk consider you walk on water. Your actions were surprising. We thought you would understand the message I gave in Exeter. That you would cooperate with us. Reluctantly perhaps, but not lose sight of the bigger picture."

He was younger than her, yet he managed to sound like a disappointed and forgiving uncle. Catrin tried to look understanding behind her mask. She was not buying at all into his outline of her naivety and guilt. Perhaps at some point, he would ask the key question.

That came next, very abruptly and quietly from the man on Atkins right, Reid Cunningham.

"Did you orchestrate the arrest of Shaykh Abrahim?"

She responded with her own question. "Do you have the written permission of the Chief Constable to interview me about the Harding investigation?"

Atkins answered, annoyed, replying crisply, "First of all, we don't need it. Second, we have the agreement of the Met; that's why you are here. You are a Met police officer and in its headquarters. What more do you want?"

As Catrin responded, the door opened. Commander Karen Moore entered alone. She sat down several seats away from them at the end of the table, making it clear she was a spectator. Moore said nothing to anyone, ignored Catrin and gave Atkins a look that conveyed she was staying.

Catrin gave her answer. "I need the permission of my former employer to speak to you about their investigation. That is a continuing part of the employment contract I signed with them. I have had no instruction. Nor have I have been part of that investigation since I left Devon."

Atkins gave her a withering look. "It may escape you, but both the Met and the Devon and Cornwall Police are in England. The minister has jurisdiction."

He turned to Moore. "Commander. I didn't expect you to be here."

Moore gave him a smile, it seemed, behind her own mask. Catrin recalled her former boss, Gerry Lauder, saying years ago that if Moore smiles at you like that, duck. The eyes were enough to show she was hunting, not being pleasant. She was wearing yet another new pair of designer glasses, Catrin saw. They made her look owlish. An angry owl, at that.

"Just observing, Nathan. Thank you."

Catrin looked at her again. Moore gave her a barely perceptible nod. That was something, at least, better than being totally ignored.

They were at an *impasse* already, on the first real question. As the seconds of silence built, Atkins didn't get angry, it appeared. He said, "In three days of interviews, we met with Superintendent Hicks and senior members of his team. We talked also to the senior management team. The only person that wasn't referred to at all was you. That is, other than to confirm you were invited to be present at the arrest in Ronaldsway. Every line of enquiry pointed to others there, but not to you. Yet you supervised the Senior Investigating Officer who led the investigation. What do you say to that?"

"I haven't spoken to them since that trip."

Cunningham said firmly, "You did; once. On your personal mobile, to a DC Ray."

So, they had checked.

She nodded, "I stand corrected. DC Samesh Ray was the family liaison officer closest to Adam Harding and his guardians. I received a card from the family, forwarded from Exeter headquarters. I wanted to verify something before responding."

"And that was?"

"Personal. Basically, that the boy was doing well. It was not related to the investigation."

To distract the line of questioning, Catrin pulled out her phone, put it on speaker and made a call. "This is Catrin Sayer, Superintendent Sayer. Would it be possible to speak to Assistant Chief Constable Billings, please? It is important."

She gazed neutrally at Atkins, placing the phone on the

table. After a moment, Billings' assistant put him on.

"Sir, it's Catrin Sayer. I am in an interview with Mr. Atkins from the Minister's office and two of his colleagues. Am I allowed to answer any questions relating to the Harding investigation?"

"No, Sayer, you are not. We deal with all questions on that investigation. He knows that. The Chief Constable made that explicitly clear to him. Is that also clear for you?"

"Yes, sir; it is. Thank you. Good day."

She stabbed her finger at the phone, cutting off the call.

Cunningham said, "We don't need it, really. Your path through this is marked by its absences rather than your presence. By the holes rather than the evidence. You, we think, were the puppeteer of this entire deceptive operation.

"From early on you targeted Shaykh Abrahim. The interview transcripts show it. You bent every line of investigation to give the appearance of focusing only on Jaber and Assad. The Shaykh became wary at first, but that strategy made him complacent. The first time Devon and Cornwall Police could arrest him, it happened. And they gave you a grandstand seat."

"They invited me to be present at an arrest of a key suspect identified during an investigation. As you pointed out, I had supervisory responsibilities for the Serious Crimes team. I accepted the invitation, in my own time and at my own expense, not as a representative of the Met. It was a courtesy."

Cunningham responded harshly. "Not what the Shaykh thought, that is clear. You and he had one interaction, we gather, outside the aircraft. From that, he had you marked as the person behind all this. He's no fool."

Catrin gave him a dismissive look and refocused on Atkins, staring him out, saying nothing.

Atkins said tersely, "Continue, Reid."

The SIS officer became more energized. "The Foreign Office inherited the resolution of that arrest. London took on the embarrassing problem of a Yemeni citizen of standing being held here. And without our knowledge, at first."

Catrin responded, prodding him. "You arranged the exchange for Assad. That is your involvement, not mine."

That angered Atkins. "We had to, to save face, and to give some justification for your unauthorised action. Other than the ring on his finger when arrested, there was no direct proof of Abrahim's involvement. None."

He paused, blinking. Cunningham took up the reins.

"British police officers arranged a public character assassination of a foreign dignitary. And did it without any evidence that would be acceptable in a British court."

He stared at her, willing her to admit to it. Catrin kept her face neutral, saying nothing. That's the sort of thing SIS does all the time, she thought.

Atkins then added, "FCO went through hoops. It was a very complicated effort, totally unnecessary if you had followed the rules."

His anger appeared barely contained.

Cunningham came back at her. "So, now the person we wanted in place in Yemen has jumped in his jet again. He is in a fancy private hospital in Pakistan, out of the loop. His health was affected by the arrest, he claimed. His credibility has been damaged irretrievably. You met Dr. Zaid during your employment. What did you tell him?"

Bury the question in the guilt trip spiel, thought Catrin. Not with me.

"You heard DCC Billings, Mr. Cunningham. If I said

anything which implicated the Shaykh; or even if it was Dr. Zaid who gave me such information, I can't reveal it to you."

"And DS Owen Tydman, what did you tell him? We know he spoke to Dr. Zaid twice shortly before the arrest of Abrahim."

Tydman was retired now. He had chosen the option, rather than stay on. She doubted that this man would get anything from him.

Catrin sighed. "DS Tydman reported to DI Kendrick, who reported to DCI Hicks, who reported to me. The investigation went on for many weeks. I have no specific recall of discussions with him."

They pressed on, question after question designed to chip at the edges of the instruction she had received over the phone from Billings.

Cunningham was the real threat. She knew that. He had the training, whereas Atkins just had the sense of power and entitlement. She had no idea what the woman was there for; she wasn't taking notes, just looking fixedly at Catrin, with no indication she was going to intervene with any questions.

Twenty minutes later, Reid Cunningham broke through her defense. It was a question that Catrin should have dismissed easily and was entirely her fault, she realised. She wanted an answer to her own question, instead of simply holding her ground. It was after a comment about London's success in getting the exchange of Assad for Shaykh Yusuf. London, not Exeter, provided the unheralded 'win', as Atkins put it.

Catrin asked, "Why did Assad return to Paris from Yemen so quickly?" She had suddenly realised a possible reason.

Atkins face made it clear that she was there to answer questions, not put them.

But Cunningham said, lightly, "Well, we hear that, thanks to the Shaykh, he will be the best paid inmate in whichever prison he ends up in here. And..."

He left it open, his expression teasing her to guess. She did, and stupidly vocalised it.

"You offered in principle an inmate exchange down the road, didn't you? Assad for one of ours. A few years in prison here to salve the wound of the people in Devon, then he will be back in Yemen."

She couldn't stop the anger rising in her voice. Cunningham pursed his lips, looking as if he didn't care. "Then he will be the best paid prisoner in a jail in Yemen, probably. For a while."

He was dismissive. "We can't get too emotional about this sort of thing, can we?"

He made it seem an afterthought. "Did you allow your feelings for the victims and the survivor to influence your own objectivity, perhaps?"

She looked at him, staring, silent for a moment.

"Objectivity?" Catrin's voice was now clearly showing her own anger. Moore came out of her silence and coughed heavily.

"Sorry," the commander said, "Nothing contagious." She was glaring at Sayer.

Catrin calmed down slightly, but not enough. "I allowed my feelings for the victims and the survivor to motivate me. I motivated the investigative team to bring the perpetrators into custody. I am proud of the work they did and my own role with the Devon and Cornwall Police. Proud of every action from the outset of the investigation to the day I left. Are there more questions?"

For some reason, Atkins seemed satisfied. "No. Thank

you. That will do."

He sat back, smiling.

Cunningham gave her a rueful smile, from one chess player to another. Her black king had toppled.

So be it, Catrin thought again, her face impassive as she kicked herself mentally.

As Catrin stood, Moore waved her back into the seat as she spoke to the third person, the woman who had said nothing.

"You are?"

"Cicely Brigham. I work with Mr. Atkins."

"Well, Ms. Brigham, pass me the recorder, please."

The woman bridled, then looked away.

Karen Moore said gently, "I will bring in two female police officers if I need to. And I have a technical officer outside, waiting there from the moment I entered. We know one of you has a live recorder. It is in here and is not ours. And I'm starting with you."

It was the tone of voice; Moore wasn't bluffing. Atkins gave Brigham a nod as Moore stood. She opened the door, admitting a young civilian technician, a woman.

As Brigham brought the recorder out of her purse, the tech took it in her gloved hand and placed it in a small case. Moore waved her out of the room and closed the door, then said, "That was a big misstep, Nathan."

She looked at the FCO staffer, now angry, then at Cunningham, who seemed amused. "Reid, we will give you your property back once our people have taken it apart and put the bits back together. The other option, Nathan – are you listening to me, Nathan?"

Atkins stopped staring into the distance and looked at Moore. His prize soundbyte of Sayer's last comment had turned into hearsay.

Moore continued, "The other option is that we keep it in that case. I will open it with the Commissioner and the Minister in the room. You can play any snippet you choose, including Superintendent Sayer's last remark. I will remind them that we had an agreement that this interview was informal, off the record."

"Now, please leave. You have been to see the wild ponies on Exmoor. We extended the courtesy for you to interview Superintendent Sayer here. Complete your formal report. Put in it one thing about Sayer not based on evidence and a lot of people here will be taking issue with it. Including me."

She opened the door again for the visitors to file out. No-one said goodbye.

Catrin stood, looking at Moore.

"What now?"

"Now you go back to your safe house. Well, no, those are for criminals in witness protection. Back to Wood Green. It serves the same purpose. I'm surprised at you. You knew Cunningham would be first rate. You were doing fine until you got nosey about Assad."

Sayer said nothing in direct response, her dejection evident. She just looked at Moore for a moment then sighed. "I'm sorry I let you down, Karen. I didn't mean to. It was best that you stayed clear. You have your own fights to handle."

"Meaning?"

"John Reed, for one. Remember? It's so well known now that people are running a book on it, even out at Wood Green."

There were changes happening in the Met, too. It was widely rumoured that Moore and Reed were candidates in line for the same key position.

Moore looked amused. "And did you bet?"

"No. Officially, gambling is not allowed, you know that. I studiously avoided hearing the rumour mill."

"Not putting money on me. Not exactly a show of confidence."

Moore scrunched up her face, changing the subject back. "This'll go nowhere. Atkins will tell the Minister exactly what he told you, that you are guilty as sin. He'll also say there is no evidence. The minister will be happy with that and move on. Puppeteer. Good description of your actions if you ask me. Don't fret it."

She sighed, 'You'll join the rest of us. Up until now, you have had only friends in the Foreign Office. Now you have both. What's on your agenda today, then?"

She was still sticking it to Catrin.

"A meeting this afternoon with a local community group on the increase in home invasions. Reassignment approvals for Covid absences. A long way from Operation Undertow."

Moore nodded her agreement to that, showing no signs of sympathy. She replied, her voice upbeat. "Look on the bright side. Wood Green is only half an hour from Spitalfields. That's not bad. The Borough of Haringey is outside the world of FCO. When I agreed to the meeting, I told Nathan that you were in exile there. The rarity of your visits to headquarters would make you feel like a tourist.

"He took that to be punishment after the crime but before the trial. Do some of the windows on the north side of Wood Green station still leak in heavy rains?"

"No, they completed the renovations some time ago. Part of the upgrade."

"Pity, that. It would have been an exciting project for you to manage. The card from Adam Harding you mentioned, the one they foolishly didn't follow up on. What did it say?"

Catrin looked at Karen and raised her eyes momentarily in a 'I don't need this' gesture. Nothing gets past Moore, as usual.

"It was a drawing by him. I had given him a set of art pens after seeing his doodles. Inside, it said, 'Thank you for everything'."

Moore waited. Catrin said nothing, so Karen asked. "The drawing. What was it?"

"Spiderman; wearing a police cap. He wants to join up."

"Not Spiderwoman speaking Welsh? With dark blonde hair, perhaps?"

Catrin didn't smile, just replied deadpan. "No. Spiderman. Adam is eleven now. There are different body lines to consider. He is still copying, rather than drawing original art."

"Well, you had better fire your sticky web stuff and flit back to North London."

Carin didn't ask, but it was on her face, Moore saw. She relented a little. "Things are starting to happen. We bide our time. You have friends in high places."

With that, Moore was out the door. Catrin sat down again, taking a moment to collect herself for the more pedestrian journey back to her office. One by road, rather than flying between buildings.

Moore's final comment intrigued her. Then she remembered a similar vague comment from the Commissioner, via Colleen.

By the evening, as she arrived home, she was despondent again, regretting the outburst at Cunningham, recalling his face, the quick flash of success in getting her to respond so openly. As she talked with Mair and then Chris he said, "There is a parcel for you, from Paris, from Isabelle, I take it."

It was a book. Not from her former art team member, but from Morely Kerswell, a new work on the life and art of Charles Catteau, a French ceramic artist. His accompanying note told her he was feeling better, able to get out and about. She knew he had been making steady progress.

Two paragraphs in the note held her attention.

Thank you for all the support you have given Isabelle in the last months. It has helped her immeasurably and, in doing so, helped me. From my first encounter with you, after the embarrassing incident of Isabelle and me falling down those stairs in London, you have shown us kindness and consideration.

You know my history, of my breakdown after years of dealing with contract killings and their perpetrators. When I recovered, and moved to David Klintz's team in art investigation, I found David to be a wonderful and sensitive manager, fair, clear, and supportive of his staff. You are from the same mould. I thank you for your friendship.

She smiled. David Klintz, the head of the FBI art investigation team was a friend, and one of her own icons. Praise indeed. As she passed the note and book across for Chris to see, the image of Reid Cunningham's brief victory smile came back into mind. This time, it didn't bother her. She had better things to smile about.

41 ST. PAUL'S

The good news the same week came for Chris, with a sweet irony, given 'Catrin's exile'; his assessment by his doctor and the interview with his human resources contact had approved his return to work, in his old position.

"I went down and talked to the team. Jasmin, the comic, changed my logon password to 'password' to make life easy, she said. They seemed happy. I think the guy who came in temporarily for me was OK."

He had a look in his eyes that made Catrin smile. "You are back," she said, softly. "That's great."

"Mostly, yes. I feel it."

He grimaced. "Now we need to get you straightened out, somehow."

She shrugged. "Self-inflicted wound. Moore is OK with me now, I concluded, although she won't admit it. That's worth something."

~~

Sandra Hunt, a retired assistant commissioner at the Met, called Catrin to suggest afternoon tea in the Crypt Cafe at St. Paul's Cathedral. The venue was close to both women's homes.

Catrin had worked for two years as Hunt's security aide during the senior officer's later years at the Met. Hunt had been the person who, earlier still, set Catrin on a 'fast track' career status.

It was a small inflection in the words 'to see how you are doing'. Catrin realised that her former boss knew of her current situation. That was no surprise, really. Sandra was well-connected to key players at the Met.

St. Paul's Cathedral, in various ways, was Hunt's second home. Unmarried, from her childhood onwards, her involvement in the cathedral provided a spiritual base and much of her social network.

And a sanctuary during troubling times. On her first meeting with the injured Constable Catrin Sayer, she had detoured there with her.

During the early days of Covid, Catrin had checked up on Sandra on a regular basis. While in Devon, that was less frequent, but tea at the Crypt seemed a good chance to catch up.

Catrin arrived early, in time for Choral Evensong. She sat with other congregants, the calm washing over her again. It surprised her that she hadn't thought of coming here earlier, once the stress of exile to Wood Green hit. Over the years, she too had found St. Paul's to be her sanctuary.

Afterwards, they met up. Sandra was using a walking stick, the aftermath of a fall and a cracked hip that happened months earlier.

After greeting each other, it was Catrin's first

comment. "You didn't say."

"You were in Devon; and busy."

Hunt's first questions were about Mair and Chris. After that, she got down to business. "Now, tell me all about it."

Catrin now saw Karen Moore as her mentor, albeit a disgruntled one. That process of guidance and trust had started with Hunt. She had no qualms about sharing her problems with her.

As the story of her case in Devon unfolded, Hunt listened attentively. Catrin saw a familiar expression on her face; Hunt was comparing versions, it seemed. When finished, Hunt moved her on to talk about the experience of the Task Force reorganisation, and her feelings after its completion, the desire to leave Devon as soon as she could. Teacups empty, she then asked Catrin to walk with her a bit.

"With this hip I shouldn't sit still too long. Nor walk for too long."

On a roundabout route to Hunt's home, they talked of other things. In Cannon Street, Catrin sympathised over the loss of one of Hunt's close friends. Her former boss stopped and faced her.

"Why do you think Aiden Jessop has been so tenacious, creating the conflict with FCO?"

It evolved, thought Catrin, but looking at Hunt's face, she saw the older woman knew the answer already.

Catrin asked, "You know Jessop? I shouldn't even ask, should I? Of course, you do. That's why my description of events didn't surprise you too much. To answer your own, though, he supported Hicks and myself to the hilt and wanted justice."

Hunt smiled. "Yes, I know Aiden quite well."

She paused, assessing Catrin, it seemed. Walking on

slowly, she looked forward as she spoke.

"Jessop and Billings went to see the Lord Lieutenant on the evening of the discovery of the murders. You didn't mention that because it was a small point, and you were giving the main events. I understand that. Was the Lord Lieutenant ever mentioned again, in an operational context, do you recall?"

Catrin thought back. "No. Not to me. Not by Billings or the CC."

"We are a constitutional monarchy, Catrin, You understand that at one level, of course. Aiden wanted justice for the Hardings, naturally. The crass stupidity of the crime and the arrogance of Shaykh Abrahim appalled him. Besides that, though, he is like I was, like I still am if I tell the truth, a servant of the Crown. We are people who do not tolerate at all the wanton killing of its appointed representatives and their kin. No matter where they are in the pecking order."

It suddenly hit Catrin. Not only Jessop, but others. Turner-Jones, for example: how she had briefed Laurie Parker for the lunch before Christmas, rather than simply cancel. Servants of the Crown.

Catrin replied, "I'm not into that, really. I gave my police oath to the Queen as the head of state, not the aristocracy bit. A Valley girl, me. You know that."

Hunt chuckled quietly. "I know. But I also know that your current feeling of failure in a professional sense, a career sense, is baseless. So, stop fretting about it – and don't deny you are, it's obvious. Karen said, 'we bide our time' you told me?"

Catrin suddenly recalled the meeting with Atkins. "She said I had friends in high places. I thought she meant her and Tom Slieman."

"Much higher again, I assure you. And here we are.

Time for me to go in and rest this hip and leg. Time for you to go and see your husband and daughter. And don't forget about St. Paul's. It is not simply a magnificent building. You know that. And let's meet more often if you have time for an old woman."

Impulsively, Catrin took Hunt's hand in both of hers, feeling the arthritic knuckles. Hunt was growing old faster than she had realised. That Catrin's parents were doing so was a reality she had absorbed. It spurred the family visits to South Wales, to let them to enjoy their granddaughter, and to let Mair know her Welsh grandparents. But for her former boss, the 'Iron Lady of New Scotland Yard' to be aging so fast, hit her.

"We will do that. I'll plan on it, look forward to it."

As she walked away, it struck her that one iron lady of a deputy commissioner had been replaced, in a sense, by the high carbon steel of another; a commissioner appointed as a Dame Commander of the British Empire.

~~

A few days later, at home in Spitalfields, Chris was clearing up after feeding Mair. Catrin had got back home earlier than he expected.

When the doorbell sounded, Mair bounded forward. Chris heard Catrin talking to someone as Mair yelled 'Moggsly'. Which surprised him. It was Paul Ngumo's nickname ever since Paul turned up at a five-a-side game one night. He had opened his kit bag, releasing the smell of cat pee. The family had recently acquired a new kitten.

Long before loss of smell was tied to Covid, Paul was protesting he hadn't noticed it. Andy Wright had entered the changing room saying, 'where did that moggsly smell come from?'.

The nickname had stuck. But how did Mair know it was Paul at the door, he wondered?

As his teammate walked through, a bright red polka dot mask over his face, he said, "Come on kiddo, it's practice night. Get your togs."

Chris laughed, "I'm not ready for that, Paul." To see Catrin appear with his kitbag packed.

She said, "You'd best get a move on. Otherwise, Paul and Tim will get done for illegal parking outside."

Paul nodded. "Tim and I aren't budging without you. The team's expecting you to turn up."

Chris suddenly smiled, putting out his two hands, palm down, flat. "I can do this."

Paul imitated him, in some long-established team ritual. "You can do this. The force is with you."

Mair giggled then said, excitedly, holding her shoes. "We are coming, with Lili and my aunties. We are the crowd."

They practised outside, in a section of a regular pitch, rather than in an indoor arena. The league wasn't playing, but the guys wanted to practice and keep the contact, the camaraderie.

Catrin watched the careful effort to involve Chris without overstretching him. She saw the smile and joy as he found that his feet had not forgotten what to do with a football.

After a while, Chris sped up, hips tilting in sudden swerve as he passed another player, a move she had seen hundreds of times.

Mair came running up. She and Lili had been playing at the edge with a spare ball. Mair ran in between Jean and Melanie, taking hold of one hand on each side. "They love him, don't they?"

Her eyes were on her father. A couple of the team also watching smiled at her.

"Yes," said Melanie, "But they are men. Like boys, they don't say that a lot to each other."

Mair repudiated the insult. "They do! Daddy says that with me all the time. And Robbie tells me that, too."

Catrin asked, "Robbie in your class, you mean?"

"Yes. I think he wants to marry me. And he likes cucumber."

Showing incredible talent as a detective, Jean looked at Mair as Catrin raised an eyebrow.

"Does that mean you are not eating cucumber, still? You are giving it to Robbie because I told Lili she couldn't eat it for you? That you had to eat your own."

Mair looked at her mother with that look; 'guilty as charged'. Not wanting to spoil the moment, the hanging judge gave her a smile, a reprieve from sentencing.

After a moment, Mair piped up again, looking at her dad. "I miss Grandma and Auntie Jen and Uncle Mason and Miss Traynor and my friends in Exeter, but I am glad we came home."

Jean bent down, picking her up, saying, 'So are we."

Yes, thought Catrin, that puts it well. Despite her exile to Haringey, it was good to be home.

42 COMMISSIONER

The Red Witch called the The Grim Reaper late on a Thursday afternoon at the end of September. Catrin took the call, wondering if it was a new problem. The rain was tipping down. It hit the large windows of her office in Wood Green noisily, but there were no signs of leaks.

For three months over the summer, Catrin had commuted from Spitalfields to Wood Green. As temporary assistant to the area commander, she dealt with a wide range of issues. Everything from local crimes to community relations and complaints against police officers had crossed her desk.

Barrington said, "It's not about the Henderson file again. I need to see you here tomorrow, at 4.10 p.m."

Catrin sighed, "I'll get stuck in the commute to Spitalfields, or getting back to Wood Green if something else comes up. How about two-thirty, does that work?"

"Four-ten precisely, please. At four fifteen, we go in to see the Commssioner."

~~

"Miss Barrington and Superintendent Sayer, ma'am."

Commissioner Worthington's assistant announced their arrival. Worthington, in uniform today, moved from her desk towards the meeting table. Catrin murmured 'good afternoon' as she took in the senior commanding officer of the Met. She could see how the woman had changed in the two and a half years since their last meeting.

Worthington was doing the same to her, it seemed.

"Sayer, have a seat for a moment. I wanted a few words with you and Colleen first. We made an undertaking to you, and you to us, when we last met. You have done your part, albeit with a few political wrinkles thrown in. It is time for me to do mine. How do you feel about the overall experience of the development track we started you on?"

Catrin had been caught out last time by this sort of broad-ranging question. She wasn't going to be so this time.

"I had a lot of different challenges, Ma'am. Both during the criminology course in Cambridge and later in Devon, during their reorganisation. I did what I thought was right, including decisions with hard, 'no-win' outcomes. When I took on the additional responsibility for the Harding case, DCC Billings told me it would widen my range of experiences. I have done that, I believe."

Worthington nodded. "If I say that at this level, there is more pain and grief than easy satisfaction, can you relate to that?"

"Yes, Ma'am. I'm proud of my work with the Devon and Cornwall team. Yet most officers there were glad to see me go once the Task Force completed its work. It meant the uncertainty was over for them."

She was now wondering what the Commissioner meant by her opening comment; 'a few words first'.

Worthington responded, with certainty. "But not the chief constable, I assure you."

She took a pause, looking at the window, reflecting on Sayer's comments. She said, to thin air, "Sometimes that's the outcome, yes."

Then she looked at Catrin. "As of today, Commander Moore reports to Assistant Commissioner Daley. She leads the reorganized group we are calling Frontline Operations. She also takes over areas formerly managed by Commander Reed, who will be leaving us, as he has accepted the post of deputy chief constable in Hampshire.

"I am moving you to the position of detective superintendent, based here, reporting directly to Moore. You will implement a new strategic approach for major organized gang crime within Frontline Operations, one focused exclusively on criminal networks with overseas connections, not the domestic gangs. The latter stay with each borough command team.

"It's a big job. A year from now, with more specific experience in that area, we'll look at promotion prospects. How does that sound?"

Cartin looked at her. "Yes. I can do that. I would like to do that. Thank you."

She stopped. Barrington had a small smile on her face.

Worthington added, "There will be overseas links, Interpol, other police organisations, naturally. One thing I want you to remember from this meeting is this; I don't want you or Karen playing fast and loose with the Foreign and Commonwealth Office. But you are not to be pushed around for political expediency, either. In giving you this job, I am sending that signal to them. You are there to work with Commander Moore and FCO as constructively as possible. Stay clear of the paths you have been travelling recently. Is that absolutely clear?"

"Yes, Ma'am."

Worthington smiled. "It was not quite the original plan we set out, was it? Months away, not longer, and back here at superintendent level. With Covid, it was the best we could do, given the circumstances. Have I met sufficiently my part of the understanding we agreed previously, do you think?"

"Yes. All three of us have, I believe. Colleen has been there for me throughout, as you said she would. I want to tell you that, also."

There was a knock on the door. The assistant popped her head in. "Commander Moore is there now."

Worthington nodded to her and stood, obviously needing to get on. "Go down and see her now. She is in her office. Colleen, you stay, please."

She stepped back, not offering her hand on parting, as last time. Covid protocols had changed their customs.

As Catrin said, "Thank you again," the Commissioner responded, "My best wishes to you. And you are right, some decisions are 'no-win' situations. But you made yours and saw them through. Make my decision about you in this role a win-win, please? I expect that of you."

Then Catrin was out the door, through the outer office and into the executive corridor, standing for a moment, contemplating her future.

43 ARRIVAL

Catrin Sayer's final official duty in Haringey was to speak at the opening of a fundraiser. It was a choral concert in aid of the North Middlesex University Hospital, a performance by the Metropolitan Police Choir. All she had to do was open the event and bring on the choir director.

It was her last evening based there. Tomorrow she would spend the first part of the morning at Wood Green closing out with the area commander. After that, she would head over to New Scotland Yard for lunch with Karen Moore, then meet her new team.

Catrin had invited Sandra Hunt to attend the concert. Chris and Mair were going also. Mair was excited to stay up late and see her mum stand at the front and talk to everyone. It was a social duty, a pleasant ending to Catrin's role in exile.

They drove together to the concert venue, the old parish church of St. Michael in Wood Green. On the way, Catrin listened to her daughter having a grown-up conversation with the former assistant commissioner. It started with, 'How did you meet my mummy?'.

That progressed to Mair showing her surprise that Hunt had been a police officer. For some reasoning in a child's mind, she had assumed that Sandra Hunt worked at St. Paul's Cathedral. It was the venue where she had most often encountered Hunt, from her days in a stroller onward.

Catrin was driving, concentrating on the evening traffic. Chris's face showed his amusement. He intervened once, after Hunt made the comment that she had worked at New Scotland Yard for a long time. Hunt was explaining that was where her mummy was going to work again now.

"Were you important, then?"

"Not so much. I was a good organizer. The police officers like your mother and the ones you see on the streets do the important work."

Chris said, smiling. "Miss Hunt was very important; she was in charge of everyone, just about."

"Like Mrs. Kariuki?" The headmistress at her school.

"Like that, yes."

Mair gave Hunt a subdued look, wondering if this woman would be as firm as Mrs. Kariuki was at times. The twinkle in the eyes of the older woman made her smile.

"Welcome to this concert by my colleagues in the Metropolitan Police Choir. The performance this evening is in support of the new haematology unit at the North Middlesex University Hospital, so it is good to see such a strong turnout, both for the choir and the cause.

"My name is Superintendent Catrin Sayer, and this is a special evening for me, too. This is my last day working at

Wood Green Police Station before assuming new duties elsewhere in the Met. It is a particular pleasure to be here tonight.

"The choir can trace its roots back to 1872. In its various forms, it has performed concerts in aid of charities regularly since then. Members are serving or retired officers and police staff. They all dedicate personal time to the joy of singing, and I am sure we are in for a wonderful evening of music. With no more ado, please welcome Constable Sefton Dean, the choral director."

As she walked off the stage applauding the entry of the music director, Catrin thought it was a fitting finish to her time in the Borough of Haringey.

After the concert, there was a melee of choir members, audience and church staff talking. The choir director approached Catrin and her family as they waited for Sandra Hunt, now lost in conversation with a retired police sergeant, a choir member.

"Ma'am, can I introduce our soprano soloist from the Schubert piece. She is from Wales also, PC Megan Taylor."

Catrin smiled at both officers, taking in the uniformed constable with a soprano voice. "You sang beautifully, Megan. Where are you from?"

"Swansea area, ma'am, nearer to Neath. I joined the Met a year ago, based in Dagenham. I did music at USW, specialising in voice, so the choir appealed to me."

The University of South Wales.

The director said, "We snapped her up. Megan heard you speak during the opener and wanted to meet you."

With that he excused himself; there were others waiting to talk to him.

Catrin kept the smile as she took in the woman,

waiting.

"I heard the accent, ma'am. Sergeant Williams at my station said you are from Ponty and started in Brixton –."

Catrin interjected, "Lambeth, actually, as a trainee, then Brixton, yes."

"I just wondered how you got to be promoted up so high, to superintendent? It's early days for me and I am settled in London now, but – I wondered how career progression really happens. I hope I am not being too forward?"

Catrin hadn't seen Hunt move from her conversation to join them until she looked to her left. Mair was beside her, looking up, waiting for her mother to answer.

Catrin gave a small chuckle and responded. "In Brixton, I was part of the uniform support team for the drug squad. I was interested in art crime – I studied art at Aber – and applied for a DC vacancy I never thought I would get. It started then. So, look for opportunities that appeal, do the courses, have the drive to try, even if it doesn't work out the first time. And look out for and listen to mentors, people prepared to help you. The experience of others will help a great deal."

Looking at the young woman in uniform hanging on her every word, she thought of herself at that age. Catrin was reminded of her own career journey with the Metropolitan Police, through joy and pain, success and failure. And it continued; tomorrow afternoon, she would walk into New Scotland Yard to meet her new team leads. They would brief her on the challenges ahead.

Her mind went back to her time in Brixton, as a constable, and to the sudden call from DCI Jane Worsely, then head of the Art Crime Unit. She recalled the drive along Dog Kennel Hill into Central London with her shift partner, Gary Day. He had told her to keep calm as she complained about having insufficient time to prepare. There was a mark on her uniform that wouldn't sponge off, and a button loose. She had just come from telling a woman that the grandson living with her had died of a drug overdose. Catrin was totally unprepared for any interview.

It seemed so long ago.

She glanced at Hunt, then back at Megan from Neath. "Megan, this is Assistant Commissioner Sandra Hunt, now retired. Why not ask her, too?"

The young soprano looked startled. She assumed the older woman to be Catrin's mother or aunt. Now she took in the amused expression on the lined face, the eyes piercing her. Megan momentarily lost her voice, trying to decide what to say to an assistant commissioner, retired or not.

Hunt saved her the trouble. "Another time, perhaps? I attend most of the choir's concerts if I can. I would be happy to talk then, if you wish?"

Megan thanked her, then Sayer, and beat a diplomatic retreat.

Chris and Catrin made their way out of St. Michael's Church with Mair ahead of them. For some reason, Mair had positioned herself so she could hold the free hand of Sandra Hunt. Hunt used the other for her walking stick and, once, quickly looked back at the couple behind her. She murmured, "A sense of deja vu, Catrin, when you were talking to Taylor?"

She doesn't miss a thing, thought Catrin.

Back in Spitalfields, she dropped Chris and Mair at the door to their building, then drove the short distance to Hunt's home. Despite the older woman's protest that she could walk, Catrin was not having that. Mair needed to get to bed and Catrin had a question she wanted to raise in private with Hunt.

Alone together, she came right out with it as they set off.

"I have this strange feeling after meeting Taylor earlier. It is as if I have arrived. Where, why, I can't say exactly, but obviously it is about my own career. I don't know why that should happen now, of all times. I have a job change, not a promotion."

She glanced sideways, seeing Hunt smile; more to herself than to Catrin. "Any thoughts?"

Hunt took a moment to decide what to say.

"We each have an intrinsic understanding of our own capabilities, I think, an inner guide. I suspect you have realised that you have fulfilled your own hopes and expectations. Taylor suddenly provided the reference point to allow you to make the comparison."

Catrin responded. "I see that, yes. Taylor made me think about my own career journey. And of the experience in Exeter supervising the Harding case. Intellectually, I know that I am now working at a different level. Exeter and Wood Green showed me that. But emotionally, it has finally hit home. Everything changes now. Did that happen to you, the experience of a sort of watershed moment?"

Hunt thought for a second. "I take it you mean the transition in the type of leadership role you now face. Yes, it did. I think it does for most people at your stage of development.

"You will no longer manage a single team, or do the case work yourself. You won't be interviewing suspects and, in your case, getting into personal danger. I remember our first meeting after your run-in with... what was his name again?"

Catrin replied, "Cheney. Colin Cheney. Dominic

Connolly's enforcer."

"Cheney. Yes."

Hunt was thinking back to the sight of her then, Catrin thought, her face badly bruised and freshly scarred. Catrin had been at the Cwmbran Kiln, suddenly confronted by an assistant commissioner. She recalled looking like a wounded deer caught in the headlights. A bit like Taylor when she realised Hunt's former role.

After a moment, Sandra spoke carefully. "No, there will be no more of that sort of thing for you. No frontline work, despite the name of the new organisation structure. Senior leadership is different."

She looked at Catrin, assessing her understanding of the comment.

"What I mean by that is I never dreamed of ending up an assistant commissioner. A senior operational officer, yes. I thought I could handle that. Advancement after that came through experience and new challenges. It evolves.

"For now, you have responsibilities for many people and several teams and... it will weigh on you. You will see people like Taylor develop. Your job is to provide them direction, appropriate training, and opportunities. You will assess their successes and failures. Some officers will develop and do well. Others won't. And the worst part of your new job will be to attend their funerals when things go totally wrong. You have already done that, I know."

Catrin was turning into Cheapside, where Hunt lived now, in an upscale apartment block. Her living room had a view of the church of St. Mary-le-Bow. They were yards from St. Paul's Cathedral.

Catrin responded quietly with, "The Malaysian officer, Sofia, killed in Nine Elms, yes."

Hunt looked at her and gave Catrin a sympathetic

smile. "The Met has thousand of police officers, but far fewer senior leaders. You can do that role; it is why I fast-tracked you and why Karen pushes you hard. It is why Commissioner Worthington has invested in you. Tomorrow will be the start of a new phase of your career. That will be as challenging as anything you have encountered, but different. And you will do well."

Catrin pulled into the drop-off zone, with its forbidding signs about absolutely no parking, and gave a nod of affirmation. "Karen will make sure I do my bit. But thank you for everything, Sandra, over the years. I am very grateful to you."

"Well, thank you." Sandra Hunt changed the subject. "Did you notice that Taylor was wearing earrings?"

Catrin grinned. "You noticed? They were what made me think of the Harding case, of another woman. The little pink sapphires."

Hunt eased herself out of the car and stood, looking across at Catrin, ready to close the door. The quarter hour chime from the clock at St. Paul's almost drowned out the first words of her closing comment.

"Given your time in Exeter, I can quite understand why. See, I could go back to being a detective, other than I wouldn't meet the fitness requirements. Goodnight Catrin. Thank you for taking me to the concert and letting me spend time with Mair."

With that, the car door closed quietly. Catrin Sayer sat there, watching Sandra Hunt walk stiffly to her building entrance and enter.

As she drove home, she hoped Mair went straight to sleep, it being so late for her. Her daughter had been wilting in the car, not quite dropping off as they worked to keep her awake until she got home.

In Commercial Road, she saw a lorry backing slowly

into a gateway, preparing to make a delivery. 'Porth Welshcakes' was written in large, stylish cursive on the side. She had seen it or similar vehicles near there before, so it was probably a regular drop. But the exchange with Sandra and the emotions arising from the discussion with the young Welsh constable were in her mind.

Porth, in the Rhondda, less than a ten-minute drive from her childhood home in Pontypridd. It was a long way from its base and made her think of her own journey. Her excitement and fears of leaving home for university. The decision to move to London, as a police cadet. And from a constable to her new role starting tomorrow, it had been quite a ride. Taking on gangs who operated globally to exploit and harm the people of London. Not directly, admittedly; she was the leader, the puppeteer, as the SIS officer called her. That was her role now.

She silently wished the lorry driver a safe journey back to Wales, as she was near her own home now.

Her husband well. Her daughter happy. To spend time with her friends on her art at the Kiln. As much as s her police work had changed, these were her anchor points.

Catrin Sayer yawned, suddenly feeling sleepy herself. She was looking forward to her bed and, after a night's sleep, a new day.

EPILOGUE

Father Budi Senen walked slowly up the path to the home of Maria Darmawan. He was a member of the clergy at the Cathedral of St. Peter, Bandung, in the Roman Catholic Province of Jakarta. The priest was pleased to see, as Maria opened the door, that the two other women were already here. He knew them as three friends, active in the parochial work of the cathedral.

It had been Anne who had requested the meeting about a personal matter, she said. She needed important guidance and asked that the meeting take place with her friends present, away from the cathedral. Her apartment was very small, so Maria had offered her home.

Anne was a single woman, from the Middle East. She had made her way to Indonesia years ago, well before Senen's appointment to the diocese. He knew that she had trained and qualified here as a nursing assistant, a personal care worker. Now she specialised with children in need of medical support. Other than her church role with her two friends, the 'A team' of the Sunday children's group, he knew little else about her.

Once the tea had been served, it was Inda, the youngest of the three women, who said, "Anne, now it's time. Tell Father Budi."

He had seen the tension in Anne during the preliminary small talk. Now the thin, middle-aged Yemeni started with, "Father, I am known here as Anne Himani, but my full name is Hanan Al Imani. I am not a single woman, but both a divorcee and an apostate of Islam. Years ago, my husband in Riyadh issued the *talaq* for my failure to provide children. In my anger and grief, I left him and my country behind rather than bear the shame of returning to my parent's home."

She paused.

Senen waited a second, then said, "You became a refugee. And you found us."

Hanan shook her head. "Not quite. I spent two months in Germany, then came here. At first, I said I was a Roman Catholic to avoid anyone who was Muslim prying into my past. Other than my sister, I have had no direct contact with my family since I left. All they know is that I am safe and well."

This time he waited her out.

"The charade, through the love of others, soon became a reality. I still needed God, I found out. The people of this cathedral supported me. That is truly when I found you all and Jesus as my saviour. However, I did something terrible at the time I left Riyadh. It has led to awful consequences.

"Nearly a year ago, a man and a child were murdered in England. I want to tell you that story and my part in it and ask for your guidance on what I should do next."

Senen looked a little wary. "You have not dealt with this at confession, I take it? You have carried it this long?"

"Other than Maria and Inda, you are the first person I have told I am an apostate. Until I told my friends last week, I have not mentioned my actions in Riyadh to anyone here."

She paused, taking a deep breath. "In Indonesia, I am entitled by law to freedom of religion, but I must not break the blasphemy laws. I would rather no-one else knows I was formerly a Muslim. One word taken wrong and – it could cause problems."

Father Senen nodded. "Go on. Explain to me your concerns."

He listened without interruption to her tale about the meeting with William Harding in the Souq Al Thumairi. Then she spoke about the events in England. As she talked about the murders and the subsequent discussions with her sister in Berlin, she had to stop for a moment to regain her composure.

"People in my family and others in the Yemeni community gossip about it among themselves. The role of the shaykh is discussed – as is my own, in starting the entire sorry mess. Some blame me, others blame only the shaykh. If I had not acted so angrily and with hatred... if only I had left the ring behind when I left... none of this would have happened."

She paused, focused only on the priest now. "It haunts my days and my nights now. Father, what should I do?"

As she stopped, the room became silent. Senen bent his head for a period in silent prayer, then sat up straight.

"If we set aside your feeling of guilt for a moment, Anne; let us pretend at least that is possible, just for one moment. Also, let us pretend you had never heard of the death of these two people and the arrest of Shaykh Yusuf Abrahim. How would you describe your life?"

Anne thought for a moment. She had not expected that

question.

"Contented; that might be the best word. I have good friends, a worthwhile job I like, and I have a faith I found that carries me. I feel the loss of family, not all the time, but often. That weighs heavily. If my family discovered I had converted, it would only bring more hurt, anger and shame, so there is no hope of reconciliation."

She shrugged. "Not happy, not sad; contented, as I said."

He pressed her. "You live alone. You have no partner in your life, or wish for one?"

She shook her head, her body stiffening. "No. Not that, no. Not allow any other man to have control of my life."

The priest nodded but dropped the point he was about to make. Anne must work with male colleagues professionally and socially, but he could see the pain of her marriage was a continuing barrier for her to any new relationship.

"That you found us, found your path to an on-going relationship with God is a blessing. Will you trust me, a man, to talk to someone about you? Anonymously, I promise. You will be safe."

Hanan smiled. "I trust you – as a priest, Father Budi."

Senen smiled. "That is a start. Now, let us talk about this guilt you feel while you are among friends; its weight and its loneliness."

Later, he would talk to her alone, he hoped, about the need for confession.

It was four days later when Father Senen called Anne, asking her to meet him next week at the cathedral, but without her friends this time. There would be a woman there, one from the British Embassy in Jakarta.

The following Thursday morning, behind the closed door of his office, Senen introduced Anne to the official. The woman was similar in age to her, well dressed in business clothes bought in Indonesia, it appeared.

Anne's first thought was that this woman knows my story. From her eyes, her expression, she has held meetings like this one before.

"I am Judith, Judith Smith, with the British Embassy staff. Anne, I would be interested to hear the facts directly. Father Senen has told me only that you believe that a ring belonged to you; the ring mentioned in the media coverage of the deaths of William and Ashley Harding and that, in selling it, you feel partly responsible for their deaths."

Anne confirmed it, then asked, "Do I need to make a deposition, or whatever it is called?"

Smith smiled briefly, "We will see, but probably not. Just tell me."

As Anne did so, she was aware that the woman made no notes and had not taken out a notebook and pen. A minute into her story, she stopped mid-sentence and asked, "Are you recording this?"

Smith seemed surprised. "Without your permission? No. I would have mentioned that at the beginning and asked for your permission to do so."

When she finished, Anne sat back, waiting for questions.

Smith asked, "Your family has no idea of your where-abouts, I understand?"

"No. For leaving Saudi Arabia the way I did I am as good as dead to them."

Smith's reaction was clear. "Please keep it that way, at least for the near future. It is important."

She took a moment, preparing her response, seeing Al

Imani's need for guidance, for resolution of her concerns.

"There is little I can say, officially. Unofficially, I can tell you that your explanation is corroborative of other information discovered during the criminal investigation. Your own is not primary evidence in the crime. Do you recall that William Harding was accompanied by another man at the souq, when you sold him the ring?"

"Yes. I thought he may have been based in Saudi. He was English but spoke Arabic."

"He was. His evidence ties in with your statement and is already on record. Also, there is an affadavit from a relative of the jeweller who made the ring. That should be sufficient for the trial. I would be reluctant to submit even a court-protected statement from you, as it would reveal your existence, if not your new name and location.

"The police officers leading the investigation were aware of Shaykh Yusuf's possible involvement early in their inquiries. Despite questioning him directly, there is no evidence of a direct link between him and the killers, Assad or Jaber. Jaber has already been convicted in the death of the daughter. Assad's deportation from France was approved last week. He and Jaber will go to trial together for the murder of William Harding in the coming months."

"Shaykh Yusuf underwent another treatment a month ago, in Lahore. There is talk that if the outcome is unsuccessful, he might still go to the USA for further surgery. They have some pioneering technique there. Our sources say that it is a last-ditch effort and that neither procedure is likely to succeed. His cancer has advanced quite rapidly, I gather."

Anne interjected, "He claims his detention by the British police caused that. It was mentioned on Al Jazeera."

Smith nodded. "Yes, that the stress of his detention and questioning contributed to his clinical deterioration. You work in the medical field, so you understand that more than I do. What do you think?"

Anne grimaced. "The impact of stress on an illness? Yes, I see that in patients. The shaykh is an elite, a VIP. Everything is done for him, so he leads a cosseted life. To be treated as a common person at a police station would be stressful for him. It is possible but... who can say?"

Smith chose her words carefully. "Please do not reveal your location to members of the Shaykh's tribe, including your own family, for your own sake. Do they know that you have changed faith, that you are an apostate?"

"No. Only my sister in Berlin does, and she understands, but has kept my secret all these years. I do know that. Here, I told no-one, except the Father and two close friends. And you, now."

"Even more reason, then. Has there been any hint of a threat by your former husband?"

Anne shook her head. "Not that my sister heard, and she is attuned. It has long been our fear. Frankly, I think he is glad to see me gone and –."

She paused, glancing at the priest.

"His own behaviours while travelling on business are not above scrutiny. If I heard that he had located me and wanted to act against me, I could make his life difficult. No, he may want me dead and think of me as such, but I doubt he would do anything."

Smith pursed her lips. "Even so, the shaykh holds a grudge. We know that. Given his actions, he may want to harm you for selling the ring in the first place."

She paused a moment, assessing the Yemeni's reaction. Anne did not deny it.

"You are at risk. Too many women in your situation

disappear or are murdered each year around the world. I am not trying to frighten you, as we know of no specific threat. But candidly put, that is the simple truth. Your best protection is your continuing anonymity."

Anne held her gaze, saying nothing. She just nodded.

Smith passed over a card. It wasn't hers, Anne saw, but an Indonesian federal government official.

"If you ever feel threatened, call this number directly. You are an Indonesian permanent resident now. You have rights. On the back is my name and telephone number. He knows it. He will call me, or my replacement, if I have moved to a new assignment.

"Try to let go of your burden, as Father Senen told you. It is not yours to carry. The shaykh will face judgement soon enough for his crimes, don't you think?"

Judith Smith stood, signalling her part in this meeting was over. She moved a step away and stopped, taking in the strain on the Yemeni's face.

"Anne, I have met other women in similar situations to your own over the years. They do not have the same story, but each one has suffered hardship and their own isolation. You have a home here, and friends, and a community. You have a truly worthwhile, rewarding profession – and your independence. That is success, believe me. No small thing at all, for you, or for anyone."

A handshake. A goodbye to the priest and the British official was out of the door.

Anne stood there, looking at the card in her hand, now with tears in her eyes.

Father Budi suggested quietly, "Shall we go into the cathedral, to pray a little? For the Harding family, perhaps, and for you?"

Anne nodded, forcing a smile. "There is a son who survived the attack, called Adam, I read. I will pray for him. And as Miss Smith reminded me, I can give a prayer of gratitude for all those who have helped me here and elsewhere, over the years."

She paused. "But before that, Father Budi, I would like to make my confession, if I may?"

NOTES

When I began the first Catrin Sayer novel, *The Chinese Sailor*, it was to tell an art crime story set in North Wales, where I lived as a university student many years ago. I wasn't even sure I could write creative fiction.

During that writing process, it hit me how a police officer's life evolves, as for any other person working in a large organisation. For some, they keep the same role or stay in the same group for much of their career. Others move within the organisation or leave it, and things change significantly for them. I wondered how my new character would develop. It took nine more novels to find the answer.

Along the way, I blithely fictionalised the Metropolitan Police Service of Greater London, inventing operating structures and groups within it. I have also taken liberties with real groups in the Met, particularly with its Art and Antiques Unit. Similarly, descriptions of other police services are fictions suited to each story. In this book, the idea of the Devon and Cornwall Police undergoing organisational change was entirely my creation.

As I wrote *The Tavistock Lieutenant*, the media coverage around the Metropolitan Police focused on its failings. Resistance to ethnic cultural changes and criminals hiding within its ranks were in the news. There was also the sudden, forced resignation of its first female commissioner. My own view of the Met is more constant, grassroots-focused, and positive. It is perhaps best expressed in Catrin's talk to a class of students in the eighth novel, *The Chiswick Chauffeur*:

"Police officers aren't heroes. Each of us has training, true, but we don't possess special capabilities to take on criminals or terrorists. We aren't any more comfortable than you around people who would kill or injure someone without a second thought. What we have, though, is something truly valuable; we support each other through thick and thin. From that bond, each of us finds the strength to do our job and, at times, keep doing it under incredibly difficult circumstances."

I have had support and encouragement from my family and friends while writing these novels. I thank all of them, particularly my wife Gill, my sister Gwen, and my brother Steve. Gill Jones, Jack Soule, Fred Grigsby, and Mike Stroud have critiqued some or all drafts of the novels. Jack has copy-edited every text. I could not have completed the series without them.

As usual, though, any mistakes and blunders you find are my own.

Allan Jones, 2022

ABOUT THE AUTHOR

Allan Jones lives in Ontario, Canada. He was born and grew up in Merseyside, England. By profession an industrial chemist, he worked for many years as a consultant on international chemical regulation. He has lived in or travelled to most of the regions featured in the Catrin Sayer novels.